Ninety-Nine Signs

BOOK 1 OF THE NINETY-NINE SERIES

ELISHEBA HAXBY

JESSE VINCENT

ABOVE THE
SUN

Contents

1. January 17, 5:02 p.m. 1
2. January 17, 6:36 a.m. 6
3. January 17, 10:29 a.m. 11
4. January 17, 11:00 a.m. 14
5. January 17, 9:00 p.m. 20
6. January 17, 9:50 p.m. 24
7. January 18, 5:00 a.m. 32
8. January 18, 6:53 a.m. 37
9. January 18, 7:02 a.m. 38
10. January 18, 9:02 a.m. 45
11. January 18, 1:30 p.m. 57
12. January 18, 4:02 p.m. 63
13. January 18, 9:25 p.m. 75
14. January 19, 8:30 a.m. 78
15. January 19, 9:00 a.m. 80
16. January 20, 5:02 a.m. 83
17. January 20, 2:45 p.m. 93
18. January 20, 9:27 p.m. 96
19. January 21, 6:00 a.m. 101
20. January 21, 3:15 p.m. 110
21. February 11, 5:30 a.m. 115
22. February 14, 3:00 p.m. 117
23. February 15, 10:00 a.m. 124
24. February 16, 7:56 a.m. 126
25. February 17, 9:00 a.m. 132
26. February 17, 4:39 p.m. 139
27. February 18, 6:14 a.m. 141
28. February 21, 2:00 p.m. 144
29. February 21, 9:11 p.m. 151
30. February 22, 5:45 a.m. 157
31. February 22, 10:30 a.m. 161

32. February 22, 12:15 p.m.   166
33. March 7, 4:30 p.m.   170
34. March 8, 11:18 a.m.   179
35. March 8, 1:10 p.m.   186
36. April 8, 8:53 a.m.   196
37. April 8, 7:48 p.m.   200
38. April 8, 7:51 p.m.   204
39. April 8, 8:30 p.m.   208
40. April 8, 9:05 p.m.   212
41. April 8, 10:06 p.m.   218
42. April 8, 11:00 p.m.   220
43. April 8, 11:30 p.m.   229
44. April 9, 9:24 a.m.   232
45. April 9, 10:04 a.m.   236
46. April 9, 10:12 a.m.   240
47. April 9, 1:49 p.m.   250
48. April 9, 3:12 p.m.   256
49. April 11, 9:05 p.m.   259
50. April 11, 9:23 p.m.   261
51. April 11, 9:43 p.m.   263
52. April 11, 10:02 p.m.   266
53. April 11, 11:00 p.m.   272
54. April 12, 9:45 a.m.   274
55. April 12, 10:45 a.m.   276
56. April 12, 11:00 a.m.   278
57. April 12, 11:37 a.m.   282
58. April 12, 12:05 p.m.   284
    Epilogue   292
    To My Dearest Hope,   297
    Dear Reader,   299
    Next in Series   301
    Levi's Journal   319

Questions for Discussion   321
Acknowledgments   323
About The Authors   325
What's Your Story?   327

Print ISBN: 978-1-7336006-2-0
Ebook ISBN: 978-1-7336006-3-7
Cover by: Get Covers

Published by Above The Sun LLC,
Eugene, Oregon

Scripture quotations or paraphrases are taken from the HOLY BIBLE, NEW
INTERNATIONAL VERSION®. ©1973, 1978, 1984, by Biblica, Inc.™ Used
by permission. All rights reserved worldwide

This novel is a work of fiction. Names, characters, places, and incidents are either
products of the author's imagination or used fictitiously. All characters are
fictional, and any similarity to people living or dead is purely coincidental.

For our families,
Who sacrifice to help
us pursue our dream

CHAPTER 1

January 17, 5:02 p.m.

TAMARA

It was not a typical drive-with-the-top-down kind of evening. The icy wind stabbed my face like a thousand razor sharp needles—painful yet somehow exhilarating. When I woke this morning, I hadn't planned on ending up here—flying down Interstate 5 in my 1985 Volkswagen Cabriolet, but here I was. Most people would have probably labeled me nuts, and I couldn't say I blamed them. It was the middle of January in Washington, the sun was about to dip behind the mountains ... but I didn't care.

I needed some kind of shock to break through the funk that had been building around my brain for the last hour. The tears had dried about eighty miles ago, and a thick fog had rolled over my mind, buffering me from the pain.

An image of Danny standing in our driveway, bare-chested, his eyes pleading with me not to go, cut through the haze.

I gunned the accelerator. My beanie blew off in the wind, and my hair whipped around my face.

I was never going back.

A serrated knife twisted deep inside my chest as tears stung the back of my eyes. I swallowed the knot that formed in my throat, forcing myself to shut down the emotion.

Danny was just like the rest of them. He wasn't worth another moment of my anguish.

My eyes landed on the charm Charlie had given me for my birthday, dangling from my wrist. "God, if you still care, will you please help? I'm sick of all this pain." It was probably futile to pray now after so many years, but a tiny part of me thought maybe he'd still listen, even after everything. A stupid notion, no doubt.

In the distance, a city came into view, and I breathed a sigh of relief.

Vancouver. Which meant Portland was close.

Soon I would be out of this state that held so many terrible memories. Maybe somewhere in Oregon I could start over and forget the heartbreak. I flipped on the radio. "1999" by Prince blared out of my speakers.

Nice. Prince was singing to me. My party *was* over, and I *was* out of time. I pushed in the car cigarette lighter and snatched up my pack of Camel 99s. I lit one up, turned up the volume, and lost myself in the sharp beats of the chorus.

"I wanna party like ... 1999!" I shouted, releasing my heaviness into the wind, letting the insanity take over.

The number ninety-nine from my smokes coupled with the lyrics lit up my brain. Was it a sign? Hope filled me for a moment, raising me above the dark clouds looming over my mind. Freedom —followed by a brief moment of clarity. Forget Danny. Forget Ocean Shores. From now on, I'd make my own destiny, "Tonight I am going to partyyyyyy!" I yelled again with the song.

Just then, a billow of smoke rose from the hood of my car.

Seriously? This was *not* happening. I punched the steering wheel and flipped on the turn signal.

Was the car on fire? My heart sped up as I merged onto the exit and took the first left, desperately looking for a place to pull over.

Smoke poured out from beneath my hood as if my car had become an active volcano. A few blocks ahead, I spotted a 7-

Eleven. I took a sharp turn across traffic, pulled into the parking lot, and turned off my car. I grabbed my purse and bolted out of the vehicle. Considering my fortune, the car would spontaneously combust and leave me not only stranded, but also without access to my funds. Circling the car, I scanned underneath for flames. There wasn't any visible fire, and the smoke had died down some since I turned off the engine.

"Are you okay?" A man stood on the other side of my car, face filled with concern. He was around six feet tall with a build that reminded me of Channing Tatum. His blue jeans and gray hoodie were snug enough to show he hit the gym quite a bit. "Kinda chilly for a joy ride, isn't it?"

"Maybe a little." I tightened my scarf and rubbed my hands together. He must have thought I was a complete maniac.

His mouth quirked up at the edges, and the smile brightened his hazel eyes. "I work across the street." He tilted his head toward the restaurant on the opposite side of the road. "I couldn't help but notice you pull in." He stepped around the car and extended his hand. "I'm Joe."

"Tamara." I shook his hand. "You wouldn't happen to know a good mechanic, would ya?"

"I do, but why don't you let me take a look at it? Could be something simple."

As Joe walked to the front of the car, I settled back into the driver's seat and pulled the small lever under the steering wheel.

He lifted the hood and disappeared behind it.

I glanced in the rearview mirror, and heat flooded my frozen cheeks. Oh. My. Goodness. It was worse than I thought.

My hair was in ratted coils, standing out in all directions like Medusa's snakes. My green eyes, usually my most striking quality, were lined with smudged mascara, making me look slightly deranged.

Okay, maybe completely deranged.

My pale cheeks seemed sunken, as if I wasn't getting the

3

proper nutrition. I'd always been told I was a pretty girl, but at that moment, I looked worse than death.

I grabbed a rubber band from my purse, raked my fingers through my hair, and pulled it up into a ponytail. Then I licked the pads of my thumbs and ran them under my eyes to remove the smudges.

One more look in the mirror showed better. Not great, but better.

I climbed out of my car and walked toward the front.

Joe was leaning over, inspecting the motor. "It looks like the radiator hose came loose and sprayed coolant all over the engine. That's what caused the smoke." He looked up and smiled. "I can jury-rig it together for now, but it will just be a temporary fix."

Literally, the best news I'd heard all day.

"You won't want to drive it far until you change out the hose."

I bit my lip and glanced to the side. Being stuck anywhere wasn't good. Having to stay at a hotel could seriously drain my funds, and I only had enough to get by for a month or so.

"Something wrong?" Joe asked, voice sincere and kind.

My eyes met his. There was something about him that made me want to tell him everything. Was it his honest face? His warm eyes?

I shut down the urge immediately. From now on, it was just me. People were all the same. They always had an angle, and in the end, they would always hurt me. I averted my gaze. "It's been a long day."

"Sorry. Let me fix this real quick, and you can be on your way."

"Thank you." I turned away before he could see the tears welling in my eyes. I pulled out my pack of cigarettes as I walked toward the back of my car. I leaned on the trunk, lit up and looked around.

There was a *Help Wanted* sign in the window of the restaurant where Joe said he worked. The green neon sign over the entrance said Highway 99 Diner. I glanced down at my pack of smokes and ran my finger over the number 99. What was it about that number?

"All right." Joe's voice interrupted my thoughts. "That should do it." He wiped his hands on the front of his jeans.

"Thank you. Can I pay you for your time?"

He looked insulted. "Absolutely not. I'm happy to help. And if there's anything else you need, you know where I work."

I studied him for a moment. "Why are you being so nice to me?"

He shrugged. "I know what it's like to be down on my luck."

As Joe walked away, my gaze returned to the *Help Wanted* sign in the restaurant window. I drew in a deep breath and took in my surroundings. I was at the corner of 99th Street and Highway 99.

A strange sensation worked its way through my entire body. Was this number leading me toward something better? Was it an omen that all of the truly awful things were behind me now? Maybe I could start all over right here. Maybe this time it would be different.

CHAPTER 2

January 17, 6:36 a.m.

TAMARA

One Year Later

A lot can change in a year's time. For me, not so much ... Sure, the landscape was different. New town, new job, new people, but that was about it. I was no longer afraid of Ryan showing up on my doorstep to bring retribution for the money I stole from him. Now I was just afraid of everyone else.

I turned into the parking lot of the Highway Ninety-Nine Diner, parked in a spot near the back and let out a deep yawn. Last night, as I tried to sleep, memories battered me like a buoy in a relentless storm. The night I left home. Fleeing from Ryan. Danny's betrayal. They all pressed down on my soul like a giant vice, crushing the life out of it.

I slammed the door on the way out of my car and drug my feet toward the diner. One of the nines in the neon sign on the side of the restaurant had burnt out.

How ironic.

Looked like my omen was a dud after all.

It started to rain, and I picked up the pace. I so did *not* want to work today. Yesterday I had pulled a double because one of my coworkers supposedly had family coming in from out of town.

More than likely, she wanted to go party it up on a Friday night but whatever. At least today was my Friday.

The smell of bacon grease, coffee, and pancakes hit my nose as I walked through the door.

Betty, the graveyard waitress, sneered. "You're late!" Betty was in her late forties, but her deep worry lines and defined crow's feet made her look at least ten years older. The bad perm and dye job didn't help much either.

I gave her a halfhearted, "sorry," and glanced around the restaurant.

A woman with a slight build sat at the bar, sipping coffee. All of the diner's thirteen tables were empty.

"Rough night?" Betty looked over the glasses that rested on her long, crooked nose, her expression condescending.

"Not how you're thinking, but you could say that. I couldn't sleep." I hurried across the room. The red-and-white tiled floor and fluorescent lights seemed as reproachful as Betty's mood.

"Okay, who is he?"

I snatched my apron from the hook behind the cash register. "There isn't anybody. I just had a lot of things on my mind and couldn't sleep. End of story." Not that it was her business either way.

"Whatever you say, honey. Next time, just make sure you get here on time."

I turned toward the kitchen and pushed through the double doors. Why was she busting my chops over a measly six minutes? She wasn't exactly Miss Punctual herself. And there was only one patron in the whole restaurant.

Joe stood off to the left of the kitchen by the time clock. He had obviously just arrived, but no one was giving him a hard time about it. He stripped off his black pea coat and gray American Eagle beanie and ran a hand through his light-brown hair. "Hey, Tam. How ya doing?" His warm hazel eyes crinkled at the edges as he smiled.

"I could use some coffee. Would you like me to pour you a

cup?" I hung my jacket and purse on a hook next to the time clock and put on my apron.

"Sure." He leaned his tall, beefy frame on the counter next to him.

Joe was in his mid-twenties and—honestly—completely adorable. Not that I thought of him like that. He had a sometimes girlfriend. One of those on-again-off-again affairs that was far too complicated to keep up with. Last I heard, they got back together, and she moved in with him, but I was never nosey enough to find out if that was true.

Yawning, I handed him a cup of coffee. "I'm so glad I have tomorrow off. It's been a long week."

"I hear that. Got any big plans?"

I yawned again. "Oh yeah, I got a hot date with my bed. Go to bed early and sleep in late. That's what I'm talking about."

He shot me a disapproving look. "Girl, you need to get a life."

The bells clanged against the door in the dining room.

"Rescued by the cling-a-ling."

Joe shrugged and raised his hands in playful defeat.

He meant well, but I didn't have the mental energy for this conversation.

Several times over the last year, Joe had butted into my personal life by setting me up with one of his friends. Each time it had been a complete disaster.

I walked out of the kitchen, grabbing a menu on the way.

Levi Taylor, one of my regulars, had already made his way to his usual seat. He'd been coming in a couple of times a week for a few months now. Usually, he'd show up around six forty-five, when it was still quiet, order scrambled eggs with diced tomatoes, and drink coffee. Lots of coffee. He didn't really say much, but I found him intriguing. Not in a physical way, even though he was quite attractive. He was in his mid-thirties with dark-brown hair, piercing blue eyes, and a genuine smile that made me feel like life could actually be better. He was always warm and friendly, but he'd never tried to pick me up like some of the other dirt bags around this place.

Plus, I was pretty sure he was married because he had a tattoo band on his left ring finger.

After he finished his breakfast, he would stay for a while, listening to his iPod, sipping coffee, and writing in his journal. Before he left, he'd write a little note for me on his ticket. It was always simple like *Hope you have a great day* or just *Great service,* with a smiley face.

I filled a mug with coffee, walked over, and set it down in front of him. "Good morning, Levi. You want your usual?"

He looked up at me and smiled. "Yes, please, and keep the coffee coming. I think I need a little extra this morning."

"Sure, I'll make another pot."

As I put in Levi's order, Joe placed two plates of food in the window. It looked like a number three from the menu. A trio of eggs, bacon, hash browns, and a triple stack of pancakes.

Taking hold of the plates, I spun around and placed them down in front of the lady sitting at the bar. "Here ya go."

She grabbed her fork and dug into the stack of pancakes as if it was her first meal in weeks.

I refilled her coffee cup and tried not to stare. It was hard not to, though. She reminded me of my younger sister.

What was it exactly? Her dark hair? Her slight build?

She looked up at me mid-bite, and I quickly turned away. Her eyes held a pain that I was all too familiar with. Images of my last night at home crashed into me, the same vivid imagery that had kept me up last night.

Memories—who needed them? Everywhere I turned lately something was reminding me of my past when all I wanted was to forget.

Around seven fifteen, things got busy, and just like that, I was running from one end of the diner to the next, trying to keep everything straight. My sleep deprivation made it a bit more difficult, but I made it through unscathed.

Mornings like this made me wish my boss would hire someone to bus the tables. It took thirty-five minutes before I had a chance to clear Levi's booth.

He had left enough money for his bill and the tip. But the note at the bottom of today's ticket felt different. It read *Keep your chin up. It will get better,* with the usual smiley face next to it.

Strange. How did he know I was having a hard time? Was it that obvious?

I looked around to make sure everything was taken care of, then ducked into the ladies' room to examine myself in the mirror. I did look a little tired but not that bad. Shrugging it off, I headed back out to clean the rest of the dining room.

CHAPTER 3

January 17, 10:29 a.m.

JOE

There was something different about Tamara this morning. I watched her through the cook's window and wondered what it was. She bustled from table to table, clearing dishes and setting new silverware rolls and coffee cups on them.

Outwardly, she looked the same as she always did, light brown hair pulled back into a loose ponytail, a few wisps out of place. Her green eyes were highlighted with smoky gray eye shadow, high cheekbones tinted with a light shade of blush.

I poured water on the grill and a steam cloud erupted. I picked up the spatula and scraped this morning's breakfast rush mess off the grill.

Over the last year, Tamara and I worked together, we had gotten pretty close. Well, as close as she'd let anyone get. Our friendship had an ease to it that didn't happen with everyone. Despite that, I didn't completely understand her. On the surface she was friendly, but she was always a bit guarded. Most of the time, it felt like I was getting only half the story.

Today, though, there was a sadness in her eyes—like something was eating her from the inside out. There had to be a way to approach the subject, but she was such a private person, if I brought it up, she'd probably deny it.

11

I gave the grill another quick wipe down and threw the towel in the laundry bucket before grabbing an extra package of corned beef from the walk-in cooler. My phone hummed in my pocket on the way back to my work area. I threw the meat in the sink to thaw and answered it.

"Hey, sweetie. You called earlier?" Susan said.

"Yeah. A couple of things. First, I wanted to see if you are going to be able to make it to the AA meeting tonight? I couldn't have made it this far without you."

"I don't know. I may have to work late."

Of course. She always worked late. And early, for that matter. "Okay, I understand." Actually, I didn't, but I didn't want to start a fight. "Is there any way you could pick up a few things for tomorrow night from the grocery store on the way home?"

"Tomorrow night?"

"Don't tell me you forgot. It was your idea."

Silence.

"The party. My sobriety birthday."

Realization seemed to dawn. "Of course, I didn't forget. It just slipped my mind for the moment. Busy day at the office."

"Three years tomorrow." I said.

"And a lifetime left to go."

If she was joking, I didn't see the humor in it. "That's one way to look at it. But in the program, we like to take it one day at a time." The sarcasm was impossible to reign in.

"I don't like your tone, Joe."

"Yeah, well you know what I don't like?" My voice started to escalate. "I don't like the way you never give me any credit. It's like you're looking for me to fail."

"Is that what you think?" Her voice shook.

I hadn't meant to hurt her. Why couldn't she understand that I'd work so hard to stay sober for her—for us? "Baby, I'm sorry. That came out all wrong. I just think maybe you should go to Al Anon or some sort of support group with me, so you can understand my disease."

"We've been over this before, Joe. You know I don't have time for that. Besides, it's not me who has the problem. Why should I have to pay for it?"

Ouch. Sad but unequivocally true. She shouldn't have to pay for my disease, but in so many ways she already had. "You're right. Don't worry about it. I'll take care of everything."

CHAPTER 4
January 17, 11:00 a.m.
TAMARA

Yawning, I glanced at the clock. Three more hours and then I'm off for—

The phone next to the register rang.

I picked it up. "Highway 99 Diner."

"Tam," a raspy voice came through the line. "It's Melissa."

Here it comes.

"I'm not feeling good. I spent half the night puking my guts out. Is there any way you can cover for me tonight?"

I knew it. She was definitely out partying last night, being irresponsible, and now I was going to have to cover for her again. "Ah, Mel, I don't know. I had a rough night too. I was really looking forward to being done at two thirty."

The line went silent for a moment. "Please, I'm begging you. There is no way I could make it through my shift like this."

Another double. Really?

"Tamara?"

Resisting the urge to throw the phone across the room, I gripped the receiver tighter. "Fine."

"Thanks Tam, I owe you."

I hung up.

"What was that about?" Joe peered through the window from the kitchen.

"Looks like I'm working another double shift. Melissa is sick."

"You're kidding."

"Yeah. She said she was up half the night throwing up."

"We both know why that was. I'll call Trudy and let her know what's going on. Maybe she can find someone else to cover the shift."

"No. I'll be fine. I need the money."

"Are you sure?" His eyebrows pinched together. "You'll be stuck working with you-know-who."

I cringed inwardly. Anthony Lombardi ... great. Wish I would have thought of that two minutes ago. Anthony was the very attractive, very conceited, very sexist short-order cook who I regret ever meeting. But worse than all that was that he was a lying, no-good sack of horse manure—and that's putting it mildly. A few months ago, he came on to me at a party, and I shut him down. His precious ego was so bruised he felt the need to tell all his buddies at work he'd slept with me. At first, I tried to deny it, but the damage was done. How does the saying go? Lies spread quicker than the truth. Joe was one of the few that actually believed me.

Anthony only worked Saturdays' and Sundays' swing shift, so I saw him once a week and rarely had to work with him. But when I did, it was pure torture.

Eight more hours. It wasn't that long. Though, at the moment, it sounded like an eternity in the netherworld.

I sighed. "I'll be fine. I don't want to get Mel in trouble. Even though she totally deserves it."

"You should take a break then. Who knows if you'll get one later. Are you hungry? I could make you something."

My stomach growled as if to answer his question. I hadn't eaten anything since waking up. "Sure, some food would be good."

"Great, what can I make you?"

15

"Surprise me. I'm going to sneak a smoke." I grabbed my jacket and purse from the hook and started toward the back door.

"You know that's a nasty habit." He flashed a crooked grin.

"Yup." I responded over my shoulder. "Maybe what you make me will be healthy enough to counteract it."

"You're awfully trusting."

I shook my head, donned my jacket, and walked out the back door into the damp air. The sun was out for the moment, but in the distance more rain clouds loomed.

I pulled out a cigarette and wiped off the chair with my sleeve before sitting down. I lit up and took in a drag. Closing my eyes, I turned my face to the sun, wishing there was a way to pull energy from it. Images from my last night at home filled my mind again. My father's accusing glare, my sister's cries in the background and the beating that ensued, my mother standing by, doing nothing to stop him.

Why did these awful memories invade every quiet moment lately?

Vancouver was supposed to be a fresh start, but it was beginning to feel more like a holding cell. A place where I was stuck, afraid to move forward, terrified to look back.

I sucked in another drag and riffled through my purse for my journal. I pulled it out and wrote a few lines as I smoked.

What am I doing here? Life seems so meaningless. Vancouver is a forsaken place, filled with nothingness, loneliness. I have hidden myself behind so many layers of pain that I can't let anyone in. I am lost in this endless purgatory. I am walking, but I know not where I go.

Oh, my word. I sounded like an emo poet. I stared dejectedly at the last line. Maybe that's what I had become—a depressed poet. I did kind of see my life through melancholy shades these days. The lines turned over in my mind several times before something clicked. I flipped to a new page and wrote.

I am walking, but I know not where I go.

I look around this forsaken place without a care in the world, wandering the ~~abandoned~~ lonely streets, without a purpose.

I slammed the journal shut. A picture dropped out of the pages onto the ground, and I picked it up. The one thing I kept that reminded me of home.

Me as a baby, about three days old. Tamara Christine Jensen, born January third, to Paul and Theresa Jensen. In the picture, my father lifted my tiny frame up high, my frilly pink dress spilling out in all directions. His gaze was intently upon me, his expression so full of love and hope, as if he believed I was destined for greatness or something.

Man, if he could only see me now. What a disappointment.

My heart writhed in pain at the thought of him seeing this pathetic existence I'd made for myself. If only I could turn my life around.

Who was I kidding? It didn't matter. I came from nothing, and I'd always be nothing. My parents both worked hard and never got anywhere. Dad was a long-haul truck driver, and Mom worked as a waitress. Dad was gone most of the time, and when he was there—

I jammed the picture in my journal and shoved it back in my purse, slamming the brakes on this jaunt down memory lane. I flicked the cigarette to the ground and stomped it out.

When I walked back into the kitchen, Joe was holding a plate containing a ginormous chicken sandwich and an equally large portion of fries. The sandwich was layered with sautéed mushrooms and onions. Melted Swiss cheese oozed down the edges. "Here you go. Joe's Surprise Special," he beamed.

My eyes widened. "I can't eat all that."

"Oh, come on." A mischievous grin lit his expression. "I'm just watching out for you. You're looking a little skinny these days."

"Ha, ha, very funny. Thanks." I snatched the plate from him and walked down the hall toward the break room. I sat down in my usual spot at the large wooden table and propped my feet up on the chair next to me. A pang budded inside me as I looked down at the sandwich.

Somehow, Joe's kindhearted playfulness made me feel lonelier. Maybe things would have turned out differently for me if I had a man like him. The guys I ended up with brought me nothing but heartache. Ryan, the drug dealer, and Danny, the cheater ... which added up to Tamara, the loner—sad girl with major trust issues.

I picked up the sandwich, opened my mouth as wide as possible, and sunk my teeth in. The first bite hit my stomach, awakening a ravenous hunger, and then I couldn't eat the rest fast enough. In less than ten minutes, I had inhaled two-thirds of the chicken burger and over half the fries.

I leaned back in my chair and pushed the almost empty plate away.

Another smoke sounded good, but a nap sounded better. Closing my eyes, I laid my head on the table.

Someone gently shook my shoulder.

Where was I?

"Tamara?"

I bolted up, mortified that I had actually fallen asleep.

Joe smiled fondly down at me. "Sorry to wake you, but things are getting busy out there."

I glanced at the clock. 12:05. I'd been in the break room for almost an hour. I yawned. "Sorry, I guess I was more tired than I thought."

"Don't apologize. I'm glad you got a long break. I didn't want to bug you, but I just sat three tables of four."

"Oh, okay. Lunch rush, here I come."

The day got progressively worse from there. When it was time for the shift change, Joe and I stood by the time clock.

Anthony always wore an unhealthy amount of Calvin Klein

cologne, so I smelled him before I saw him, which gave me just enough time to brace myself for a disgusting mixture of awkwardness and aggravation.

He walked up, wedged his way between us, and snatched up his time card. "Where's Melissa?" His short, spiky black hair jetted out in all directions.

"Sick. I'm covering for her." I said as politely as I could, but it was hard not to let contempt seep through my tone.

He turned toward me, his gaze slowly making its way up my body. An expression best described as sardonic crept over his face. "She looked just fine at Dickie's last night when I left her and Mark." He shook his head and turned back to the time clock. "Tamara, you really are too easy."

Joe's hands tightened into fists, and he stepped toward Anthony. "That's enough."

"Oh." Anthony's eyes widened in mock horror. "What, is she your girlfriend now? You gonna beat me up?"

Joe's face reddened, and a vein pulsed on his forehead. "If that's what it takes."

Anthony threw his head back and guffawed. "You don't scare me, Phillips." He jammed his card into the slot and walked away as abruptly as he came.

What was that all about? Joe and I were friends but defending me like that to Anthony was way more than I ever expected.

Our gazes locked for a brief moment. "You shouldn't have to put up with stuff like this."

I shrugged and looked away quickly. "I'll be fine."

He hesitated for another moment, exhaled, and punched out.

CHAPTER 5
January 17, 9:00 p.m.
TAMARA

Will this day never end? I refilled a coffee cup and imagined inhaling a drag of a smoke. It had been hours since my last break, and man, I was having a serious nicotine fit.

Melissa was probably curled up in front of the TV, feet propped up, catching up on *Grey's Anatomy*, while I dealt with Mister Attitude in the kitchen and a restaurant full of ungrateful customers.

I finished the rounds with the coffeepot. Everyone had food and all drinks were full.

Time to sneak a few drags.

I hurried toward the back, but before I reached the door, the bells clanged.

All I needed was a few minutes, but clearly, I wasn't going to get even that. Irritated, I hustled back into the dining area.

The new customer had already seated himself at a booth next to the door.

I approached the table with a menu and a glass of water. "Good evening, would you like to hear about our specials?" I asked, mustering up all the false cheerfulness I could.

The young man looked up at me with a flirty smile. "Actually, I'm more thirsty than hungry. Do you have a full bar here?"

I couldn't help but give him a genuine smile in return. He was cute. And those eyes—what a stunning shade of blue. "Sorry, sir, all we serve is beer and wine, and we have a two-drink limit." It seemed awkward calling him sir. He couldn't be much older than me.

His smile faded. "I guess beer will have to do. How about a Corona?"

"That we have. Be right back." I felt his eyes on me as I walked away. Was he checking me out? I grabbed the bottle, popped the top off on the way back to the table, and set it down in front of him.

He glanced up, his eyes sparkling with amusement. "Um, can I get some limes?"

"Oh," I stammered, feeling the blood rush to my face. "Sorry. It's been a long week."

"No worries. I'm sure there is some way you could make it up to me." He winked.

I turned away, speechless, face blazing. What was that supposed to mean? How did he think I could make it up to him? This is not where I saw my night heading.

But I kind of liked it.

My heart clenched. What was wrong with me? More than anyone, I knew what kind of pain going down this road could bring. Do *not* think about those sultry eyes and flirtatious grin.

After cutting fresh limes in the kitchen, I went back into the dining room.

He stood by the jukebox, scanning the music selection.

I walked slowly toward him, nervously taking my turn to look him over. He was about five foot eleven, with an athletic build, broad shoulders, and wavy dirty-blond hair. He wore faded blue jeans and a vintage Iron Maiden T-shirt.

He punched a button and "Long Day" by Matchbox 20 bellowed out of the speakers mounted on the wall.

Before I had a chance to look away, he turned around and caught me checking him out.

He flashed me that same grin as before, lifted his beer to his mouth, and took a swig.

The muscles in my stomach tightened. Man, he was attractive.

Shut it down, Tamara.

"I guess you won't need these, then?" I lifted the small platter of limes and gestured toward his almost finished beer.

"Sorry, couldn't wait. I was really thirsty, remember? I'll use them for the next one." He looked down, eyeing my nametag. "So, Tamara, what time do you get off?"

I hesitated. The truth felt dangerous but lying wasn't an option. He would probably still be here when I got off work. "My shift ends at nine thirty."

If he felt my reluctance, it didn't slow him down. "Do you want to do something after work? You look like you could use a drink."

"I don't think that would be a good idea."

He tilted his head to the side. "Why not?"

"I don't make it a practice of going out with complete strangers. I don't even know your name."

"Kyle. So that takes care of that problem." He set down his beer.

I looked away from him to hide a smile. "I don't know."

"Oh, come on. I've had a long week too, and it would be nice to have some good company." He put his hands up in front of him. "Look, I promise to be a perfect gentleman." He leaned closer and winked. "I won't do anything you don't want me to do."

In spite of myself, my heart sped up and heat flooded my cheeks. Why was this guy affecting me like this? There was no way he could be Mr. Right. After everything, I was positive there was no such thing. But he was Mr. Right Here Right Now, and I could use a drink after the day I've had. "Give me a minute, would you?"

He leaned back, a smile playing across his lips. "Sure, as long as you grab me another beer on your way back."

"You got it." I retreated to the back of the restaurant and lit up a smoke.

The cold air felt good on my face as I paced back and forth, fighting the inward battle. Going out with this guy was a huge mistake, wasn't it? For one, I didn't even know him. For two, men couldn't be trusted. I took a long, contemplative drag of my cigarette.

But what was the big deal? It was just a drink or two, and he didn't seem creepy. Actually, he seemed like a nice guy. An extremely attractive nice guy.

My lips curled into a smile.

The smile turned into a grimace as I thought about the alternative. Another lonely night in my dumpy apartment, reliving all my painful regrets.

Having a drink with a hot guy sounded more appealing by the second. It had been a while since I had gone out. It had been over a month since I'd even had a drink. The more I thought about it, the more I could taste that Long Island Iced Tea sliding down my throat. I was tired of thinking and sick of being alone.

I flicked my cigarette to the ground and pulled Kyle's ticket from my apron pocket.

Meet me by the red Cabriolet at 9:45. I wrote on the back. I didn't want anyone to see me leave with him.

The rumor mill already had plenty of material to toss around.

On the way back into the dining room, I grabbed another Corona and popped the top off. Foam spilled over the lip as I set the bottle firmly on the table next to the ticket that I had written on. Then I turned to walk away.

"My ticket already? What if I wanted another beer?"

I looked over my shoulder with a slight smile. "Two drink limit, remember?"

CHAPTER 6

January 17, 9:50 p.m.

TAMARA

Kyle was leaning on my car when I walked out of the restaurant. It always took at least fifteen minutes extra to wrap things up. This time it took twenty because I had to make the proper adjustments to my hair and makeup.

"You made it." Kyle seemed relieved. "I was beginning to think your boyfriend in there was going to come out here and stir things up."

"My boyfriend?"

"The guy in the kitchen kept giving me dirty looks. I figured he had a thing for you or something."

"Oh, that's Anthony. Don't mind him. He's a ..." I couldn't think of a descriptive enough word to show my disdain for him without using expletives. "Who cares about him? Where do you want to go, and are we taking my car or yours?"

"Yours might be a little easier to maneuver around town." He pointed across the street to a semi.

"You're a trucker?" It sounded more like an accusation than a question. I should've known. The Highway 99 Diner was located across the street from a truck stop.

He crossed his arms. "Do you have a problem with that?"

"It looks like I'm breaking another one of my rules."

"Rules?" He lifted an eyebrow. "Seriously?"

I put my key in the lock of my car. "Yes, I don't go out with strangers or truck drivers."

He narrowed his eyes, and his mouth curved up into a cocky smirk. "It's high time you throw caution to the wind."

"You know, I think you're right." I opened my car door, climbed in, leaned over, and unlocked his.

The radio blared too loudly as I turned the key. I reached up quickly and turned the music down to a reasonable decibel level. "Sorry, rocking out helps me wake up in the morning."

He slid into the seat next to me. "It's all good. I like loud music. But what are we listening to, the oldies' station?"

"Hey, lay off my station. It's the best of the 80s, 90s, and whatever."

He raised his hands in playful surrender. "No messing with the music."

"So, what are you in the mood for?"

"You tell me. It's your town. I don't know Vancouver at all."

I put the car in reverse and backed out of the parking spot. "Well, we could head to Portland and go to the Invasion Cafe. It's a gay bar."

"Oh, that's funny." He shifted a little in his seat. "Please tell me you're joking."

I couldn't help but laugh. "Just checking. You never know. But, seriously, we could go to Dickie's. It's kind of like the bar in *Coyote Ugly*. Hot chicks dancing on bars and stuff. It's usually really hopping on a Saturday night."

"That sounds a little more up my alley, but I was thinking something more low-key."

"Low-key, huh?" I bit my lip and mentally ran through the list of bars I was familiar with. "How 'bout the Grand Cafe? It's like two bars in one. They have a dance floor downstairs and a place to karaoke upstairs."

"Sounds perfect. Want to get something to eat first?"

I hadn't eaten since lunch, but I wasn't really hungry.

"Actually, I'm more thirsty than hungry." I turned my head slightly to check his reaction.

His grin widened. "All right, then."

I merged onto the interstate and hit the accelerator.

Kyle reached over and turned up the radio. "I love this song. 'Sister Christian' by um." His forehead creased as if he was thinking hard. "REO Speedwagon."

"Nice try, but you are way off. It's Night Ranger."

"No, it's REO Speedwagon."

"Oh yeah? I bet you a shot of Patrón that it's Night Ranger."

"You're on."

The banter continued like that as I drove. By the time we arrived at the bar, I was pretty sure he owed me three shots.

When we walked in the door, two girls that looked like sisters were singing a decent rendition of "Sweet Child O' Mine" by Guns N' Roses.

Kyle looked over my shoulder as I pulled up the songs we were arguing over on my phone.

Right on all three of them.

"Ha! Pay up, sucker." I jabbed him in the arm as we headed to the bar.

Smirking, he rolled his eyes and waved down the bartender.

Across the room, there was a guy who, from the back, looked like Tommy, one of the cooks from work. Not good. All I needed was more evidence to implicate me as the diner tramp.

"Bartender, can I get three shots of Patrón and a rum and Coke?" Kyle pulled out a credit card.

Across the room, the man turned. Not Tommy.

I breathed a sigh of relief. But what if I did run into someone from work? I should have thought of that before bringing Kyle here.

I was so stupid sometimes.

I slammed my hand on the bar. "Make that two rum and Cokes." Time to get this party started. All I needed was a few drinks to calm my nerves. And more importantly, temporarily numb the empty chasm that had taken up residence deep down in the dark parts of my soul.

"Whoa, girl, pace yourself."

I threw down my first shot. "Don't worry about me. I can handle my liquor."

"I'm sure you can, but four shots of alcohol in less than twenty minutes is not a good idea for anyone." He picked up one of the shots and gulped it down.

"Hey! That's mine. I won it fair and square."

"Believe me, I'm doing both of us a favor. I told you I wanted some good company tonight. Holding your hair back while you puke your guts out is not what I had in mind for our first date."

First date? If he was a trucker just passing through, wouldn't this be our only date?

The bartender put two highball glasses in front of us.

"Okay, but you owe me one later." I downed my second shot. Kyle took my hand, led me to a table and pulled out a chair for me before he sat down.

I hung my purse on the back of the seat and sat.

Kyle looked around the room. "You come here often?"

"Not really. Only a few times."

A man with a mullet, wearing acid-wash jeans and a black sleeveless shirt, walked by us. He made his way to the center of the floor and picked up the microphone.

I leaned toward Kyle. "Check this guy out."

He smirked. "We're about to be serenaded by Joe Dirt himself."

I choked on my drink. "Ten bucks he sings something white trashy."

"You like to gamble, don't you? Maybe we should have gone to the casino."

"No, you're wrong about that. I only like to bet when I know I'm right."

"Oh, confident, aren't we?" He leaned in, his eyes amused. "What's your idea of white trashy?"

"I don't know. Quiet Riot or Motley Crew?" I took a large gulp of my drink.

"I'm in." Kyle brought his glass to his lips.

In the background, mellow whistling and hand drums came from the speakers.

"No way!" I slammed my drink down, mouth wide open.

The man's voice was smooth and husky as he sang "Don't Worry, Be Happy."

"Ah." Kyle leaned back, a smug grin breaking across his face. "Pride cometh before losing your tail."

"Whatever. That's not how the saying goes."

"Wanna bet?"

I narrowed my eyes at him.

"Don't be a sore loser."

"Okay, fine." I riffled through my purse, pulled out a ten, and slid it across the table.

"How 'bout you just get the next round?"

"Deal."

We sipped our drinks and made fun of the different singers, each of them at varying levels of intoxication, trying to imitate their favorite artists. There were a few decent performances, but most of them totally sucked.

Kyle gulped down the last bit of his cocktail.

"You ready for another drink?" I asked.

"Absolutely."

"Want the same thing?" I stood, feeling a bit woozy. Maybe I should order a side of fries and a glass of water and sit the next round out.

"Actually, I think I would like a Long Island."

"Okay. I may grab some food. Do you want something to eat?"

"Nah, just the drink."

"Be right back." I headed toward the bar.

"Tamara," a woman's voice called.

I scanned the crowd but didn't see anyone I recognized. Possibly my paranoia was playing games with my head.

"Tamara."

This time it was louder and closer. I spun around and standing right behind me was the last person I expected to see. It took me a minute to put it together, because it felt so out of place.

"Tamara. I thought it was you. Oh, my goodness, chica, I can't tell you how happy I am to see you." She threw her arms around me, giving a heartfelt squeeze.

My blood ran ice cold and my body rigid. What did she think she was doing?

I grabbed her arms and yanked them off of me. "Shelby Turner, what are you doing here?"

Her eyes grew wide, as if she were shocked at my reaction. "We're on our way to California. Doing a little road trip."

"We?" A lead anvil crashed against my insides. "Danny?"

Understanding filled her expression. "What? No! Tamara, I'm so, so sorry. I never got a chance to apologize. You don't even know how sick with worry I was when you took off like that, and Danny—"

"Don't you dare talk to me about Danny!" My hands tightened into fists. "You can take your apology and shove it! I will never forgive you for what you did!" I wanted to pull her out of the bar by her blonde locks and ruin her beautiful features with my bare hands.

"Is everything all right?" Kyle rested a hand on my shoulder.

"Sure, everything is fine," I said through clenched teeth, glaring at Shelby.

"Okay ..." Kyle moved to my side, putting his arm around me. "You gonna introduce me to your friend?"

"I don't have any friends here." I turned to walk away.

"Tamara, please," Shelby begged.

"I get the impression that she doesn't want to talk to you," Kyle said as I left. I was almost to the door when he caught up to me and took hold of my arm. "Hey, what's going on?"

"Just give me a minute." Outside, I bummed a smoke from a guy standing by himself.

Pall Mall. Not my favorite, but better than nothing. My pack lay on the table inside. In the same building as Shelby.

The guy tried to make small talk with me for a moment before flicking his cigarette to the ground. A friendly nod later, he went back into the bar, leaving me to my nasty thoughts.

What? Was this some sort of sick cosmic joke? I looked toward the sky and took in a forceful drag. Revisiting my past was something I was trying to avoid, and now here it was slapping me in the face. I mean, what were the odds that Shelby, who lived hundreds of miles away, would be at the same bar I hadn't even planned to go to? Way too small of a world, I guess. I took one more long pull from the cigarette, hoping it would have some sort of calming effect.

It didn't.

I was just as ticked off as I'd been five minutes ago. I flicked the cigarette to the ground and stomped it out, imagining it was Shelby's face.

Kyle walked through the door, two shots in hand. "Okay, I gave you eight minutes. Are you all right? You looked like you were about to rip that girl's head off." He held one of the shots toward me. "I thought you might need this."

I took the small glass, embarrassment washing through me. "You must think I'm psycho or something. I just was not expecting to see her tonight."

"Do you want to tell me who she is?"

"Long story, but let's just say she is my ex-best friend from a different life and the reason I'm now in Vancouver, but I would rather not talk about it."

A crooked half-smile crept up his face as he lifted his shot into the air. "Here's to keeping the past dead and buried."

I clicked my glass to his. "I will definitely drink to that."

We both downed our shots. The liquor tasted strange, almost bitter as it went down my throat.

He came closer and put his arms around me.

Letting him hold me was a mistake, but his touch was like finding water in the middle of the desert—refreshing yet invoking a deeper thirst. For a moment, I basked in the feeling, breathing him in. He smelled like musk mingled with alcohol. I looked up.

His eyes locked on mine. "You know, you're kind of cute when you're angry." He leaned down and pressed his mouth against mine. His hand came to rest ever so gently on the base of my neck and his lips parted. The warmth of his breath sent a current surging through my body, and I let go of all thoughts of resisting.

I slid my free hand up his neck and through his hair. For a long moment, I was so lost in the kiss that I forgot why I was outside in the first place.

The door opened behind us, and a boisterous group of people came out of the bar, laughing and carrying on.

I backed out of Kyle's embrace.

Shelby was leaving the bar with a guy I'd never seen before.

Anger quickly resurfaced.

Kyle put his finger on my chin and pulled my face back to his. "Forget about it. It's not worth it." His lips met mine again. "Let's go dance." He wove his fingers through mine, led me back into the bar, and down the stairs.

I felt a little dizzy as I followed Kyle's lead out to the dance floor. He steadied me as we swayed back and forth to the music. Closing my eyes, I rested my head against his chest. With the buzz of the alcohol swirling through my veins and Savage Garden's "Truly, Madly, Deeply," playing in the background, I could almost pretend my past didn't matter. All the demons were muted and for this glorious moment I could actually forget.

CHAPTER 7
January 18, 5:00 a.m.
JOE

The song "I Can See Clearly Now" blared out of my radio alarm clock. Stretching, I smiled through a yawn and let the music play. It's one of those songs that reminded me of childhood. Whenever I had a bad day, my mom would push the furniture to the side, pull out her vinyl Johnny Nash album, and turn the record player up as loud as it could go. Then she would drag me into the middle of the living room and make me dance with her until we were both laughing so hard, I couldn't remember what I was upset about in the first place.

As the memory faded the lyrics spoke to me in a fresh way. This song put into words exactly how I felt lately, like my life was finally coming into focus—the rain clouds were gone, and the sun was shining, even if it was the middle of January in Washington.

Yawning deeply, I reached out to pull Susan close.

She wasn't there.

I turned on the light and scanned the room, my gaze landing on the yellow notepad on Susan's nightstand.

Susan was an insomniac. Many times, she would be up by four a.m. just because she was restless. More often than not, I'd find her in the office pouring over work stuff. I hated it because I loved snuggling up to her first thing in the morning. But that was

Susan, a very driven person. I rolled over to her side of the bed and saw a short note written in her elegant penmanship.

Hey, sweetie, I woke up and couldn't sleep, so I went for a jog.

Since I had the house to myself, I cranked up the radio and, like a complete dork, danced around the bedroom. I sang along with the music as I climbed into the shower. I grabbed the overpriced spiced ginger soap Susan recently purchased and lathered myself.

Susan had a high regard for the finer things in life, which was fine by me because her upper management job at Macy's supported it.

I rinsed off quickly and stepped out of the shower, snagging the white towel that hung on the hook next to the tub. I dried off and wrapped the towel around my waist. The bathroom mirror had completely steamed up, so I used Susan's blow-dryer to make a circle big enough to see myself trim my beard. If Susan had her way the beard would be gone, but I preferred a bit of scruff. Not to mention, I looked like a fifteen-year-old without it.

Michael Jackson's "Billie Jean" began to play.

I snapped my fingers to the beat, snatched up the hairbrush, and sang into it, sliding my feet backward into the bedroom. Mid-moonwalk, my foot hit the area rug, my body lurched, and I barely grabbed the towel before it dropped to the floor.

"Nice save." Susan's voice rang out over the music.

I spun around.

She leaned in the doorway, looking sexy in her tight yoga pants and oversized sweatshirt. Her full lips were curved slightly, and her dark eyes danced with amusement.

When Susan was all done up, she looked like she belonged on a runway, but I liked her best the way she was at that moment: no makeup, no designer clothes, hair damp with sweat from her workout. She seemed more real this way. More natural.

She sauntered toward me and gave me a quick peck. "Now that's something you don't see every day."

"You caught me. I'm a closet Michael Jackson groupie."

"It's okay, I won't tell."

"Better not! I can't let information like this get out."

"Silly man." She leaned in for another kiss. "You better finish getting ready for work."

Glancing at the glowing numbers on my alarm, I cursed under my breath. I opened the dresser drawer and grabbed the first clean thing I found. Faded blue jeans and a white V-neck T-shirt.

Susan scrunched her face up.

"What?"

"Are you really going to wear that?"

"Baby, come on." I tilted my head to the side. "I work in a greasy spoon, not the Hilton."

"Whatever." She rolled her eyes and walked into the bathroom.

As I drove to work, I couldn't help but think about the last three years and how much things had changed. More like how much *I* had changed. It was nice to be able to look in the mirror and actually like the man reflecting back at me. Flashbacks of shameful memories from the life I had before I got clean and sober occasionally hit. However, it had become easier to deflect those painful thoughts because that's not who I was anymore. Susan didn't seem to see that, though. If she did, she would have made it to the meeting last night. Why couldn't she see how hard I had worked to get here?

Pulling into the diner parking lot, I noticed Tamara's Cabriolet. Strange. Had she been called in to work again? Poor girl had been working far too much lately.

Instead of entering the restaurant through the back door, I walked through the front.

Tamara wasn't there.

Betty, paced behind the bar, hand on her forehead.

"Hey, Joe." Betty spotted me as soon as I walked in. "My daughter just called. There's an emergency with my granddaughter. I need to go meet her at the hospital and the new girl isn't here yet." Her voice grew more frantic as she talked. "Do you mind if I take off before Jennifer gets here?"

"Yeah, sure, go. And keep me posted."

She gathered her things and motioned toward the only patron in the place. "He hasn't ordered yet."

"I got it, Betty. I'm sure Jennifer will be here soon."

"Thanks, Joe."

What a morning it was turning out to be. Betty's grandchild was in the hospital. Jennifer was late. And where was Tamara? A wave of anxiety hit me. That was definitely her car in the parking lot. Had something happened to her?

I crossed the room and grabbed the coffeepot, trying to shrug off the worried feeling. I poured myself a cup before walking over and refreshing the coffee of the customer. "Have you decided what you want yet, sir?"

He peered up from behind his menu. "Yes. I'll take a western omelet, hash browns, and rye toast."

"All right, I'll go get that started for you." Ten minutes later, I placed the food in front of the man and turned to the clock.

6:45.

Not good. Jennifer should have been here by now.

I called her number from the kitchen.

No answer.

Great. Just perfect. The breakfast rush could arrive any moment, and there was no way I could run this place myself. I didn't want to disturb Trudy with all she was going through lately.

There was always Tamara.

She would come in.

She deserved to be left alone after how hard she worked yesterday and the day before, but it gave me an excuse to make sure she was all right.

I took a deep breath and dialed her number.

Straight to voicemail.

My stomach churned harder. Not only did that mean I was stuck here by myself, but there was also no way for me to know if she was okay.

CHAPTER 8

January 18, 6:53 a.m.

TAMARA

My eyes jerked open to the sound of a car door slamming and panic flooded my mind. Where was I? It was dark, which made it even more disorienting. There was a small window by my feet, and a streetlamp accompanied the morning light.

Déjà vu.

For a moment, I was eleven years old and in the back of my dad's semi, except in the present there was a guy lying next to me.

Oh man, not good.

I was in Kyle's semi, parked right across the street from where I work.

How exactly had I gotten here? Claustrophobia choked my senses. This couldn't be happening. Why was I naked? Seriously? I hadn't planned on sleeping with him.

I had to get out. I scanned the area. Where were my clothes? The rapid eye movement made my head spin, and an intense wave of nausea overtook me. Even so, I was able to locate everything except my shirt. Desperate, I grabbed the first shirt I could find and threw it on. I almost tripped on the way out of the truck. Apparently, I was still drunk, but I didn't care. I had to get out of here.

CHAPTER 9

January 18, 7:02 a.m.

JOE

Three orders. No big deal. I could cook three orders in my sleep. If no one else came in for a while, I'd be fine. But where was Tamara? It didn't make sense that her car was here, but she wasn't. Was she in danger? Had she been abducted? Vancouver could be a dangerous place. The other day I read an article about human trafficking in this area.

I shook my head. Snap out of it, man. Tamara was fine.

Me, on the other hand ... Who was I kidding? There was no way I could run this restaurant by myself.

The hanging bells clanged against the door.

Unbelievable.

We needed to have a better back-up plan for these sorts of situations. As much as I didn't want too, I had to call Trudy.

One ring.

Two rings.

Three rings.

Voicemail.

Really? This was not the way today was supposed to go.

"Hey, Trudy, give me a call. We've got a situation. Jen was a no show, and I can't get ahold of Tamara, call me as soon as you get this."

The hanging bells crashed again.

I imagined ripping them off the door. After slamming my cell phone down, I hurried back into the dining area with the coffeepot. I entered the dining room and stopped mid-step.

Levi Taylor.

So did *not* want to see him right now.

Or ever in normal life.

A few years ago, my sponsor suggested I go through counseling to work through some emotional hang-ups. The counselor I ended up seeing happened to be Levi.

This man knew practically everything about me, and he was sitting in my diner after I had been trying to avoid him. He'd been coming in quite a bit lately, and I would always hide in the back.

I took the orders of the other customers before heading toward Levi's table. "Good morning, sir." I said, pretending not to know him.

"Well, good morning." His expression held a hint of amusement.

Was he enjoying making me squirm? Maybe it was his way of punishing me for not coming to his office anymore. "Would you like some coffee?" I placed a menu in front of him.

"Sure, some coffee, and scrambled eggs with diced tomatoes."

"All right, sir. It may take a few extra minutes. The waitress didn't show up this morning."

"Tamara?" He twisted in the booth to look out the window. "I just saw her."

"No, not Tamara. Wait. You saw her?" I followed his gaze.

Her Volkswagen was gone.

"What was she—?"

The bell clanged against the door. A large, well-dressed gentleman entered, followed by his wife and two children.

"I better seat them."

"Take your time."

"Thanks, Levi." I accidentally let his name slip.

The corners of his mouth twitched, then he looked down and opened his journal.

Twenty-five minutes later, everyone was taken care of, but my mind was still puzzling over Tamara. Levi had seen her? At least I knew she was alive. That was a relief, but something still seemed off to me.

On my way back into the kitchen, my phone rang.

Tamara?

Nope. Trudy.

"Hey, Joe," she said, voice groggy. "I just got your message. I will be on my way as soon as possible."

"Please hurry."

"Will do. I'm sorry," she said through a yawn. "I thought Jennifer was a keeper."

"Yeah, me too. See you in a few."

While the restaurant was slow for the moment, I looked around the kitchen. The graveyard shift cook had failed to load up the refrigerators and the little containers. I stocked everything and then scraped and cleaned the two large grills, the whole time my stomach bunching up in knots as I thought about Tamara.

I needed answers, and as much as I didn't want to talk to Levi, I had to know what he saw.

The diner eventually cleared of everyone except for him. I headed to his table with a fresh pot of coffee and offered him a refill.

"Yes, please." He set his pencil down and looked up from his journal.

"Hey, do you mind if I ask you something?" I filled his cup.

"Not at all."

"You said you saw Tamara earlier?" I slid into the booth across from him.

"Yeah." He shifted in his seat and hesitated before he spoke. "I probably shouldn't have said anything."

"Oh, come on, Levi. It's not like she's one of your clients." My eyes bore into his. "What was she doing?"

He glanced around the empty restaurant and leaned toward me. "I have to say, it seemed odd. She stumbled out of a tractor trailer right before I came in."

"A semi?" That was not like Tamara. The slow burn in my stomach that had nagged at me all morning ignited into a wildfire. "What did you do?"

"Nothing." His face flushed. "She staggered to her car and drove off."

"She *staggered* to her car, and you just let her drive away? What if she was hurt?" I dialed Tamara's number.

It started ringing.

A good sign.

But then it rang and rang and rang.

Finally, her voicemail picked up. "It's Tamara's phone. You know what to do."

I stood up. "Hey, Tam. It's me again. I'm worried about you. Call me as soon as possible. If you don't, I'm coming by your house when I get off today."

Why was I so upset about this turn of events? Just yesterday I told Tamara she needed to get a life, but for some reason my stomach turned in on itself over the situation.

Levi leaned forward. "I'm sorry. It just all happened so fast and—"

"I just don't get it. Aren't you supposed to help people? Don't you have some sort of oath to uphold or something?"

"This really isn't about Tamara, is it?"

"Don't do that. Not here. I have to go call my boss."

"Sure, but Joe?" He took out a card from his wallet and held it out. "Just in case you ever need to talk."

I looked at it hard for a second, my mouth twisting sardonically. It was Levi's way of saying I still needed help.

Maybe he was right. And Susan too. Maybe I hadn't changed as much as I thought.

I snatched the card and walked away. Back in the kitchen, I called Trudy. "Where are you?" My voice nearly broke.

"I'm pulling in now. I picked up Frank and Richard on the way. You sounded pretty stressed out, so I rallied the troops. They'll take care of the kitchen while I run the floor. You can go home earlier than you planned."

I let out a deep sigh. Getting off early gave some relief, though my chest still felt tight. At least I'd be free to go check on Tamara, but what would I find? Was it even right to just drop by unannounced? I guess at the moment I was too concerned to care about boundaries. "Thanks, Trudy. Something came up."

"Perfect, but before you go, I need to talk to you."

"Understood."

After she hung up, I grabbed my coat and waited in the dining area.

My phone rang again.

Betty, with an update. Everything was going to be okay with her grandchild. Apparently, her daughter was a new mother and freaked out at the slightest things.

Trudy walked in, Frank and Richard in tow. Trudy was in her early fifties, with a hefty build and dark-brown hair that she always wore up in a loose French twist. She was usually upbeat and energetic, but today her shoulders drooped, and tiredness weighed down her features.

Guilt punched me in the gut. She had a lot going on right now. I wished I hadn't had to wake her. But there wasn't another option.

"Joe, can I speak to you in my office?" Her voice seemed strained.

"Of course." I followed her down the hall to the small office wedged behind the storeroom and closed the door behind us.

She kept her back toward me, silently staring at the wall. Finally, she turned, dark eyes full of tears.

"What's going on?"

"I'm running this place into the ground is what's going on." She buried her face in her hands.

Trudy had been like a second mom to me. Three years ago,

when everyone else turned me away, she talked her jerk of a then-husband into giving me a job. Last year she finally left him and was granted the diner in the divorce. Though it would have been a better deal for her if she knew how to run it.

I placed my hand on her shoulder. "This is just a hiccup. People are unreliable sometimes. You're doing the best you can."

"It's not just the Jennifer thing. I have no idea what I'm doing. I need help."

"Then I'll help you." Ideas had been floating around in my mind for a while about how things could improve.

She looked up at me with mascara running black rivers down her face. "You will?"

"Of course." I grabbed the box of tissues off her desk and offered it to her. "Anything you need."

"Are you sure?" She pulled out a tissue and blotted her eyes and nose. "It will mean a lot more hours. Will Susan be okay with that?"

"She'll be fine with it." At least I hoped she would be.

Trudy pulled herself together. "Look at me. I'm a mess. Didn't you say you needed to be somewhere?"

My mind instantly shifted back to Tamara. "Actually, yes." I followed Trudy back into the dining room. I was almost to the door when a guy with messy, dirty-blond hair stumbled in, reeking of alcohol.

"Excuse me," he said to Trudy. "I'm looking for Tamara. Is she working today?"

She eyed him up and down. "Today is her day off. Is there something I can do for you?"

"I need to get ahold of her. Could you give her my number?" He grabbed a napkin off the counter and scribbled something down.

"Not gonna happen," I muttered under my breath and strode toward them.

He held the napkin out to Trudy.

I snatched it from his hand. "Actually, I'm on my way over to her house right now. I can give it to her."

"Who are you?" He lunged toward the piece of paper in my hand.

I held it out of his reach. "Tamara's friend."

"Okay, 'Tamara's friend,'" the little man said with air quotes. "Just make sure she gets it. I need to talk to her."

"Sure. I'll let her know." What had Tamara been thinking? The dude looked like a sleaze.

I turned and headed to my car, his phone number clutched in my hand. Acid churned in my stomach as I drove away. He probably had a girl lined up in every town he stopped in. Tamara definitely did *not* need to be involved with a guy like that.

I crumpled the napkin and threw it out the window.

CHAPTER 10

January 18, 9:02 a.m.

TAMARA

When I got back to my apartment, I popped a few sleeping pills and went straight to bed. Sleep was peaceful at first—pitch-black nothingness. But then I began to dream an ominous force was chasing me down a dimly lit corridor. Violent accusations echoed off the walls behind me. Adrenaline pulsed through my limbs, fueling me with strength to move faster.

Suddenly, a light shone bright at the end of the corridor.

I ran with all my remaining strength toward it, but a door slammed in front of me, locking me out.

A man cloaked in black appeared before me.

I screamed and turned back, but he was there too, as if he were all around me. I looked away from him, but only darkness surrounded my vision.

Bam, bam, bam.

The sound came from behind the door. Terror rippled through me. I had to get through, but it wouldn't budge. Tormenting cries filled the air, overtaking me. My knees buckled, and I fell to the ground.

Bam, bam. Someone pounded on my apartment door, shaking me awake.

Even through the foggy haze of consciousness, I suddenly became aware of every part of my aching body.

Bam, bam.

The noise was like piercing needles in my hungover brain. I rolled over and put the pillow over my head.

Who would want to see me at this hour? Kyle, maybe?

No. Of course not. He didn't know where I lived.

Why was I such an idiot? How did I get in the back of Kyle's semi? I glanced under the blanket. Why was I wearing Kyle's T-shirt?

I recoiled mentally. Which meant he had my shirt. Which meant there was proof that last night had happened. Which meant there was one more mistake to add to my list.

I hated the list.

"Tamara, are you in there?" A man's voice echoed through the door.

I stuffed my face deeper into my mattress, trying hard to block out the world.

"Tamara." The voice persisted.

Like the dream, it seemed to surround me. I just wanted everything to go away.

"Tamara. Tamara."

I rolled over and climbed out of bed, feeling disoriented. Something felt different. As if last night's mistake had been bigger than most.

It was probably just the nightmare still looming over my mind like a nebulous shadow.

"Hold on. I'm coming." I made my way to the door. "Who is it?"

"It's Joe."

I froze. Joe? What would he be doing here? Did he know about Kyle? The thought sent my heart racing.

No, of course he didn't. I'd been careful.

I opened the door a crack. "Joe? What's going on?"

"Are you okay?" He hesitated. "You look awful."

"Don't you have a way of making a girl feel good?" I muttered.

"I've been trying to call you."

"I turned my cell to silent when I got home. I needed to sleep without interruption." I gave him a pointed look, hoping he would take the hint. Visitors weren't welcome at the moment.

"Oh, yeah, sorry." His face reddened. "Uh, can I come in? I'm worried about you."

I swallowed hard, a pit opening up in my stomach. He had to know something. But how? "Joe, thank you, but I really would rather you didn't. Don't worry about me. I'm okay." I forced a smile.

"Tamara, please." His tone lowered. "I need to talk to you about something."

My heart sank. Against my judgment, I stepped away from the door to let him enter. "Give me a minute?"

"Take your time." He set his keys and cell phone on the wooden chest that doubled as my coffee table.

I ran my fingers through my tangled hair as I crossed the small room. Closing myself in the bathroom, I looked in the mirror. My hair went every which way, and there were dark circles under my bloodshot eyes. I splashed water on my face and grabbed the Neutrogena to wash away last night's filth. I ran a hairbrush through my hair and threw it up in a ponytail before applying extra concealer to the dark circles. I dabbed on cover up and brushed on mascara. They did wonders to my appearance, but I couldn't help feeling embarrassed that Joe had seen me before my little routine.

Placing my hand on the bathroom door, I hesitated. The puzzle clicked into place. My car. My stupid, stupid car had still been in the diner parking lot when Joe got to work.

No, the car wasn't stupid. I was. Why hadn't I parked it behind Kyle's semi? Oh, that's right because I had no idea how I got there. My head pounded and my hands shook. I grabbed the Tylenol and tried to unscrew the top as I walked back into the living room. Childproof lids should be optional for people who don't have kids. "Dumb thing won't open," I groaned.

"Here, let me help you." He took the bottle, unscrewed the top with ease, and handed it back to me. "Just gotta be smarter than the inanimate object." He flashed a crooked smile.

My eyes narrowed. "Very funny." I shook a few pills into my hand on my way to the kitchenette and poured a glass of water. "Cut me some slack. I just woke up. My brain is not fully awake."

"Uh-huh." He nodded as his grin widened. "You just keep telling yourself that."

"So that's how it is? You came over to mess with me first thing in the morning while I don't have all my wits about me." I popped the pills in my mouth and took a big gulp of water. "You could have waited till Wednesday for that."

Joe's expression grew serious.

"What?"

He was quiet for a moment, hazel eyes deepening with an emotion that was hard to read. "It's hard to explain. You've seemed down lately. Yesterday at work, you just seemed sad, distant, almost lost." His gaze held mine for a beat too long.

My stomach clenched into a knot. Hopefully the feeling of panic wasn't apparent on my face. "I thought I did a pretty good job, considering the circumstances." I crossed the room, sat down on my small love seat, and motioned for him to do the same.

"You did fine." He settled in next to me. "You kept all your orders straight. You were friendly and pleasant, but it was deeper than that. There was an emptiness behind your eyes, like something was eating you from the inside out. Then you had to work another double with that creep, Anthony. I just had a bad feeling about that."

So, all this was about how I was at the diner yesterday? That I could handle. "I appreciate the concern. Maybe I was a bit off, so thank you for letting me know. I'll work on it." I stood, hoping to end the conversation.

"I wasn't finished."

"Oh." Blood rushed to my face. He knew about last night. There was no other explanation. I sat back down.

"I know it's none of my business but when I came in to work today, I saw your car in the parking lot. You weren't in the diner, so I called you a couple of times. No answer." He turned and looked me in the eyes.

It was okay. All he had were his assumptions. He didn't have to know what really happened.

What would he think of me if he did?

He'd probably judge me. My heart broke a little at the thought, but I kept a poker face.

"Later, Levi Taylor showed up. He let it slip that he saw you stumble out of a semi-truck across the street."

I sucked in a sharp breath and leaned forward, arms crossing over my abdomen—holding myself together. A lock of hair fell loose across my face. This was so much worse than I thought. Not only did Joe know about Kyle but Levi did too. I might as well engrave a scarlet letter to my forehead and call it good. "Levi Taylor saw me climbing out of Kyle's semi? Could someone please just shoot me now?"

"Oh, come now, Tamara, don't beat yourself up." Joe swept his hand over my back.

A lonely tear slid down my cheek. My gaze met his.

He tucked the lock of hair behind my ear. "It kills me to see you like this."

His words affected me deeper than I expected. "Why do you even care?"

Pain and empathy flashed in his eyes. "I just do."

"You really shouldn't." I looked away, breaking the intensity of the moment. "I'm so not worth it."

"Why do you do that?" He sounded almost angry.

"Do what?"

"Put yourself down like that. Because I think you *are* worth it, okay?" His voice was thick.

"You don't even know me." As I said this, protective walls

49

erected around my heart. I wasn't ready to let him past my barrier and I didn't want to have an emotional collapse in front of him.

"You're right, I don't know you. I mean, I do, but not really. I know you're a good person, and you have a good heart, but you keep people at arm's length." He fell silent, closed his eyes, and took a deep breath. "I just want you to know that I'm here for you, if you do want to let someone in."

We sat in silence for a moment. I'd never seen Joe like this before. I was used to the happy-go-lucky, laid-back side of him that he showed at work, or occasionally outside of work. Here I was, accusing him of not knowing me, but maybe I didn't know him. He was definitely more insightful than I had given him credit for. And maybe, just maybe, he did know me.

"You're right, Joe. But I keep people out for good reasons. Believe me, you don't want to know what's in me. It's not pretty." My voice cracked on the last couple of words.

Joe placed his hand on my back again, this time with more caution. "Hey, it's okay," he said tenderly. "We all carry stuff inside that's not pretty. And we all have been hurt by people we trusted. But it's a bad idea to keep it bottled up. You should talk about it. Believe me, it can help."

"What, to like a therapist?"

"I meant to a friend. Say me, for instance."

He deserved a lot of credit. He was being sweet, kind, and an all-around good guy. And I was— being a complete jerk.

I reached over and grabbed my pack of cigarettes. "You want one?" Though Joe wasn't a smoker, it seemed polite to offer.

He shook his head.

"I can guarantee you don't want to know my stuff." I walked to the window next to the bed, opened it, and lit up. "You say I'm a good person, but you have no idea the things I've done. You just don't know what it's like to screw up like I have. The worst mistake you probably ever made was putting cheddar cheese on a Reuben."

He laughed a humorless laugh. "Is that really what you think?

You act like you're the only one that's been through anything."
He grabbed his keys off the wooden chest and fiddled with the
different circles linked together, as if he was distracting himself
from something that hurt.

Had I offended him? I let the silence drag out for a moment.

"Tamara, I'm an alcoholic."

What was he talking about? He'd never touched alcohol when
I was around. I snuffed out my cigarette and sat back down next
to him. "You don't drink."

"Not anymore, because I do stupid things when I do."

"There is no way you've done anything worse than me."

"How about murder?"

My heart stopped for a second. "Murder?"

"Abigail Marie Phillips. At least that's what Kayla wanted to
name her. She was my girlfriend at the time." He fidgeted with the
keys, keeping his eyes on them as he spoke. "She was conceived
after a party. We were both drunk." Joe finally looked at me, eyes
welling. "Kayla wanted to keep her. She was so excited when she
told me the name she'd picked out. But I wasn't ready for a child.
I was only nineteen. I could barely take care of myself." He
swallowed hard and set the keys back down on the table. "I
pressured her into having an abortion."

"Joe." I said his name softly as if to cushion my words.
"That's not murder."

He wiped his eyes. "It sure felt like it at the time. It's possibly
the most selfish thing I'd ever done. The guilt ripped me to shreds,
and then tore us apart. That was when I started drinking heavily. I
dropped out of college and made a complete mess of my life."

I stared at him for a long moment. Who was this guy? Why
did he seem to genuinely care about me? Yesterday he had
defended me to Anthony, and now he was here in my apartment
spilling his deepest secrets.

"I've been clean and sober three years. And it's because I have
people in my life that cared enough about me to reach out and to
love me, even in my most ugly moments."

My chest tightened with longing. What would that even feel like? To have someone love me like that?

"If you don't want to talk about it, I understand. But it can help."

"I'm not sure if anything can help me."

"It never hurts to try." His mouth curled a tiny bit, and my heart softened even more.

"You said the other day that you could tell something was wrong?" I reached for another smoke.

"Yes."

"The night before, I couldn't sleep because I kept thinking about my last night at home when I was a kid." I lit up the cigarette and inhaled a long drag. My heart hurt at the thought of talking about it. How crazy that something that happened years ago could still feel so fresh. My mother told me once that time healed all wounds, but if she were in front of me now, I'd call her a liar. Time hadn't healed this wound. In fact, it was just as swollen and oozing as the day it was inflicted. "That's when everything really changed for me. I mean, life had always been hard. One of my earliest memories was sitting on the couch, squished between my siblings, blaring the television to drown out my parents fighting. But I kept quiet and did what I needed to do to fend off the abuse. I learned young that if I did everything right, I'd get hit a lot less."

Joe placed his hand on my arm, warm and comforting. His hand felt like the only thing that anchored me to the present moment.

The rest of me was a sixteen-year-old girl, lost and broken, trying to sleep in a house full of noise. If I let go, I could still hear the slamming of the door and my father's accusing tone.

"That night, I was almost asleep when my father's voice boomed through the house ranting about how someone was going to pay. I knew in my guts someone was about to get beat. I figured it was one of the boys. They always were getting in trouble for something. I shoved the pillow against my ears and tried to ignore it."

For a few seconds, I zoned out on my cigarette, watching the smoke twirl upward and then disappear. Joe stayed silent, holding the space for me. Like somehow, he knew I needed the momentary reprieve from the painful memory.

"That was when I heard my sister's trembling voice. She said she didn't know where it came from and that it wasn't hers. I couldn't believe it. My father had beaten my brothers for years, and I had even been hit on occasion, but I'd never seen him lay a hand on Dakota before that night. She was the baby of our family."

Joe's gaze was full of empathy, as if he could feel my pain as I shared it.

I closed my eyes for a moment and all I could see was my sister. What I would give to turn back the clock. I swallowed back the emotions that were trying to come.

"'Don't you lie to me!' My dad yelled, but the sound of him hitting her seemed louder than his voice. I had to do something, Joe. I couldn't just lay there and hear her be beaten half to death." I couldn't stop the tears from spilling from my eyes now.

Joe's arm came around my shoulder.

Warmth washed through me, and suddenly all I wanted to do was curl up in his arms.

"I bolted up in bed and ran down the hall before I could think better of it. The scene was horrific. My dad's hulking frame towered over Dakota as she stood crying, blood dripping from her chin. Mom stood off to the side, hand over her mouth, eyes wide in terror. As usual, she wasn't doing anything to stop him. Something inside of me broke. Dakota was too small to take what I knew my dad was capable of. He held up a tiny plastic bag containing a yellowish powder. I'd seen her hanging out with a rougher crowd lately, but I didn't think she was dumb enough to do drugs. Dakota denied it was hers, but something in me knew that she was lying. I felt so guilty. If only I had kept a closer eye on her, it wouldn't have happened."

"But you were a child too."

I jammed my cigarette into the ashtray. Back then it didn't matter that I was a child. I had to save my sister. Bracing myself, I had stepped into the dim light of the living room, unable to stop the lie that was forming on my lips. "I told him it was mine and took the beating for my sister. After all, it was my fault."

Joe sucked in a sharp breath. "Tamara, how can you say—?"

I held up my hand. "Save your judgments until you hear the rest of the story. I ran away that night to my boyfriend, Ryan's house. I couldn't handle facing my dad after that. I mean, I'd been beaten before, but this was more. I had always been the 'good one.' But from that moment on, if I stayed, I would be treated as 'the one who brought drugs into his house.' The abuse would have only gotten worse for me.

About a month into shacking up with Ryan, I found out he was the drug dealer that had been supplying my sister."

Joe's eyes widened, but he said nothing.

"The night I found out about it, I waited till Ryan was asleep and stole a bunch of money from his wallet to survive on. That night I looked for my sister at my parents' house, but she wasn't there. I searched for Dakota for hours, but in the end, I had to leave town before Ryan found me. I abandoned my little fourteen-year-old sister to a life of abuse and drugs."

"It's not your fault, Tamara. You need to let go of the guilt."

"I wish I could believe that, but I should have stayed. I should have tried harder to save her."

"I understand why you would feel that way, but at the time you did the best that you could."

Suddenly I was more aware of his hand resting on the middle of my back. "You think so?" I asked, leaning toward him.

"Absolutely."

"Thank you for listening." I tipped my head onto his shoulder.

He lifted his arm and put it around me.

"I think I do feel a little better." I basked in the warmth of his touch as he traced circles on my arm.

A conflicting mixture of comfort and guilt worked its way through me. It was nice to be held by someone I felt safe with. But at the same time, it felt wrong, too intimate for people that were just friends.

Joe's phone rang and he jumped, then answered it.

I sat up and scooted over a tad, putting an appropriate distance between us.

"Hey, baby." He listened for a beat. "Yeah, I'm out and about right now. I'll head home soon and get it started." He listened intently for a few moments. "No, thankfully Trudy sent me home early. I have so much stuff I've got to do for tonight."

Obviously, he was talking to his girlfriend, Susan, but it seemed like he was trying not to tell her he was at my house.

"Okay, hun. I'll pick some up on the way home. Yeah, love you too." Joe hung up and looked toward me. "Sorry about that."

"No biggie." I shrugged. "So why didn't you mention where you were?"

"You noticed that, huh?"

"Yup."

He raked a hand through his hair and blew out a sigh. "I don't know. Susan gets a little weird sometimes, and I didn't want to start a fight. But you're right, I should have just told her."

"I'm sorry. I shouldn't have asked."

Joe stood and grabbed his keys. "What are you doing today?"

"Nothing, really."

"You should hang out with me. I'm having a get-together at my house later on, and I could use some help getting things ready."

"But you just said ... Susan? Wouldn't that make her uncomfortable?"

"Come on, I don't want to leave you here by yourself. And

plus, there's a guy I want you to meet." An impish smile spread across his face.

I smacked him on the arm. He couldn't be serious after the last date he set me up on.

"I'm joking, but I could use some help, and Susan is working until four." Joe reached his hand out to help me up.

"You're not going to take no for an answer, are you?"

"Nope."

"Fine." I took ahold of his hand and pulled myself up. "What's the occasion?"

"It's kinda my birthday."

"Your birthday? Isn't your birthday in May?"

He laughed. "May 18th. This is my sobriety birthday, three years today."

"Oh, wow, I didn't realize. That's awesome, Joe. Good job."

"Thanks." He tilted his head toward the door. "We should get going. I have a ton of prep work still to do once we get back to my house."

CHAPTER 11

January 18, 1:30 p.m.

TAMARA

On the way to Joe's house, I stopped by Dutch Bros. and ordered a 911. Six shots of coffee to get me through the next five hours or so. Caffeine was possibly running a close second when it came to favorite vices, behind my smokes. Who needed sleep when I could just dose up on caffeine?

Joe lived in a two-story townhouse in a nicer part of town. The decor was modern and chic, but kind of stiff. I was scared to touch anything for fear of breaking it. It did *not* match his personality.

"Nice place." I should *not* have let him inside my dumpy apartment. Sipping my coffee, I followed him down the hall.

"You like it? Susan does all the decorating."

Portraits of him and Susan, mounted in elegant glass frames lined the walls. In the pictures, Joe almost looked as if he was playing dress-up in someone else's life. Both he and Susan reminded me of someone you'd see in a Banana Republic layout in a fashion magazine. Susan was gorgeous, of course. Jet-black hair in a sleek cut that framed symmetrical features and dark eyes. Her full lips smiled down at me as if I was a welcomed guest, but there was something about her that said she could rip me up and throw me out with a grin still on those lips. Had Joe completely thought through inviting me over?

Suddenly, I wasn't so sure about meeting Susan. Especially not in this context. Here I was, in her house, alone with her boyfriend. Somehow, it just felt wrong.

"She has good taste." I said politely, if not completely genuine. I chewed on the edge of the coffee cup to keep from saying something I might regret.

"I'll give you a tour later, once the food is prepared."

"Susan will be home in a few hours, right?" Was I even dressed nice enough for this gathering? I had thrown on black jeggings, an oversized hoodie, and knock-off UGG boots. The guests I imagined in this house wore things like sweater vests and cardigans. Maybe I could help Joe and fake an illness before Susan or any of their guests arrived.

"Yup." Joe flipped on the lights.

The kitchen was spacious, with plenty of counter space and an island in the middle of the room. The cabinets were black; the countertops, saffron and ebony marble.

I draped my purse over the back of a chair and set my keys on the island.

Joe opened the door of the stainless-steel fridge and pulled out a bundle of celery stalks. "Can I trust you with dicing the veggies?" His lips twitched at the edges.

"I think I can handle it." I tried to take the celery out of his hand, but he kept hold of it for a few extra beats. Was he flirting? What a stupid thought. What was wrong with me? Why was I reading into his actions all of a sudden? *He's just a friend, Tamara.* He had a beautiful girlfriend, who he had a wonderful life with. He was too great of a guy to throw all that away, flirting around with a girl like me. I didn't have a thing on Susan.

Joe moved to a hanging basket full of avocados, squash, and onions. He picked out an onion and grabbed two cutting boards on the way back to the island. He slid one down in front of me and laid the other kitty-corner to it.

He was just acting like his happy-go-lucky, playful self. Nothing had changed.

Or had it?

Knock it off, Tamara.

Acting confident in my cooking skills, I rinsed the celery in the sink. Truthfully, I was pretty incompetent in the kitchen. My diet—when I wasn't at work, eating what Joe cooked me— consisted of things that could be microwaved and fast food, primarily Taco Bell and Subway. I wasn't going to admit that to Joe, though. I had already shown enough weakness for one day. I set the celery on the chopping block and whacked off both ends of the stalks.

"Trudy asked me to help take over some of her managerial duties today."

I stopped mid-chop. "Joe, that's great." The words tasted like a lie. Working with Joe was pretty much the highlight of my week. I didn't want things to change, especially not after this morning. "So." I glanced down at the celery. "Does that mean you won't be working as a cook anymore?"

"Everything will pretty much stay the same for now. I'll just be working more hours."

"Oh." I let out a breath I hadn't realized I'd been holding. "You already work full-time, though."

Joe set the onion on the cutting board, lopped off both ends, and cut it directly down the middle. "I know, but I could use the extra hours, plus its good management experience."

"True. And Trudy definitely needs the help."

We exchanged a knowing glance.

"What are you doing?" Joe's eyebrows pinched together.

"What?"

"You're mangling the celery."

My shoulders inched up toward my ears. "Yeah, I really don't know what I'm doing."

"Let me show you." Joe stepped around the island. "First of

all, there is a proper way to hold a knife." He gently curled his hand around my hand holding the knife.

Butterflies swirled around in my stomach. Why did I like the feeling of his touch?

Susan would definitely freak out if she showed up right now.

"Oh, is there?" I slid my hand out from under his. "School me then, Yoda." I smirked sarcastically.

His grin mirrored mine as he picked up the knife and cleared most of the celery, leaving only two stalks.

"Okay, this is how you were holding it." He grabbed the knife, his grin spreading wider across his face. "It's fine to hold it like this if you want to look like Norman Bates from Psycho."

"Wow, that bad, huh?"

He pointed the knife toward the already cut celery. "Just ask the celery. It was screaming-in-the-shower terrifying."

I laughed and punched his arm. "Are you going to tease me all afternoon, or are you going to show me how to do this?"

He spent a few minutes instructing on the do's and don'ts of slicing and dicing and then turned the knife back over to me.

Hours later, I lounged on a stool at the island as Joe prepared the final dish. I checked the clock. 3:26. If I left in ten minutes, I would be gone fifteen minutes before Susan was scheduled to arrive, and I wouldn't have to deal with any weirdness, a.k.a. neurotic-jealous-girlfriend drama.

Actually, Susan was probably a nice person—or why would Joe be with her?—but that didn't mean she and I were going to be BFFs or something. Besides, after today, I was pretty sure Joe had already taken that position.

Joe stood crosswise from me, stirring eggs into a brownie mix. "Why is it that brownies always taste so much better before they're cooked?" Joe dipped his finger in the mixture, brought out a glob of chocolate goo and licked it off.

"You're hilarious."

"I'm serious. Why do you think people want to lick the spoon?" He dipped the plastic spatula into the batter. "Here, try it." He lifted a scoop out of the bowl and brought it close to my mouth, but instead of giving me a taste, he smeared the chocolate mixture across my face.

"Oh no, you didn't!" I sprang up from my seat, yanked the spatula out of his hand, and chased him around the island.

He turned, caught ahold of me, and unsuccessfully tried to wrestle the spatula out of my hand.

I attempted to break free from his grasp, but he had me in a bear hug from behind. I couldn't help but crack up. I struggled for another minute to reach his face with the spoon and finally dabbed him.

He roared with laughter and loosened his grip.

Someone cleared their throat loudly.

Susan? So. Not. Good.

She stood in the doorway, arms crossed, face creased into a scowl.

Joe straightened up. "Hey, baby. This is Tamara. She was just helping me get ready for the party."

"Is that what they're calling it these days?" Her gaze darted back and forth between the two of us.

Tension wrapped around me like a straitjacket. This was exactly what I'd wanted to avoid. I knew that look she gave us. It was the same look I wore the day I caught Danny with Shelby.

But I was nothing like Shelby.

I racked my brain for an excuse to leave the room. "Hey, nice to meet you, Susan. I was just about to head out for a cigarette." I grabbed my purse from the back of the chair and flung it over my shoulder.

Joe threw me a cheesy grin. "You might want to wash your face first."

Anger radiated from Susan's severe eyes.

She had every right to be ticked off. I can just imagine what she must be thinking. I walked toward the door, wiping the chocolate off my face with my hand.

As soon as I crossed the doorway, Susan tore into Joe. "What is going on here?"

"Calm down. Nothing is going on, okay?" Joe's voice elevated. "Like I said, she was helping me out. We were just messing around. It was harmless."

"It didn't look harmless to me." Her tone became sharper.

"Relax." Joe's said, his voice low.

Closing the door behind me, I could no longer make out the words. What was I thinking? I should have given myself more time. If I had just left fifteen minutes ago, none of this would have happened.

I rounded the corner and pulled out my smokes. I ran my finger over the 99 emblem on the front of the pack. That number once had seemed like a symbol of hope. Now it ridiculed me, reminding me how this was the way my life really was. Always in the wrong place at the wrong time.

How could Susan even be the least bit insecure? She was even prettier in person than in the pictures on her walls. If Joe was going after me, that would be like trading in a Maserati for a jalopy.

I had to get out of here and forget today ever happened. All of it. Even the good parts. Especially the good parts. Being close to people was dangerous. I was on my own in this world.

I turned toward my car and dug through my purse for my keys.

Where were they?

I opened my purse farther and looked harder.

No.

I had left my keys in the middle of the kitchen island.

CHAPTER 12

January 18, 4:02 p.m.

TAMARA

Joe's frustrated voice carried to the porch as I stepped up. "You're being ridiculous. I'm not going to stop being her friend."

"I wasn't born yesterday, Joe! I saw the way you were acting with her!"

Maybe I should just call a cab and get my car tomorrow, after things had cooled down. Gnawing on my lower lip, I stared at the doorknob. No. That would be cowardly. Not to mention I didn't have the extra money for a taxi. I pushed the door open and took a few steps down the hall.

"Can we please just let it drop for now? Everyone is going to be here in less than an hour."

A loud crash came from the kitchen, like someone had thrown a dish.

I hesitated mid-stride. Maybe if I just tiptoed backward—

"You obviously care about your friends more than you care about us. I am sick of being in second place." Susan rounded the corner.

Perfect. She probably thought I was there the whole time, eavesdropping. "Oh, um." I stumbled over my words. "I am so sorry. I was about to go."

She scowled in my direction and pushed passed me out the door.

Had I just caused a breakup? Joe didn't need this right now—not today. I wanted to get my keys and bolt, but could I leave Joe alone after all of this? Would he even still want me here? "Joe?" I crept down the hallway toward the kitchen. "I just need my keys."

Chocolate goo splattered the island, and broken shards of glass combined with the sticky mixture speckled the floor.

Joe stood at the sink, filling a bowl with steaming water. "I'm so sorry, Tamara," he said, voice full of humiliation. "I just don't think sometimes."

My heart sank, heavy with the hurt apparent on his face.

Had Susan thrown the brownie mix at him?

"Hey, none of that." I wanted to reach out to him and comfort him the way he'd comforted me earlier, but if Susan came back, that would make things worse. I glanced down the hallway toward the door and then over at my keys.

Could I actually leave him with this mess? Worse than that could I leave him in the middle of his pain?

"We don't usually fight like this." Joe's eyes stayed on the bowl overflowing with water in the sink. "I don't know what to do."

His tone reminded me of the way my mom acted after a fight with my dad. Always trying to make him look better. It never worked for her, though. Just like it wasn't working for Joe now. Susan was angry, understandably, but she'd taken their fight too far. "It will work out," I said, but inwardly I wasn't sure I wanted the words to be true.

"Do you want to know what's really messed up?" His gaze met mine, his expression tortured. "Within an hour my house is going to be filled with people celebrating my three years of sobriety, and all I can think about is how good a drink sounds right about now."

I walked across the kitchen. As much as I wanted to leave and pretend this day never happened, I couldn't. Joe needed me.

"Susan will be back, and for right now, I'm here for you." I turned off the faucet, took the bowl of water away from Joe and dumped a little out. "Let's just get this place cleaned up for now." I grabbed a washcloth from the sink.

"See? That's what I love about you. You're so laid-back," he said with a half-smile, the comparison clear in his voice.

"I am laid-back about some things, but if you tick me off, I can be pretty scary. I almost punched a girl in the face last night at the bar." I ran the washcloth along the wall and wrung it out over the water.

"I would've liked to see that. Somehow I just can't imagine you in a bar fight." Joe fetched another washcloth and cleaned the mess on the floor.

"I may be little, but I pack a punch."

"I'm sure you do." Joe smiled.

"What, you wanna go?" I put up my fists. "I had to fight my two older brothers growing up, so I'm pretty sure I can take you down."

"Step off, girl." His grin widened. "We've got work to do."

"Fine." I straightened. "You're just scared."

"You may be right." Joe grabbed the broom out of a small closet and swept the glass into a pile. "How many siblings do you have?"

"Three brothers and a sister. Five of us."

He quit sweeping for a moment, a thoughtful expression lining his features.

"What?" I wiped the last of the chocolate off the wall.

"It seems the more I learn about you, the more there is to know."

"Oh, come on." I placed the washcloth into the bowl and brought it to the sink. "After this morning, you know everything there is to know about me."

His eyes narrowed into slits. "That's doubtful."

"Whatever, what about your family?" I held the dustpan steady for him as he swept glass shards into it.

Joe took the dustpan from me, dumped the glass into the garbage and gave the floor another wipe with the washcloth.

"Do you have any siblings?"

"Nope. It was just me and my mom growing up. My dad was never in the picture." Joe washed his hands and then grabbed a few plates of food from the fridge.

Sad. But what was worse—having a father like mine or one that didn't care enough to stick around? "That must have been hard." I followed his lead into the living room where he placed the food on a beautiful glass table.

"Not really. My mom was good enough to fill the role of both parents. Besides, she ran away from my dad when she was pregnant with me because he beat her."

I gasped. "When she was pregnant? That's terrible." We walked back into the kitchen for more platters of food.

"When I was thirteen years old, she finally told me the story. But she also made it clear that she had forgiven him long ago, and she begged me to do the same."

I thought about the people who had hurt me. Could I even consider forgiving them? The anger that I held against them gave me strength to keep running. Yet there was something compelling about the idea. Honestly, though, that kind of forgiveness didn't seem humanly possible.

"She sounds like an amazing woman."

"That was the biggest thing she taught me. She always said, 'God has forgiven me of so much, who am I to hold a grudge?'"

"So, she's religious?"

"I guess you could say that. She practically raised me in church. Sunday mornings, Wednesday nights, if the doors were open, we were there."

I took a deep breath. I'd faced my fair share of heartache in my short life, and I tended to blame God for it.

Joe seemed deep in thought as he arranged the last of the food, placing the biscuits between the smoked salmon dip and mini sandwiches.

Was he thinking about his mom? His absent, abusive father? Or Susan? Was she coming back before the party started?

I wanted to ask him what was on his mind but bringing up a painful subject right before everyone was supposed to show up didn't seem like the best idea.

I reached for a cracker, topped it with dip, and shoved it in my mouth. "Yum." Joe was a good cook, sure, but I had only experienced his diner food, which was pretty basic. The spread before me now was a gourmet feast. "You are a fantastic cook. Why are you wasting your talents at the diner?"

He shrugged. "Guess I like the environment."

"The environment?" He had to be joking. The best part of the Highway 99 Diner were the customers, and he was stuck in the back most of the time.

He smiled apologetically, as if trying to avoid the question.

"Seriously, though, where did you learn to cook like this?"

"My mom taught me." He took a seat on the couch. "She was a cook too, but in a much nicer restaurant."

"I have got to meet this woman." I plopped down on the couch next to him.

"I wish you could, but ..." He turned toward me. "She died in a car accident a few weeks before my eighteenth birthday."

My heart constricted. "Oh, Joe, I'm sorry." I took hold of his hand.

His gaze fell on my hand, and his fingers curled gently around mine. "I still miss her every day."

Joe and I both knew what it was like to stand alone in the world. But I had run away from my family, while his had been taken from him.

"It happened almost nine years ago now, but it still hurts to talk about it." A glistening tear ran down his face unto his manicured beard. Reaching up, I removed it with a fingertip, and an electrical current passed through me. I searched his eyes. Had he felt it too?

The only thing I saw was the inner storm he was struggling to hide.

The doorbell chimed.

Joe closed his eyes, clenched my hand a little tighter, and let it go. With a sigh, he got up from the couch and disappeared down the hall.

"Hey, hey." A familiar voice echoed.

I couldn't place it, though.

"Congrats on the big day, man. Three years. Good job!"

"Thanks, Caleb."

Oh, wonderful. Of course, he would be here. Caleb was Joe's best friend, and one of the people that he had set me up with. He scored zero on the attraction scale. Not that he was ugly, just too skinny for my taste. A nice guy, but we had very little in common. Though he had spilled a glass of red wine on my favorite dress, he still tried to get together again, leaving me messages a couple of times. I had never returned his calls, which made seeing him now uncomfortable.

His voice drew closer. "Can't stay long. I have a date with this blonde girl named Jessica. Just met her at the gym and ..." Caleb's words trailed off when he focused on me in the living room. He shot Joe a questioning glance.

I rolled my eyes toward the floor. So awkward.

"Tamara, you remember Caleb."

"Yes, of course. Caleb." I gave an uneasy nod.

"Tamara." He nodded back, then turned to Joe. "Where's Susan?"

Joe scratched his head. "I'll fill you in later, but the story I'm going with right now is that she was called back to work unexpectedly."

Caleb looked toward me again, this time with suspicion. "She isn't going to be here tonight? Man, that's harsh. What did you do?"

Joe glanced at me, then back to Caleb. "Long story and now's not the time."

The doorbell rang again.

Why had Joe looked at me before saying that? Caleb must be thinking I was a homewrecker or something.

One by one the guests arrived, and Joe's house filled with people. Some I knew. Most I didn't. Several of the guests asked about Susan. Each time Joe made the same excuse, saying she got unexpectedly called in to work. A pang of guilt hit my stomach, every time he said the words. Should I still be here? If it weren't for me, she would be with him and he wouldn't have to lie.

Melissa showed up with her boyfriend, Mark. Even though there was a part of me that was still irritated with her for the two double shifts in a row, she was a welcome distraction from the guilt.

"Tamara," she said, eyes lighting up.

Mark stood beside her, barely acknowledging my existence.

"Thanks for covering for me last night. I was in bad shape." She looked just fine now, for being as sick as she'd said she was. In fact, she looked great. Her golden hair was pulled loosely up into a half-ponytail, and wispy strands fell softly around her oval face. She wore a clingy, scoop-neck sweater, skinny jeans, and black boots with six-inch heels.

I thought about calling her out on her miraculous recovery, but I figured I'd better play nice for the moment. I didn't need any more drama today. "It's all good. I need the extra cash."

"I get that."

I smiled and hoped it didn't come across as curt. Fact was, she didn't 'get' it at all. Melissa didn't know what it was like to need money. She was a junior at the University of Portland, and her rich dad paid for practically everything she needed, from her Mini Cooper to the upscale apartment she lived in near campus. Then there was Mark, her doting boyfriend, who had graduated from the university last year with a degree in business and worked as a financial consultant for an investment firm.

Honestly, I didn't even know why she worked.

Mark leaned over and whispered something in Melissa's ear.

She giggled and turned her full attention to him.

Suddenly I felt too exhausted to carry on false pleasantries with people I had very little in common with. I excused myself and searched for Joe. Last time I'd seen him, he was heading toward the kitchen, so I made my way in that direction. I rounded the corner and there he was, back toward me, refilling a bowl of dip.

"Hey, Joe, I should probably get going, just in case ..." My words trailed off. Man that sounded bad. Hopefully nobody had heard me. "I'm so sorry."

"Yeah, so am I."

I wanted to hug him and assure him that everything would be okay, but, knowing my life that would be the moment Susan decided to come home and things would blow up again.

Joe was better off without me.

"See you Wednesday." I waved and headed down the hallway without giving him another look.

I took the long way home, this time with the top down. Anything to take my mind off the last twenty-four hours. I couldn't believe I had gotten myself into this kind of mess. All of it on the tail of yet another colossal mistake. If I wouldn't have gone out with Kyle last night, Joe wouldn't have shown up at my house, and all the chaos that followed would have never happened. Why did drama follow me wherever I went?

Oh, I knew! Because I was stupid enough to let someone in again. When would I ever learn?

I pulled onto I-5 and pushed on the accelerator. Sometimes I felt like my life *was* cursed. Joe was only trying to be a good friend, and by the end of the day, I had pretty much ruined his relationship. I thought of the terrible dream I had this morning— the one with the dark force chasing after me. Who had been the man in front of me? Joe? Kyle? Or something more symbolic?

Maybe *I* was the darkness. I was the common denominator in all of it.

I pressed harder on the gas.

Flashing blue and red lights appeared in the rearview mirror.

"Seriously? Here's the cherry on top of my crap sundae," I muttered, pulling to the side of the road.

An officer as tall as Michael Jordan approached my car, waving a flashlight. He stopped beside the driver-side door, his massive frame towering over me. "Ma'am, do you have any idea how fast you were going?" He said deep voice full of authority.

No, but I'm sure you're going to enlighten me. I shook my head. "Officer, I apologize, but I thought I was going the speed limit."

He rested his hands on his hips in an intimidating stance, looking like an unfriendly version of the Jolly Green Giant. "Well, let me inform you that you most certainly were not. Do you see that sign right there?" He jerked his head toward the speed limit sign I had the misfortune of pulling over in front of. "What does it say?"

"Fifty-five miles per hour," I answered, my voice small.

"That's right, but I clocked you going seventy-four." He leaned over and peered into my eyes. "Have you had anything to drink tonight, Miss?"

"What? No!"

"May I see your license, registration, and proof of insurance?" He shined the flashlight around the inside of my car. Probably looking for drug paraphernalia.

I handed him my license first and dug through the glove box for my registration and proof of insurance. When I turned back toward him, he was studying my license. "Tamara Jensen?" He examined the photo for another moment before taking the rest of my information. "All right, Miss Jensen, just sit tight. I'll be right back."

I drummed my thumbs on the steering wheel as I waited for the officer to return. "God, please, I can't afford a speeding ticket."

Another police car pulled up behind the first one.

I cursed under my breath. This was not a good sign. They didn't usually send multiple cop cars to a routine traffic stop.

Two officers approached my vehicle this time. The second officer was much shorter and rounder than the first.

"Miss, step out and make your way to the back of the vehicle," The taller officer said.

My heart thundered inside my chest, and fear surged through my entire body as I opened my door and climbed out. Were they going to arrest me?

Unbelievable.

The officers followed me to the back of my car.

"Please stand on one leg with the other leg six inches off the ground and then count by ones starting at one thousand," the stout officer directed.

I carried out his instructions flawlessly, but inwardly I was fuming.

"All right, walk in a straight line, nine steps, placing one foot directly in front of the other. Then turn and walk back in the same way," the officer commanded.

Again, I did exactly what he said.

When they had finished their ambush of humiliation, they slapped me with a $187 speeding ticket. Which I guess was warranted considering how fast I was going. But a sobriety test— really? They obviously didn't think it was 'normal' to drive with the top down in the middle of winter.

Defeated, angry, and half-frozen, I put the top back up on my car, got in, and blasted the heater the rest of the way home.

Pulling into my assigned parking place, I thought about Joe and the expression he wore right before I left. It was probably a mistake, but I wouldn't be able to sleep tonight if I didn't at least make sure he was okay. I pulled out my cell.

Hey Joe, I hope you're okay. I'm here if you need to talk.

I hit send and waited. Unease bit at my stomach as I stared at the phone. What if he blamed me for tonight? What if he regretted reaching out to me? What if he stopped being my friend? I put my phone in my pocket and sat there for a long time, my imagination conjuring up images from this morning's dream. Why would I be thinking of this now? Did it have something to do with Joe? I didn't think so. I tried to shake the thoughts away, but I kept seeing myself running, trying to escape the darkness— and then feeling the horror, as I realized there was no way out. Maybe this was my destiny, to always be on the run.

Finally, I climbed out of my car and headed to my studio. I walked in and turned on the light. The gloominess of the dingy opaque walls added to the depression of my mood.

Despite spending a considerable amount of time and energy trying to transform my apartment into a home, it still felt more like a dungeon. No matter how many lights were on, it seemed dark. It smelled of musty carpets, cleaning products, vanilla candles, and cigarette smoke. The musty scent lingered no matter how much I scrubbed or how many candles I lit.

The gray loveseat was off to the left with a wooden chest in front of it. A small colorful cut of fabric draped over the chest and a saucer with a half-burnt candle sat in the middle of it. For the most part, the studio was clean, but the blankets on the daybed were in a balled-up mess.

I set the ticket on my makeshift coffee table and walked into the bathroom. I opened the medicine cabinet, grabbed the bottle of sleeping pills, shook three into my hand, and washed them down with a glass of water. On the way back to my bed, I snagged my journal.

January 18

Aren't dreams supposed to fade over the course of the day? Here it is, nine in the evening, and this nightmare only gets more vivid. Maybe it's my subconscious trying to speak to me. Maybe it's telling me it's time to move on. I have to consider all of this is related. In my dream, I was running for my life, fleeing from a haunting force. When I was about to escape, a man cloaked in darkness appeared before me blocking me from moving forward.

His presence was so intense it was like he was in front of me yet all around me at the same time.

I tapped the end of the pencil on my temple. Could it be that no matter how hard I tried and no matter how far I ran there would always be darkness hovering over my life?

I grabbed my phone. Joe still hadn't texted back.

Joe, again, I'm sorry. I hope you and Susan work things out. Please let me know what happens. I'm here for you.

I regretted hitting send as soon as I touched the icon. If Joe wanted to talk to me, he would have texted me back before. Now I seemed overly concerned, maybe even clingy. Worse yet, Susan may have come back and seen the texts from me before Joe did.

I looked down at the last couple of lines in my journal. Words formed in my mind and inspiration hit. Dark inspiration, but inspiration nonetheless. I flipped back in my journal a few pages and added the lines to the poem I had started the other night.

A man stands in front of me,
> *And all around me at the same time*
> *I look at him, but only darkness surrounds my vision.*

I glanced back at my phone.
Still no reply from Joe.

CHAPTER 13

January 18, 9:25 p.m.

JOE

Ignoring the beep from my phone, I stormed out the front door and jumped in my Jeep Cherokee. Fighting with Susan was not how I wanted this day to end. Not only did she take off right before my party, but she came home afterward to yell at me more about Tamara. She even threatened to leave me again. Slamming the stick into reverse, I peeled out of the driveway. If that was the way she wanted it, maybe I was better off without her.

I sped through a yellow light, made a left on Burnside, and pointed the Jeep back toward the 7-Eleven a few blocks away.

Three years sober, and I couldn't remember the last time I wanted to drink this badly. How could this day have ended up like this? I had woken up feeling amazing, like I could overcome the universe, but now here I was, driving way too fast through a residential area. My phone dinged again, but I didn't care. I couldn't handle any more theatrics today. Now was the time to forget everything. I pulled in beside the store, unbuckled my seatbelt, and opened the car door. The ache in my throat pulled me toward the beer cooler in the rear of the store.

Back in the day, I would've gone for something hard, but it was too late, and the liquor store was closed. I snagged a forty-ounce Milwaukee's Best.

Just one beer. The tone of my thoughts was black as coal. What a sick, minimalistic justification. Milwaukee's Best was the cheapest beer with the highest percentage of alcohol. This one bottle equaled almost four cans. Not enough to get me drunk, but enough to take the edge off.

One is too many and a thousand is never enough. The words of my sponsor rang through my head. I slammed the beer down on the counter, squashing the voice before it had time to root itself inside my conscience.

The cashier, a slender woman with a nose too big for her face, looked up at me.

I tried to smile to put her at ease, but it felt more like a grimace.

She averted her eyes and scanned the beer. "Three seventy-nine, please."

She didn't even card me? I suppose it didn't matter to her if I was in self-destruct mode. I handed her four ones. She dropped two dimes and a penny in my hand with a timid smile.

"Have a nice night."

"Thanks." I grabbed the beer and forced myself to walk calmly out the door. I sat in my car for a while, the unopened beer between my legs. Two sides of myself screamed at each other, like a couple of ladies in a catfight.

It's just one drink, the addict inside of me coaxed. *No one would ever know. You really want to tick Susan off, don't you?*

But Susan wasn't the only reason I'd gotten sober, though, she played a huge part. Years ago, when I was still a miserable drunk, I had cheated on her. When she caught me, she left me, which was the wake-up call I needed. I'd hurt her deeply, but I couldn't imagine my life without her. I promised myself that day that I would die before hurting her again. But I had also gotten clean for myself. I couldn't stand the person I used to be, and I didn't want to become him again

Don't do it, the other side of me seemed to plead. *Remember Abigail. Remember how you hated who you were while drinking.*

"God, help me," I cried out, tears of desperation filling my eyes. So many things built pressure inside my chest. The fight with Susan ... memories of my mom ... confusion about Tamara ... "I don't want to do this." I slammed my palm against the steering wheel. "Why is this so difficult? Why can't I make things right with Susan? Why did you take my mom from me?"

Would he respond—this God I wasn't sure I believed in?

I quieted myself, tracing the circle of the lid of the beer with my finger. Would he send some sort of sign or divine intervention?

'Cause all I felt were tears drying on my face and blood pounding in my ears. I opened the beer. The sweet fumes of alcohol filled the car.

I thought of having to face Susan when I returned home. Would she want to yell at me more, or would she have taken all of her stuff to a hotel? The thought of losing her made me sick, but the thought of facing her anger made me sicker. Either way, it would be much easier to be completely drunk. I brought the bottle to my lips, visualizing myself emptying the nectar down my throat and forgetting this whole night.

Tamara suddenly crossed my mind. What would she think of me if, after three years of being clean and sober, I went and ruined everything? Every wall that I pushed past today in her life would mean nothing if I did this. If for nothing else, I needed to be strong for her.

I forced out the serenity prayer, something that had always helped me in my darkest of moments. "God, grant me the serenity to accept the things I cannot change, the courage to change the things I can, and the wisdom to know the difference."

Using every bit of willpower I had in me, I rolled down the window and dumped the beer onto the pavement.

CHAPTER 14

January 19, 8:30 a.m.

TAMARA

Why can't I sleep? I slammed my bed in frustration. My interaction with Joe still plagued my thoughts. I rolled over again to check my phone one more time.

Why couldn't I let it go?

My eyes adjusted to the soft blue glow of the screen.

Nothing. It had been over ten hours since I messaged him and still nothing. My stomach hurt—a mix of sleeping pills, party food, and anxiety.

I stared at the last sentence I had texted, reading it again for, like, the eleventh time.

Please let me know what happens. I'm here for you.

The problem was I knew what happened—I happened. I just wish he would tell me something.

Even if he didn't want to see me again. The silence was killing me.

I looked at the clock. 8:30. He'd surely be up by now. This was probably a bit stalkerish, but I dialed his number.

It rang. Which meant his phone wasn't dead and my messages had gone through. It rang four more times and went to voicemail.

"Hey Joe, I hope everything is okay. Call or text when you have a minute." There. That was it. The ball was in his court now. If he wanted distance, that was up to him.

If only I could get some decent sleep and forget yesterday. I downed a few more sleeping pills, threw a pillow over my head, and forced myself back to sleep.

CHAPTER 15

January 19, 9:00 a.m.

JOE

The next morning, I woke up on Susan's three-thousand-dollar, white sectional couch with a backache. How could something so expensive be so miserably uncomfortable? Facing Susan had been worse than I thought. When I returned home, she was angrier than ever. We fought for nearly three more hours with no resolution. I tried my best to reassure her nothing was going on with me and Tamara but didn't get through. She wanted me to agree to stop being Tamara's friend.

Which I couldn't do even if I wanted to. We worked almost every shift together.

I rolled over and punched the pillow Susan had thrown at me the night before. How could I even begin to distance myself from Tamara? I couldn't abandon her after everything she'd told me yesterday. After banging down the walls of her heart and practically forcing her to open up to me. Ditching her now would be cruel. But playing around with her the way I did yesterday was out of line. If I had walked in and Susan was acting like that with another guy, I would have probably beaten the sense out of him and asked questions later.

But that wasn't the point.

The point was that Susan, after all this time, still hadn't

stopped punishing me for my past mistakes. I wish so badly I could hit the rewind button and take back that stupid, drunken mistake. What I needed more than anything with Susan was a clean slate. A new beginning.

I blamed my mother for this idealistic thinking. She used to say there was always a way to have a fresh start. She'd begin each day in prayer, saying God's mercies were new every morning. When she talked about it, her face lit up as if she really believed it.

That might work for me if I could prove to Susan that I was a new person.

Maybe if I had a devout faith like my mom, I would be stronger. But when my mom passed away, my faith died with her. The day of her memorial was the last day I stepped foot inside a church. How could a loving God have let her die? My mom served her God faithfully for years, but in the end, He chose not to save her.

When I got clean and sober, trusting God was the hardest part. The first step of my program was admitting my problem was bigger than myself and then surrendering to a higher power. I did it grudgingly, hoping it was true. My drinking problem was, and still is, too big for me to control.

Unfortunately, I had always been more like my father—he was the lying, cheating alcoholic. How was it possible to be so much like someone I had never met?

I wasn't like him in one aspect, thankfully. I would never hit a woman.

Guilt washed over me as I thought of Susan. My infidelity all those years ago had caused a strong, confident woman to be damaged and insecure. I had wounded her, and it was up to me to make her better. The problem was, how?

For the last three years, I'd tried with everything in me and hadn't gotten very far.

I rolled off the couch and stumbled to my feet.

I didn't know how to make things right between us, but I had to try.

I tiptoed up the stairs, then into the bedroom and stood for a moment, admiring her beauty, the way her dark hair fell across her angelic face. My heart softened as I took in her quiet vulnerability. How could I fix us?

What would Mom say? I chuckled under my breath. She would have kicked my butt a long time ago for living with a woman out of wedlock. "Living in sin," she would've called it.

Perhaps that was it. Marriage might be the answer. Maybe it would help Susan to get over her insecurities if she knew how committed I was to her.

Susan's eyes sprung open as if she'd heard my thoughts. She looked around the room and rested her gaze on me. The line of her mouth curved into a slight smile, letting me know the storm was over. "You know it's creepy to watch someone while they sleep."

"You just looked so beautiful. I couldn't help myself."

She raised an eyebrow. "Mister Phillips, are you trying to sweet-talk your way into my bed?"

"Maybe, is it working?"

She pulled back the blankets and patted the mattress beside her.

I crawled in and pulled her close. "I'm sorry. I really should be more sensitive."

"I'm sorry too." She nuzzled her head into my chest. "I shouldn't have taken off. It's just that, when I saw you with that girl..."

I brought my hand under Susan's chin and tilted her head up to look her in the eyes. "You have nothing to worry about. Tamara is just a girl I work with." I leaned in and kissed her tenderly. Why did those words feel some much like a lie?

CHAPTER 16

January 20, 5:02 a.m.

TAMARA

My eyes popped open the next day a half an hour before my alarm went off. I immediately checked my phone again.

Zero missed calls, zero voicemails, and zero text messages.

Joe hadn't called me back or even texted me for the whole day yesterday. Staring at the blank screen on my phone, uneasiness pricked at my insides. Maybe Susan came back, and they'd been so busy making up he didn't have a spare minute to let me know he was okay. That would be a good scenario, except for the fact that Susan hated me.

Joe had told Susan he wouldn't stop being my friend, but what if she forced him to choose? My heart ached at the thought.

Good thing today was his day off, as I couldn't handle the full force of his rejection yet.

I threw my phone aside and pulled the covers over my head. Levi Taylor darted into my thoughts. Heat tinged my face. He would no doubt come into the diner today, and I'd have to face him. Why did he, of all people, see me scrambling out of Kyle's truck? What a nightmare. My pulse sped up as I bounced back and forth between the two dilemmas—Joe and Levi. I rolled out of bed, ran to the bathroom, and splashed water on my face.

Get a grip, Tamara. I stared at my reflection in the mirror.

There wasn't any reason to freak out. Why would I even care what Levi thought of me? I didn't even know him.

Besides, what was the big deal? I was twenty-two years old. Was I not allowed to make a few mistakes on the way to growing up? And this thing with Joe would probably just blow over. Being all doom and gloom and stressing out about it wasn't going to help anything.

I splashed my face again and grabbed the Neutrogena. Might as well get ready for work.

When I showed up to the diner twenty minutes early, the restaurant was completely empty except for Trudy, who sat at the bar rolling silverware into napkins. "Well, good morning, Tammy girl," she said. "You're here awfully early." Trudy was raised somewhere in the South and still had a slight accent that got thicker when she was trying to make a point.

"Yeah, couldn't sleep. What are you doing here?"

"Trish called in sick last night, and I couldn't find anyone to cover for her. It's hard to find good people for the graveyard shift." She chuckled. "What am I saying? It's hard to find good employees, period." She glanced around with hyper alertness, rolling the silverware with shaky hands. "I hear you got stuck working two doubles last week."

How much coffee had she drunk throughout the night?

"I don't mind." I shrugged. "In fact, you should have called me this morning. I would have come in earlier."

She stopped mid-roll. "You're kidding, right? Girl, if I could have ten more employees like you, this place might actually run smoothly."

I didn't really know how to respond, so her words hung in the air, creating an awkward silence.

"You should get some rest." I picked up a few napkins from her pile and placed a knife and fork in the middle of one. "I can take it from here."

"You sure?"

"Yeah, I got it. It's not like much is going on."

"All right, darling. I guess I'll scoot on out of here, then." She stood up from the bar. "You have a good day, Tammy girl. And thanks for all your hard work around here."

"Not a problem," I said, feeling awkward again.

I made my way back to the kitchen to get my first cup of coffee.

Tommy, the graveyard cook, was finishing up some last-minute prep work for the day shift. "Hey, Tamara," he said with a smirk. "How was your weekend?"

What was that in his voice? Did he know something? "My weekend was fine." I was probably being paranoid, which was a symptom of a mental disorder. "Pretty uneventful."

His smile grew bigger. "That's not what I heard."

Okay, so maybe I wasn't being paranoid. Heat flooded my face. "What exactly did you hear?"

"Betty told Anthony that you came into the diner with some guy Saturday night. She said you were drunk out of your mind."

Dumbstruck, I stood there, blinking rapidly. I came into the restaurant that night? What the freak? What else did I do that night that I couldn't remember? "You know what? You tell your buddy Anthony to mind his own business. And as for Betty, she needs to learn how to keep her big mouth shut!"

"Sheesh, Tam, calm down. No big deal, right? So you got a little action this weekend. Good for you, is what I say. If anybody is talking, it's because they're jealous. And you can tell Anthony yourself. Frank has jury duty today, and Anthony's covering, remember? Frank's been complaining about it all week."

I hadn't thought life could get worse, but it had. God must have been playing another sick joke on me. I flashed Tommy a fake smile. "Awesome," I said sarcastically, then headed out back and dug through my purse for a smoke.

A few minutes later, Anthony's Camaro pulled into the parking lot.

Taking a frustrated drag, I prepared myself to work with him.

He climbed out of his car and walked toward the front of the diner.

At least he hadn't come this way. I lifted my cigarette to my mouth and cursed under my breath. I'd already smoked it down to the filter.

I threw it to the ground, stomped it out, and picked up my pack of Camels. Part of me wanted to smoke another one, just to delay the inevitable, but another five minutes wouldn't help that much, and there were probably things that needed to be done inside. I shoved my smokes into my back pocket and made a beeline to the dining room.

Tommy and Anthony stood close together in the kitchen, talking quietly between themselves.

My stomach twisted into a knot. Surely, they were gossiping about me. *That is it!* Fuming, I pushed through the double doors. Why did Anthony have to know about my drunken mistake?

He'd probably use it as proof to back up his lies about me.

I was so ready to get out of this miserable place. I'd been feeling the itch for a while, but now I was beyond done.

The door bells clanged against the glass.

Levi Taylor.

He crossed the room and sat down in his usual seat.

I grabbed the coffeepot and made my way toward him, painfully aware of my stomach making its way through the Boy Scout rope-tying handbook. I pasted on the most sincere smile I could muster. "Good morning, Levi. Do you want your usual?"

"Yes, please." He smiled genuinely up at me, and some of my anxiety melted away. I had been so afraid that he would judge me, but I didn't get that vibe from him at all. Just the same kindness and warmth I always felt.

"I'll bring that right out." If this had worked out so well, maybe all the stuff I was stressing about this morning would turn out okay too. Once I put Levi's order in, I looked around to find something to keep me busy.

The silverware and napkins were still at the bar where Trudy had left them, so I did some rolls.

Ten minutes later, the bell rang from the kitchen. As I picked Levi's order up from the window, Anthony sneered at me and shook his head.

Anger flared in me for a moment, but being the mature adult I was, I ignored him and walked away. I placed Levi's food down in front of him. "Anything else I can get you?"

"Nope. Just my check when you have a minute."

"You got it."

"No hurry, though." He took another sip of his coffee.

On the way back to the register, I picked up all the half-empty salt and pepper shakers. What a slow morning it was turning out to be. Tuesdays were always kind of quiet, but this was ridiculous. After a few minutes of busywork, I picked up Levi's ticket and headed back toward his table.

"Thanks, Tamara."

Something about those simple words made my heart expand.

"You're welcome. Let me know if you need anything else." I walked back toward the silverware.

What was it about this man that affected me? Did he have something I needed? A pang of sadness washed through me. Even though I felt a connection to him, we were worlds apart.

If I could only break into his world ... but how?

Somehow it felt like he was trying to break into mine. That's what his little notes seemed like—a way of reaching into my world.

A loud crash echoed from the kitchen.

I leaned my head around the swinging door. "Is everything okay in here?"

Anthony stood in the middle of a pancake-batter puddle, which was rapidly spreading across the floor. He glared at me. "Yeah, everything is fine."

"Whatever, just checking." I went back to my busywork, trying not to allow Anthony's rudeness to bug me.

Only seven thirteen a.m. I snuck another smoke break. By the time I returned, Levi had gone. I grabbed a bleach rag on the way to his table and cleared it.

The ticket was a bit odd this morning. On the first line, *trailer park* was scratched out. On the second line, *wooden pew*, with another scribble line through it.

An image of me as a little girl hiding under a church pew ran through my mind. I pushed away the thought. There wasn't any way Levi could know about that.

Underneath was the normal note. *Hope you have a fantastic day.* With the usual smiley face next to it.

I shoved the ticket in my pocket and shrugged off the strange feeling that the scribbled out list was about me.

The rest of the morning stayed completely dead.

The only busywork left was filling ketchup bottles, a task I had put off because it required going into the kitchen and possibly running into Anthony. So far, I had done a decent job of avoiding him. I let out a deep sigh and prayed a quick, desperate plea that he'd be too busy to notice me.

As I turned the corner, Anthony came out of the cooler.

Another unanswered prayer.

A disdainful smirk etched itself across his mouth. "So, Tamara." He crossed his arms and cocked his head to the side. "I hear you got something to say to me."

"You heard wrong. I can't think of a single word I'd want to say to you. You have to care about someone at least a little in order to talk to them."

His dark eyebrows furrowed, and he scowled.

"You know what is wrong with girls like you?" he asked, voice full of venom.

Girls like me? What an arrogant dirt bag. "I really don't care about what you think."

"Whether you want to know or not, the problem is that you have no respect for yourself. When you don't have respect for yourself, it makes it impossible for others to have respect for you."

Heat pulsed through my veins. After the way he had lied about me, he had the nerve to lecture me about respect?

"You know what? I'm so sick and tired of your self-righteous, egotistical attitude. You act so high and mighty, but you're nothing but a lying sack of dog vomit. You just stay out of my face, and I will stay out of yours. If you don't, I'll call Trudy and file an official complaint."

"Ooh …" He raised his hands in the air next to his face and wiggled his fingers. "I'm so scared. I'm sure she would love to hear about your little incident the other night."

"You wouldn't."

"Why don't you give her a call and find out?"

"Just stay away from me, Anthony." I pushed past him, grabbed the ketchup, and stormed back to my side of the restaurant.

The diner stayed slow for the rest of my shift. Serving a total of six tables all day, including Levi's, gave me entirely too much time to stew on the confrontation with Anthony.

Maybe I really should pick up and leave Vancouver. There was nothing good for me here, and it seemed to be growing worse by the moment. My job was falling apart. I still hadn't heard from Joe. More than that, Anthony was right—I was the one who brought all this misery on myself.

At the end of my shift, I counted my measly tips as Melissa entered the diner, face lit up with a huge grin.

Her blonde ponytail bounced as she skipped through the glass door toward me. She pranced over, threw her arms around me, and pulled back, leaving her hands on my shoulders. "Guess what, guess what, guess what?" Her eyes glimmered with delight.

"Uh, you won the lottery and you never have to work here again?" Not that I cared at the moment.

"No. Even better."

"Just tell me."

"Come on, Tammy, you're no fun." She wriggled her left hand in front of my face, revealing an excessively large, princess-cut diamond ring. "Mark proposed to me this morning. Isn't that unbelievable? And there's more. He got this incredible job offer in New York. We're moving there next month."

The room closed in around me. I should have been happy for her, but all I could feel was a growing ache in my heart. A chasm had opened inside of me, and it was all I could do not to fall in.

Melissa's voice carried on, but it sounded as if she were talking underwater. Something about Mark bringing her breakfast in bed and proposing to her. I couldn't make out the words.

She quieted after a minute. "Earth to Tam."

Somehow, I worked up a smile. "That's amazing, Mel. I'm so happy for you." She was so high on life, the falseness in my voice didn't burst her bubble.

"Oh!" Her eyes widened, and she covered her mouth with her hand. "Maybe you could be in the wedding. You would have to come to New York, of course, but." She paused, seeming to switch trains of thought. "Oh my goodness, Tam, can you believe this is happening?"

Nausea turned my stomach. "I can't wait to hear all the details, but I have an appointment I have to get to." I gave her a hug.

"Thanks, Tamara. I'll tell you all about it tomorrow."

"Can't wait." I grabbed my twenty-four dollars and ninety-nine cents' worth of tips.

Ninety-nine cents? Really? I was so sick of that stupid number. Every time I saw it, it made me think of my lonely, miserable, pathetic life. I pulled a penny out of my pocket, put it in the till with the other change, and snatched out a dollar. I shoved the tips in my pocket on the way to my car.

Tears streamed down my face, blurring my vision, making it difficult to put the key in the ignition. Hopefully Melissa wasn't witnessing this absurd display of emotions.

I shoved the car into reverse and peeled out of the parking lot. There was something about seeing her so overjoyed that made my depression even more depressing. Why did girls like her get life handed to them, while I worked so hard yet had nothing?

A horn honked beside me.

I jerked the wheel back into my lane.

A few blocks ahead, an open parking spot seemed to be calling to me.

I pulled the car into the spot, leaned my head over the steering wheel, and let the angry fit of sobs take over.

Eventually, I pulled myself together and glanced around. I was parked between two churches: Hope Chapel and First Baptist.

A sign right next to my car said *God loves you.*

My heart hardened. "If this is the way you love me, God, why does it hurt so much? If this is your love, please stop. I don't know how much more I can take. You know, I'm not even sure I believe in you anymore." The god I believed in was angry, distant, and did not care about my pain.

Tap, tap. A tall bald man leaned toward the window of my car.

I hesitantly rolled it down a few inches.

"Are you all right, miss? I didn't mean to startle you." He wore black slacks and a gray Oxford shirt.

"No, I'm fine. Just waiting for someone. They'll be here any minute." I'd been lying so much lately it was becoming a habit.

He stood there for a long moment, eyes deepening with concern. "My name is David. I work on the pastoral staff here." He motioned toward Hope Chapel. "Actually, I'm a counselor." He opened his wallet and took out a card. "If you ever need to talk to someone." He slid the card through the gap at the top of my window.

I took it. "Ah ... thanks."

"What did you say your name was?"

"Oh, I didn't say. My name is Tamara." How much of my breakdown had he seen? I must've looked a complete mess. My eyes felt puffy and burned from the excessive tears. "You know, I think I'm actually in the wrong spot. My friend should have been here by now. I better get going."

He hesitated. "Okay, well you have a blessed day. I hope you find who you are looking for."

I smiled weakly, feeling guilty for lying to this nice stranger. "Thanks. Nice meeting you." I turned the key in the ignition and glanced in the rearview mirror.

Levi Taylor pulled up right behind me.

Why was Levi here? Was he stalking me now? Is that how he knew about my childhood?

No, that was stupid. If he was following me, he probably just wanted to make sure I wasn't doing anything reckless, which was far worse than stalking. I didn't need a chaperone.

I flipped on my signal and sped out of there before he had a chance to get out of his car.

CHAPTER 17

January 20, 2:45 p.m.

LEVI

As I pulled up in front of David's church, the conversation I had with Sarah earlier weighed heavy on my mind. I turned off the car and waited for David to notice me. He seemed deep in thought as he watched a small red car drive away. I took the moment to gather my thoughts, wishing the tightness in my chest would ease.

My father's voice rang loudly through my mind like a church bell swinging back and forth. *If you have something weighing you down, you just need to release it to God. He's the only one that can really help you with the obstacles you face.*

For the most part I agreed with my dad, but I had already released my burden to God a thousand times. I had prayed earnestly and quoted all the Bible verses I knew pertaining to my situation.

Take delight in the Lord, and he will give you the desires of your heart ...

Whatever you ask for in prayer, believe that you receive it, and it will be yours ...

His promises were clear. If I was faithful to God, he'd be faithful to me, so why hadn't he been? I was doing everything on my side, but it didn't seem like God was living up to his end of the bargain.

I exited the car, but David didn't notice. He was caught up in the moment he'd had with whoever just drove away. That's what I loved about the guy, he genuinely cared about people. I'd envied that about him ever since we'd met six years ago while working on our masters' together. He had a deep pocket for emotions but never let the pains of previous clients or his own personal life seep over into other sessions, something I'd always struggled with.

After graduation we'd lost touch, but three months ago, when we ran into each other at the grocery store, he spoke like we'd seen each other yesterday. Then he blatantly declared us meeting up again after so many years was not a coincidence, but a divine appointment orchestrated by God.

All I could do was laugh.

David didn't believe in coincidences or dumb luck. He believed in angels, demons, and God's divine will. I also considered myself a man of faith, but sometimes he could lay it on a bit thick. Still, he had been a great friend and a sympathetic ear when I needed it the most.

I reached through the car window and pushed on the horn. "David! Come on."

Gasping, he took a step back and clasped his hand over his chest. "Holy biscuits, you scared the ever livin' out of me."

"Sorry." I chuckled.

"That's okay, Taylor." Smiling, he came over and gave me a hug. "How are you, my friend?"

"Just fine." I stepped away and opened my car door.

He rounded the car and climbed in, cramming his tall frame into the passenger seat of my Honda Accord. "You know what they say about paybacks."

"That's right." I snickered again as I got in. "But it was worth it. I needed a good laugh."

"Yeah, what's going on?"

David already knew my situation in its entirety. It had been an ongoing conversation between us since we reconnected. "Oh, you know, same heart ache, different day of the week."

"More stuff with Sarah?"

"Yeah."

"I'm sorry. Would you like to talk about it?"

"Seems like lately that's all I do. Either I'm talking to you or talking to God. Right now, I wish I had some answers. Or some sort of breakthrough."

"Yeah, sometimes talking is overrated. Why don't we grab something to eat?"

"Food sounds good." I checked my watch. Sarah wouldn't be home for a few hours. "Where do you want to go?"

"Let's go to that diner you keep talking about." A strange expression crept over his face. "I have a feeling about something."

"Oh, yeah?" I put the car in gear and drove toward the Highway 99 Diner for the second time that day.

CHAPTER 18

January 20, 9:27 p.m.

TAMARA

Smoke from the cigarette in the ashtray drifted up toward my apartment ceiling as I glared at Levi's note in my hand. The scribbled-out list really bugged me.

I brought the list closer and focused on the words.

Trailer park and *wooden pew.*

Why would he have written those words? And why would he have crossed them out? Was he trying to play games with my already messed-up mind?

There was no way he could know that when I was a little girl, I lived in a trailer park next to a church.

Did he think I was trailer trash? Him and the whole diner. Not only trailer trash but a slut too. By now Betty had told everyone she'd seen me with Kyle.

The trailer trash part was obvious, but the wooden pew?

When my parents fighting got really bad, I would sneak away and hide under the wooden pews in the drafty church. Images of me, freezing cold, crying under those dank pews, begging God to make the fighting stop overwhelmed me. As much as I prayed, the fighting never quit. Eventually, I stopped praying or even believing that God ever heard me in the first place. If Levi did somehow know about that time, why would he want to bring it up?

I grabbed my phone and scrolled through the names. My finger hovered over Joe's number, but he didn't want to talk to me. Why had he bothered to pretend to care? I didn't need him. My wounded heart threw an irregular beat. Who was I kidding? I couldn't go on like this. It was as though I had fallen into emotional quicksand. The more I struggled to get out, the deeper I sank. I threw my phone aside and pulled out my journal.

January 20

Why do I want to run so badly? Why am I so confused? I wish life could magically work itself out and everything fall into place the way it's supposed to, but I have come to realize it doesn't happen like that.

The road is always hard, the emptiness is always there. The feeling of being lost never ceases to exist. This darkness that has been with me so long has somehow become a part of me. I'm scared to face it, but I cannot escape it. I don't want to live this life anymore. The darkness is too much. The confusion is too hard to bear. I can't make sense of it. I have been here before, many times ... this feeling, this place ... and I don't want to stay. I want to run.

I pushed my journal to the side, heart heavier than when I started. What if all of this could end right now? What if I just stopped living? There wasn't a single reason to keep going.

I peeled myself off the couch and crept toward the bathroom. I flipped on the light and stared vacantly at myself in the mirror. Who was this person that gaped back at me?

No one I recognized.

I opened up the cabinet door and grabbed the sleeping pills. Emotions clawed and beat against my insides. Loneliness, disappointment, anger, regret—they all had a name and a face. My father and the way he abused me. Ryan and the crazy life he introduced me to. Danny's empty love and ultimate betrayal. Charlie had been the one flickering candle in the storm, but even he had a strike or two against him. His later generosity made up for it, but who really knew. If I would have let him in, would he have eventually crushed me like Danny? And now Joe, making me open up to him and then ignoring me. My life was too messy for him, so he had tossed me aside like everyone else.

And now I was alone ...

All of it seemed to lead to this one pathetic moment. Things were never going to change. If I ran from this place and never looked back, I would still take the pain with me.

But this small container of innocent little pills might offer me a real way out. I would never have to think or feel again. I could just disappear.

Gripping the top of the bottle, I twisted.

If I did this, who would find me? Would it be my landlord, coming to collect rent?

No, too long from now.

Would it be my neighbor, once my body began to smell?

Maybe ...

My phone buzzed from the other room. Hesitantly, I walked over to see who it was.

A text from Joe.

Hey Tam, sorry it took so long to get back to you. Things have been crazy. Just wanted you to know I'm thinking about you.

As I looked at the message, my heart stopped. Joe was thinking about me? After nothing for so long, now this? I didn't know how to take it, but it changed everything.

I knew then who would find me.

If I didn't show up for work tomorrow, Joe would come looking for me. The thought of Joe finding my lifeless body made me cringe. I couldn't do that to him. Especially not after him telling me about his tragic past.

I had been sinking into the dark waters of my soul, and his words were a lifeline pulling me to safety. As much as I hated him for not returning my messages until now, I couldn't write him off as not caring, and that was enough.

I set the pills down and crossed my room. I opened the window and put my head outside. Taking in a long, deep breath, I filled my lungs with the cold night air. Images of me under the church pews came to mind again, but this time they carried a different feeling. In those moments, a presence had wrapped around me like a warm blanket, protecting me from the bitter cold. I sensed that same presence now.

Was this presence bigger than the darkness I'd been running from?

A shiver ran down my spine. The darkness was so thick, black, and all-consuming. But if I looked long and hard enough, I could find my way toward the light. I closed my eyes and imagined three beacons standing around me. The first one was Joe. The second one, Levi. I didn't know who the third one was, but he was there.

I closed the window. How had I come so close to doing something so irreversible? Whether I had the guts to go through with taking my life or not, I was extremely thankful for Joe's text. And in a strange way, Levi's note too.

A simple prayer rolled off my lips. "God, grant me the serenity to accept the things I cannot change, the courage to change the things I can, and the wisdom to know the difference."

I ran to the bathroom and dumped the sleeping pills down the toilet. I wanted to live. I had dreams to fulfill, desires yet unmet. For a moment, I had lost sight of that. With more force than necessary, I slammed the cabinet shut.

The mirror broke, cracking, spider-webbing out in all directions.

My distorted image stared back at me in shock. Was that what my heart looked like?

A shattered mirror, a broken reflection.

I played the words over and over in my mind and looked around for my journal. It was still open from my hopeless writing earlier.

A shattered mirror, a broken reflection.
  The pain in this life causes this faulty perception.

The broken mirror reflected the broken parts inside of me.

From love to loss, from hope to despair,
  Empty promises and unfulfilled dreams.
  My heart awakes with a silent scream.

Not a bad start. Maybe I would finish it another day. Curling up in bed, I closed my eyes. As I lay there, more lines sprang up inside me. I tried to quiet my mind and sleep, but before I could stop myself, I had the light back on and was writing more.

Is this real what I see?
  Or just a faulty perception
  A broken reflection.
  I cry and I plead: deliver me
  From this faulty perception, this broken reflection.
  I am so sick and tired of this self-rejection

I read the poem again and again. Could all the pain I had been through someday turn into something that could touch others? I took in a deep breath, overwhelmed by the thought of my pain impacting other people's lives. Gently, and with a smile, I closed my journal, pulled up my blankets and adjusted my pillow.

CHAPTER 19

January 21, 6:00 a.m.

TAMARA

As I turned the key in the ignition, music rolled out of the speakers. "Lullaby" by Shawn Mullins. I must have heard this song a thousand times, but this time the words wrapped around my heart, squeezing every last bit of depression from it. I cranked the radio up and sang along. For the first time in as long as I could remember, I actually believed those words. Everything was going to be all right.

I was looking forward to seeing Joe today, Levi too, and even facing the haters at the diner. I had made the choice to live last night, and that decision seemed to outweigh what others thought of me. Joe was doing what he needed to be happy, Levi was too innocent to be a crazy stalker, and the rest? Well, if they hated me that was their problem.

I backed out of my parking lot and sang along with the song. It felt good to actually sing the lyrics out loud. I had to tell someone now.

I picked up my phone, and a pang wrenched my stomach. The only person I could think to call was Joe, and I couldn't call him this early. Susan might answer. Just like that, the elation was gone, overshadowed by the depression cloud. I mentally reached out, but the feeling of peace eluded me.

Turning down the radio, I berated myself for not being more emotionally stable. Wasn't one of the symptoms of bipolar disorder high highs and low lows? Whatever my mood swings meant, it couldn't be good. I rolled down my window and lit up a smoke.

When I arrived at the diner, Joe's car was nowhere to be seen. Near the back, where the employees parked, there was a white Mercedes with the lights still on.

I pulled into my normal spot, about three car lengths down, and glanced through the window. My stomach tightened as recognition dawned.

Susan's car, with Joe in the passenger seat. He and Susan seemed to be in an intense conversation.

A fierce desire to step between them rose in me—a strange need to protect him. But Joe could obviously take care of himself. Ignoring the impulse, I dug through my purse, acting as if I were fishing something out of it.

After a minute, Joe stepped out of the car and walked into the restaurant.

Susan backed out of the parking lot.

Once I was sure she was gone, I went inside. I waved a quick hello to Trisha, one of the graveyard waitresses. Her eyes were puffy, and she sneezed as I hurried past her toward the kitchen. I didn't want to catch her bug, but more importantly, I was anxious to see Joe.

He stood by the time clock, just about to punch in.

"Good morning," I said cheerfully. I was sick of all the heaviness. I wanted things back to the way they used to be before the incident with Susan.

"Hey, girl," he replied with his usual warmth.

His smile lit up my insides like a candle in a dark room. "Would you like a cup of coffee?" I asked, slipping into our normal morning routine.

"Yes, ma'am. I was up kinda late last night." He walked across the kitchen and rummaged through the small metal refrigerators.

I poured us both a cup of coffee and tried to ignore the questions that were assaulting my brain. Why was he up so late? Was it because he and Susan were fighting? Or because they were making up?

"Remember how I'm taking over managing a bit?"

I nodded.

"You're training a new girl today. Her name is Claire. She should be here around seven."

"Why do I always get stuck training the newbies?" I handed him the cup of coffee.

"Because you're the best, most reliable waitress we have." He blew away the steam and took a sip.

"You trying to butter me up or something?"

"Just calling it like I see it."

The bell clanged from the dining room.

"Duty calls." Picking up the coffeepot, I pushed through the double doors.

A young woman wearing black jeans and a short-sleeved blouse with a thick belt that rode high on her waist, waited in the dining area.

"May I help you?"

"Yes, I'm Claire." She walked toward me, reached out her hand, and gave mine a firm shake. Her dark hair was pulled into a high ponytail, with two small ringlets, coiled perfectly, hanging down to frame her narrow face. Up close, she was a bit older than I first guessed, probably late twenties. She was pretty, with a petite build, and large brown eyes with the slightest crow's feet beginning to form around them. "I'm here for training."

"Joe told me you were coming. I'm Tamara, and I'll be showing you the ropes. Do you have any experience with waiting tables?"

"Oh yeah, this is old hat for me. For the last couple years, I've done mostly bartending. But I'm needing to get out of that scene." She grabbed ahold of one of her perfect curls and twisted it around her finger. A tattoo of a vine wrapped around her wrist, and a name I couldn't read wove through it. "You know how it is."

"Yeah, I hear you." Her honesty was refreshing, and it was nice she had experience. It would make my job easier. I pointed her toward Joe so she could fill out her paperwork and timecard.

The doorbells jingled, and I turned.

Levi. He smiled and took a seat at his normal table.

I crossed the room, coffeepot in hand. "Your usual?"

"Sounds great." There was something different about him this morning. His presence alone caused the peace I had felt in the car earlier to resurface. Without thinking, I closed my eyes and stood there for a moment, soaking it in.

"Tamara? Are you okay?"

I opened my eyes and shook my head. "Um ... yeah. I was just remembering something." My face burned as I walked away.

What was that about? I was definitely losing it. I put Levi's order in and tried to brush off the whole incident. There was no use giving it much attention. Just more of my emotional instabilities. I walked into the kitchen in search of Claire. She stood next to the employee time clock, listening to Joe explain how to use it.

"All right, Claire, you ready?" I motioned for her to follow me to the dining room.

She followed me out.

I pulled out a ticket book on the way to the cash register. "So, we pretty much do everything old school here, all by hand, no computers, and this thing." I slapped the register next to me. "Well, it's a dinosaur."

She laughed as the bells clanged against the door.

Four hungry-looking men walked in.

I picked up four menus and a pitcher of water. "Grab the coffeepot and follow me."

Three sets of people came in over the next few minutes.

Claire shadowed me, taking note of how I did things.

Throughout the little rush, I couldn't help but sneak glances at Levi. One time when I looked toward him, it seemed as if he was talking to the empty booth in front of him. Then he scratched his head, laughed out loud, and wrote something down.

I chuckled. Maybe I wasn't the only one going crazy.

Five more groups of people came in, and I started to feel flustered. "Okay, Claire, until this rush is over, how about you fill coffee cups and clear tables?"

She nodded and walked toward the nearest booth.

Finally, the craziness subsided, and I helped Claire clear the rest of the tables.

Levi had left sometime near the end of the rush, so I hurried over to his empty table before Claire could, just in case he'd left a note. There was five fifty for the eggs, a dollar forty-nine for the coffee, and two dollars for the tip. I turned the ticket over.

Everything is going to be all right.

My eyes welled up with tears, and my hands shook.

How in the world could he have known about my experience this morning? Maybe he was a stalker after all, but I had only ever felt good vibes when he was around. Was he an angel?

What a stupid thought. He was probably listening to the same radio station I was this morning and thought of me.

I shoved the ticket and cash into my apron and glanced around the room.

The few remaining patrons were eating, and Claire was across the room clearing the last dirty table.

Time for a break. I strode toward Claire. "You smoke?"

She shook her head. "I quit a couple of weeks back. It's tough, but I'm hanging in there."

"Good for you. I've tried to quit. It didn't work out so well."

"Just wait till you have a two-year-old scowling at you every time he sees you light up."

"You have kids?"

"Yup, one boy." A proud smile brightened her face. "He's the love of my life and very hard to resist." She pulled out her cell phone, swiped her finger across the screen and turned it toward me. "Here's a picture."

He was adorable, with a full head of sunshine-blond hair and a smile that illuminated his big brown eyes and dimpled his cheeks.

"Very cute."

Her grin widened, and she slid the phone back into her pocket. "I'm sorry, I'm just a proud momma. Didn't you say something about a smoke break? Go ahead, if you need one. I can hold down the fort."

"You sure?"

She rolled her eyes and motioned for me to go.

I flashed a grateful look and headed out back.

The air outside was thick with moisture, and ominous gray clouds gathered in the sky. I lit a smoke and sat, hoping the rain would hold off until I finished.

The door opened behind me with a creak, and Joe sat down in the chair next to me, close enough that our arms were touching.

A tingling sensation worked its way through me. For a second, I indulged in the fantasy that he felt it too, and that there was no Susan.

I ran my finger over the number on the front of my cigarette pack and smiled. Lately I'd begun to believe my number had led me to more heartache. But in this moment, feeling nothing had changed between us after the other day, hope filled me once again. "Joe, do you believe in signs?"

"What do you mean?"

I held up my pack of smokes. "Would you believe me if I told you this number led me here?"

His eyebrows shot up. "Do tell."

"I'll give you the edited version." I sat up and turned to him. "I had just left Ocean Shores after yet another awful experience. I didn't have a clue where I was going. Vancouver came into view as I reached for my smokes. The number 99 jumped out to me. Then I flipped on the radio and Prince's song '1999' was playing."

"Nice." Joe laughed. "Gotta love Prince."

"Right?" I took a drag of my cigarette. "So there I was, jamming to Prince, for the first time that day feeling like things might work out, when smoke began billowing out from my hood."

"That was the day we met. I remember coming to help you."

"Yes. When you left, I noticed all the 99s everywhere. The diner, the intersection, my pack of Camels. It felt like it had to mean something."

"Like what?"

"At the time, I thought it was an omen leading me to something better. There's been moments since, though, when I've thought it led me to a dead end."

"I think you're right about it being a good omen."

My gaze met his. "If nothing else, it led me to you."

His countenance clouded over, and he averted his eyes.

Oh man, that was too much. Hopefully he wouldn't read into my words. "Did I say something to upset you?"

"No. You just made me think of something." He picked up my lighter and fidgeted with it. "I was hoping to ask your opinion about a decision I've made."

"About?" I threw my cigarette to the ground and stomped it out.

He shifted in his chair, flicking the lighter several times before he spoke. "I was thinking about asking Susan to marry me."

"What! Why?" I blurted out. Suddenly it hurt to be this close to him. I stood, took a few steps, and leaned against the side of the diner. Looks like they weren't breaking up after all. I should be happy that I hadn't caused permanent damage in their relationship, but this felt worse.

The emotion creeping over Joe's face seemed like sadness. "Susan and I have been together off and on for six years, and we've been through a lot together. If it weren't for her, I don't know where I'd be. And maybe—" He shook his head. "I don't know."

This couldn't be happening. Had the world gone mad? Why did everyone feel the need to get married all of a sudden?

"Look, Joe, it's your life, and I am obviously the last person who should be giving love advice, but you should do what makes you happy. I mean, does Susan really make you happy? I've never even heard you say you were in love with her."

Pain shadowed Joe's eyes. "Someone once told me that love was not just a feeling or an emotion but also a choice. I choose to love her. She deserves that much."

"Who told you that? Dr. Phil? Does that go along with his fake-it-till-you-feel-it garbage? I don't buy that for a second. When you love someone, you feel it."

"You don't have to be a jerk about it."

My heart dropped. I hadn't meant to hurt him. "Listen, I know it's not really any of my business. I just didn't like the way she treated you the other night."

"It's not always like that. And believe me, she had good reason for the way she reacted."

I didn't care what kind of problems the two of them had. It didn't give her an excuse to abandon him that day.

Claire stuck her head out the door. "Hey, guys, I just sat three tables."

"We'll be right in. Just get them some water and menus." I told her.

"Already did."

"I'll be there in a minute."

She bit her bottom lip and closed the door.

I looked down at Joe. "Can we finish this conversation later?"

He shook his head. "No need."

"Okay. I'm sorry if I hurt you."

"Don't be. I asked your opinion, and you gave it. I respect that. It doesn't mean I'm going to change my mind." Joe stood, his face hard. "You should probably get to those tables."

Was he dismissing me? My chest felt tight. Why did I have to be so honest? I should've been more supportive of his decision. I walk back into the dining room, swallowing the lump forming in my throat. So much for things going back to normal between us.

CHAPTER 20

January 21, 3:15 p.m.

JOE

After grabbing my bag, I exited the bus and hoofed it toward the gym. Probably not the best idea to try to fit in a workout between shifts today, especially without my car. I tried to be patient with Susan since everything recently was my fault. But her insistence on driving me to work this morning to keep me from sneaking off with Tamara—or whatever deviant thing she imagined was a tad extreme.

I pushed through the fitness center's door and walked toward the men's locker room.

"You're late!" Caleb playfully scolded as soon as he saw me.

"Yeah, bro, sorry. I had to ride the bus."

Caleb shot me a confused glance. "The bus? What, is your car broke down?"

"Long story, too long." I looked down at my watch. "We need to get started if I'm going to get back to work on time."

We hurried into our normal routine for the day—chest and shoulders. After the military press, we made our way over to the bench. I placed ten more pounds than last time onto the barbell and laid on the bench, while Caleb spotted me.

"Can I get your thoughts about something?" I pushed up on the bar.

"What's up?"

After several reps, I set the bar in the holder and moved off the bench. "Can you believe Susan and I have been together for almost six years?"

Caleb removed some weights from the bar and took his place on the bench. "Yeah. She's quite the woman."

"What's that supposed to mean?" I released the weight a split second before Caleb was ready.

"Nothing." Caleb grunted, pushing the weights up. "What's with the attitude?"

"Sorry. It's just that I'm thinking about marrying her."

"Hot diggety!" Caleb nearly dropped the weights on himself.

I quickly grabbed the bar and placed it on the rack.

"That's fantastic news." He got up and slapped me on the back.

"You really think so?"

"After everything you've put her through, that girl deserves a ring. It's like I always told you, man, crap or get off the commode." Caleb had a way of simplifying life with crude yet somewhat enlightening statements.

"So, does that mean I am finally crapping?" I added weights to the barbell and lay back down.

"In a sense you are, but in a good way. Why? Do you feel like you're crapping?" His voice grew serious.

"Literally or figuratively?"

"I don't know. Both, I guess. You don't seem happy."

I finished my reps and sat up. "It's just a big step, and the way Tamara responded ..."

"Tamara?" Caleb's eyebrows pinched together. "What do you mean?"

I glanced at my watch again. "I don't know, man, but I got to get back to work soon."

"All right, whatever." Caleb started his last rep. "You better not just leave me hanging on this Tamara thing."

I had brought it up. I might as well spill my guts. "What do you think it means when you tell a girl that you're planning on marrying someone, and she gets angry?"

"Hormones?"

I rolled my eyes. "Not funny."

"What? Tamara's kind of a moody person. She may get her monthly bill a couple times a month, if you know what I mean." Caleb pushed the weights up a final time and placed the bar on the rack.

"She is not that bad." I grabbed a few sanitary wipes and cleaned the bench. "You're just mad that she didn't like you when I set you two up."

"That's not true. Yes, I was bummed she didn't want to go on a second date, and yes, it's a pity I spilled wine all over that very nice dress she wore. But she seemed, uh, she seemed ... What I'm trying to say is that she's a pretty girl, but there was just something sad about her."

I grabbed my towel and walked toward the shower room. "She's just misunderstood. She's had a tough life. We hung out all day a bit ago, and now I understand her a lot better."

He threw me a skeptical glance but didn't say anything.

After a quick rinse, we both made our way toward the hot tub.

Caleb settled into the hot water across from me. "So what did Tamara say?"

Talking about Susan and Tamara in the same apparently-never-ending conversation had my insides humming in an extremely uncomfortable way. "She said it didn't seem like we were in love and brought up that stupid fight we had the day of the party."

"But didn't you guys make up?"

"Yes. Not that everything is perfect yet, but we're getting there." I leaned back and tried to relax.

"Why do you care what Tamara thinks? If you love Susan and things are good, who cares if Tamara doesn't see that?"

I wish I knew. It shouldn't matter, but it did.

"You know why she got mad? She's jealous. Dude, that girl has the hots for you."

My heart sputtered. "Tamara? No." I tried to say it smoothly, but it came out sounding awkward.

"You're in denial, man. There's more, isn't there?" His words hung in the air like an accusation.

I didn't want to have this conversation with him. He knew me too well for me to hide what was going on inside my head.

"Isn't there?"

"There might be something, okay? But I don't know what it is, exactly. Things are always so easy between us. When I am with her, I feel more alive."

"Oh man, this is worse than I thought. You want my advice? Stay as far away from Tamara as possible. Susan's beautiful. With her you know what to expect. Of course, you're attracted to Tamara, but you have something great right in front of you. A bird in the hand is worth two in the bush."

I turned toward him, mouth gaping. "A bird in the hand? What does that have to do with anything?"

"How does it not?"

I raised my hands in the air, exasperated. "You know, I have to be honest. I never knew what that statement meant."

Caleb's mouth tilted into an arrogant grin, and his eyebrows rose as if he were going to take great pleasure in schooling me. Whenever he explained his know-it-all sayings, he spoke to me like I was a two-year-old. Half the time he gave really good advice, but the other half I wanted to punch him in the face.

"Well, Joe, let me enlighten you. It is an old, medieval proverb that means it's better to hold on to something you already have than to pursue something you may never get."

Caleb was right. I may have my doubts about marrying Susan, but with her, I knew what I was getting into. "Susan and I are strong. Our relationship isn't perfect, but what relationship is?"

"Exactly, there is no such thing. Take my advice about Tamara. With her you're just borrowing trouble."

His opinion held merit, but there wasn't any way to avoid Tamara even if I wanted to. She worked almost every shift I did. "So, will you be my best man?"

Caleb laughed. "You're putting the cart before the horse, aren't you? You got to ask her first. Who's to say that she'll say yes?"

"Oh, she'll say yes." I flexed my arm. "No woman can resist this."

He punched my shoulder. "You just keep telling yourself that, bro."

CHAPTER 21

February 11, 5:30 a.m.

TAMARA

Over the last few weeks, I did my best to keep my mind off the negatives. I ordered a GED book off the Internet, so I could study, and enrolled in an online poetry class. Writing seemed to be the best way to work through my emotions, and for the most part, I did feel better.

Yet for some reason, I was tired all of the time. Even when I went to bed early, it was like I couldn't sleep enough. Then again, the sleep that I did get was restless and filled with all sorts of strange dreams and nightmares.

Earlier this morning, I had dreamt I was a little girl of about six or seven, standing in the middle of a playground. The day was bright, the sky a perfect shade of blue. Children played all around me, but I stood there, motionless, paralyzed by the sense of being completely alone in the midst of the crowd. I wanted to call out, but I couldn't think of anyone that would hear me.

Then, out of the corner of my eye, I spotted my older brother, Josiah. It had been years since I'd seen his face.

Relief and excitement flooded my senses. I ran to him and threw my arms around his neck.

He picked me up and spun me, squeezing me so tightly I could barely breathe, then he put me down.

"Tag! You're it." I touched his arm and ran away.

Josiah ran after me, laughing and teasing under the monkey bars, up the ladder, and down the slide. When we got to the merry-go-round, he pushed me around and around.

At first it was fun, but then I got dizzy. I asked him to stop, but he pushed faster.

"Please," I begged. "I'm going to get sick."

"You're fine," he said, his smile so bright that I almost believed him.

I tried to smile back, but my stomach whirled with nausea.

The sky darkened overhead, and Josiah's smiling face became contorted and demonic.

Suddenly, I was no longer a little girl, but my present age.

The demon gave another big heave, and the merry-go-round spun so fast I could barely hang on.

A dark vortex opened up in the earth, sucking at me.

I couldn't hold on much longer ...

I jerked awake, heart racing, a cold sweat beading upon my forehead.

For a few merciless seconds, the room continued to whirl around me. The nausea tore at my stomach, and it was all I could do to make it to the bathroom before vomiting.

An hour or so later, I still lay by the toilet, the vertigo swaying the room back and forth.

How could I go to work feeling this way? I crawled toward my phone and clicked on Joe's number.

"Tamara?" he answered after one ring.

"Yeah, Joe, it's me. I'm sick. There's no way I can work today."

"I'll call Claire." He was silent for a moment before saying softly, "You feel better. Is there anything I can do?"

"No, I just need to rest." I hung up, went back to bed and slept for the rest of the morning.

CHAPTER 22

February 14, 3:00 p.m.

JOE

I sat in the jewelry store parking lot, taking a few moments to myself before heading back to work. The white gold, diamond-encrusted band and diamond solitaire shimmered in the sunlight, and I sucked in a sharp breath. Buying a ring on Valentine's Day seemed a bit cliché, but this was the first time in weeks that I had a spare moment. Also, it was the first time in weeks Susan had given me my driving privileges back.

Man, that sounded bad. What was I, a child? But I guess I deserved it. Hopefully this ring would finally end her insecurity. Hopefully this ring would show Susan that she was the only woman for me. Hopefully this ring would shine brighter in her heart than my past mistakes.

Was that even the right reason to ask her to marry me? But that wasn't my only motive for wanting her to be my wife. Susan and I had built a life together. I loved her, right?

Seemed like I should feel more excited, though. Shouldn't I be elated?

Perhaps that was fairy-tale thinking.

What did I want—to be her knight in shining armor? To carry her off into the sunset and live happily ever after? I laughed at the thought. Susan had never needed to be rescued a day in her life. She was the one who had rescued me. We met when I was twenty-one in my full-fledged party days. To put herself through college, Susan bartended at a pub I used to frequent.

At first, she hadn't responded to any of my advances. She was beautiful and carried herself with a confidence that made her feel out of reach. It took a while, but eventually I wore her down. And because she made me work for it, I fell for her all the harder.

I snapped the jewelry box shut and started my car. This was the right move for us. What did it matter the reasoning behind it? We'd been together for six years, for the most part. We'd lived together for the last few months. This was the next step in the progression of things.

So why did I feel so unsure? I tossed the ring case into the glove box and drove toward the diner. Susan was, without a doubt, the best thing that had ever happened to me.

Thoughts of Tamara interrupted, and I mentally recoiled. Lately she'd been turning up all over the place in my mind, and today was no different.

She had called in sick again this morning, and everything in me wanted to go check on her.

Was Tamara the cause of me doubting my choice?

Ridiculous.

Tamara was all sorts of wrong for me. Somebody with my kind of past needed someone like Susan. There was something attractive, though, about Tamara and the fact that she wasn't all put together.

It would be nice, for once in my life, to be the strong one. To be the savior. To be the one to take care of her. To be the one who brought her soup when she was sick or made her laugh when she was having a bad day.

My heart sputtered and my face heated up. It was messed up to even be thinking like this. Even worse was that it affected me this deeply.

I flipped the turn signal on and merged onto Highway 99.

Maybe I should talk to Trudy about switching schedules so Tamara and I would work opposite shifts. But Trudy would want an explanation, and I couldn't tell her why.

I pulled into the parking lot and shut off the engine.

Maybe I could just be mean to Tamara. Do something really terrible to make her hate me.

I exited the car and slammed the door. Who was I kidding? I could never do that. She needed me.

Those words impacted me way more than I wanted them to. Tamara needed me.

"Hey, Joe, glad you're back," Claire said as I walked into the kitchen. "I'm taking off."

"Thanks for covering for Tamara again. I couldn't have done it without you."

"She would've done it for me. I can't believe she's still sick." She put her time card in the slot, and the machine clicked.

"Yeah." Should I go check on her? Tamara had never even called in one day this whole year she'd worked here, so four days in a row was worrisome. "I hope she's okay."

"I'm sure she will be. Have a good night." She waved and then disappeared out the back.

As much as I had fought it over the last few days, it was time to go check on Tamara.

I looked at my watch as I walked up the sidewalk to Tamara's apartment. If I stayed for less than a half hour, I could make it home before Susan, and I wouldn't have to lie. I hated lying, and I hated sneaking around.

Yet here I was, sneaking and planning to lie by omission.

I stepped up to the door and knocked.

"Come in." Tamara's muffled voice came through the door. "It's unlocked."

I pushed the door open and walked in.

Tamara sat on the couch, her slight frame hunched over, head buried in her hands.

My heart dropped into my stomach. "What's going on?" Maybe she was really sick, like with cancer or something.

She was completely still.

A slender, white, plastic stick sat on the wooden chest in front of her. Two bright pink lines glared up at me from the stick. I didn't need to ask what two lines meant. I dropped down next to her and gently placed my hand on her shoulder. "Just know, whatever you decide, I'm here for you."

She looked up at me, grief-stricken eyes locking on mine, her expression a mixture of horror and regret. "What choice do I have?" Her voice quivered. "I can't have a baby. I can barely take care of myself."

"Tamara ..."

"No, Joe. Don't say anything. I've already made up my mind." She dropped her head back into her hands. "I can't believe this. I've been taking birth control pills for years. I've gone over this again and again. It must have been those two double shifts in a row. I was so busy, I must have forgotten. I'm such an idiot." Her voice cracked, and her body convulsed as she fought against tears.

How could I make her understand that doing this, taking this life, would hurt far more in the long run? How could I convince her without sounding like a hypocrite? She already knew that I'd walked this road before. "Tamara, I'll never fully understand what you're going through, but I hope you give this time. Don't rush into anything. You don't have to do anything right away."

She sat up, wiping the tears from her face. "I know you mean well, but I just can't deal with a pregnancy."

"You can do this. You don't give yourself enough credit and I'll be here. I can help you." My voice had a pleading edge to it.

"Right, because Susan would be perfectly fine with you helping me raise my illegitimate child."

She was right. I was making false promises. Promises that were impossible to keep.

Tamara reached for her phone and typed something in the search engine. "I am going to make the appointment this second." She froze a darkness overshadowing her eyes. "This number 99 is leading me straight to hell." Tamara's face had gone white.

What was she talking about? I looked over her shoulder.

Google showed the address of the clinic: 10733 99th street.

"There's more than one clinic, Tamara. Just because that was the first one you saw doesn't mean anything."

She gave me a hard, empty stare and dialed the number.

We sat in silence as the line rang.

"Hello, I need to schedule an appointment for an ... an abortion."

More silence as she listened to the person on the other side.

"I'm not that far along. The first day of my last period was in the beginning of January. I took the test today."

More waiting.

"Okay, Tuesday at nine a.m." Tamara wrote down the time and day on a piece of paper in front of her. "Thank you so much." She hung up the phone and looked up at me. "Tuesday, they are doing a walk-in clinic. I could be there a while because they take patients in the order they come. If I made an appointment, the soonest was six weeks out." Tamara lit a cigarette. "But if I wait, the procedure is more invasive. It's much better if I do it early on." She ran her free hand through her hair. "Honestly, I just want to get this nightmare over."

"Can I have one of those?" I pointed at her pack of cigarettes. I wasn't a smoker, but my nerves where shot.

Tamara frowned but pulled a cigarette out of her pack and handed it to me.

I lit up, inhaled too hard and started hacking. It was totally stupid, but it broke the tension.

"You're too funny." Tamara nudged me with her knee, grabbed the cigarette out of my hand, and snuffed it out. She took hold of my hand and squeezed it firmly. "You always have a way of making me feel better. Thank you for being here for me. Even if you don't agree with what I want to do, will you take me Tuesday? I don't want to be alone."

I didn't want any part of it, but I couldn't find it within myself to tell her no. I wrapped my arms around her, drawing her close. "You know I will."

She pulled back. Her eyes pierced into mine, and a magnetic pull radiated from her.

I raised my hand to her face. The heat of her skin kindled something deep inside of me. So badly I wanted to be there for her, for all of this.

Her wild green eyes were full of intensity.

I swallowed back the desire building in my throat. For a moment, I traced the outline of her cheek, while everything else in my life fell off the periphery of my conscience. I began to lean in.

My phone buzzed in my pocket, rescuing me from the huge mistake I was about to make.

I kissed her forehead as I rose. "I gotta go."

"I know." Tamara turned her head away.

"See you in the morning." I bolted out the door.

My stomach recoiled on itself as I looked at my cell phone. I had known it would be Susan, but her name on the screen allowed the full force of my self-reproach to hit me.

Nothing actually happened, but in this case, almost was too close.

This time I couldn't excuse my behavior with alcohol.

Perhaps that's what Tamara was—another addiction. Another desire that threatened the life I had built with Susan. She was certainly intoxicating enough.

Closing my eyes, I relived the moment—Tamara's eyes burning into mine, the feel of her skin underneath my hand, her lips inches from mine. I shook my head as the overbearing weight of guilt worked its way through me.

This had to stop. Tamara wasn't an addiction. She was a person, a good person, who needed a friend.

But being her friend was no longer an option for me. She wasn't safe.

I would help Tamara through this week and then distance myself from her. As soon as I could, I would talk to Trudy about trading shifts. It was the right thing to do—for everyone involved.

CHAPTER 23

February 15, 10:00 a.m.

LEVI

In psychological terms, bipolar disorder refers to a condition defined by severe mood swings. Times of extreme elation followed by a dip in mood so low one may find oneself suicidal.

I wasn't by any means suicidal, but lately I'd experienced my share of ups and downs. This morning particularly, I was on a severe down as I slipped into the pew next to my wife, Sarah. I leaned over and kissed her on the forehead, preoccupied with my inner turmoil. My sadness deepened as I looked around at the church I grew up in. It was the same beautiful building, with all the familiar faces, but lately I felt like a stranger in their midst. Did I even belong here anymore?

Sarah stood and sang along with the choir, lifting her heart in worship. Her honey-blonde hair rested gingerly on her shoulders, accenting her high cheekbones and jade eyes. She was lovely. Flawless. A picture of elegance and strength.

As I closed my eyes, I imagined the way I'd found her a few days before, balled up on the bathroom floor, head pressed to her knees, arms buckled around her legs.

She hadn't looked so strong then, but to her credit, she'd just heard the news.

The doctor had given her no hope.

I nearly pushed to my feet, but instead I buried my head in my hands, letting the tears roll down my face. *God, I don't understand. Please help me understand.*

The music stopped, and Sarah sat next to me, her hand resting on my back. Her touch was so comforting.

But I should have been the one comforting her. I had tried the first day, when I picked her up off the bathroom floor and carried her into the bedroom, holding her for the remainder of the afternoon as the crying came and went.

"Let's turn to Acts 15:2," My father, Pastor Taylor addressed the congregation.

I did my best to pull my emotions together and sat up stoically. For the next forty-five minutes, his voice was only background noise. Words I couldn't make sense of. Or maybe I just couldn't hear another sermon about God's will and His divine plan.

Dad concluded the sermon with an invitation. "The altars are open if anyone would like to come and pray."

Sarah strode toward the front of the church.

I remained glued to my seat. My pain, coupled with hers, made it too hard to stand. I took in three deep breaths and whispered a quick prayer. "God, help me."

Sarah faced my dad, and his hand rested on her shoulder.

It's going to be okay. A faint whisper deep inside my heart.

In the same moment, peace gently flooded over me, giving me strength to stand. I made my way toward Sarah and wrapped my arms around her. "I love you so much."

Sarah buried her head in my shoulder. "It's going to be okay," I said and somehow was able to believe it myself.

CHAPTER 24

February 16, 7:56 a.m.

TAMARA

I walked over to Levi's table and refilled his coffeepot. He looked up at me, his eyes probing me as if I were a glass house with all of my sins laid bare.

"Thanks, Tamara." His smile seemed forced. How could he make me feel so exposed? Could he possibly know what was going on with me?

A couple and their young child were sitting at a table in the middle of the restaurant. They set down their menus, and I walked over to take their order.

"I want Cheerios," the little girl said.

The mother laughed. "They don't have that on the menu, sweetie."

The child started to cry. "But I want Cheerios."

"Hey, it's okay." I said, faking a smile. "We have something better than Cheerios. You see that guy over there in the window?" I turned around and pointed at Joe.

The child stopped crying and cautiously turned her head to the kitchen. "Who is he?"

"He's the cook. And not only that, but he's the best cook I know."

The little girl moved her gaze between Joe and me several times and then shook her head. "My mommy's the best cook."

Both of her parents chuckled.

"You got me there. I'm sure your mommy is a real good cook. But I promise our cook can make the best pancakes you ever tasted."

The child's face lit up. "I love pancakes."

"One triple stack coming up, then." I glanced over at Joe again. He waved at the little girl and then our eyes met. His expression crushed me. It wasn't judgment. That I could handle. There was a depth of caring in his eyes that I didn't deserve. Even more than that, it was evident he believed with everything in him that I should have this baby.

He had walked down this road before, and in his mind, he had made the wrong choice. Which to him meant I was making the wrong choice too.

I jotted down the rest of the family's order and put it in the window. Avoiding any further eye contact, I scurried to the back of the restaurant. Smoking made the nausea far worse, so I just sat down and took in a long breath. I regretted not grabbing my jacket on the way out here. The damp air was cold and seemed to seep into my bones. A part of me wished that I could have afforded to not work until my appointment, so I wouldn't have to deal with moments like this. Or the smells that were making me queasy.

But being by myself, cooped up in my gloomy apartment, was far worse than dealing with Levi's and Joe's looks of concern. Being home was like being chained in a dungeon with a crowd of angry onlookers shouting words of condemnation. My mother's voice was the loudest in those dark moments.

When I was twelve years old, my mother made me watch this video called *The Silent Scream*. It was a documentary created to expose the horrors of abortion. The images of the fetus being ripped apart limb by limb, thrashing around trying to escape the suction device, mouth opened wide in anguish, would forever be etched into my conscience.

In my mother's mind, abortion was murder. Plain and simple. She saw it as her duty to educate me on that fact. "It goes against nature," she'd say. "It's a natural instinct to protect your child, not kill it." How ironic that she didn't protect me from my father's abuse.

My mother would've called my plan murder, but I saw it as a mercy killing. Yes, I would be snuffing out this life that was growing inside of me but in the long run, I would be sparing the baby all the pain I would bring upon it.

Did that justify my actions, though? I wasn't so sure.

Maybe if I could get ahold of Kyle, things would be different. If I wasn't so alone. I didn't have what it took to be a mother, not by myself. Wasn't it wrong to bring a child into the world when he or she wouldn't be taken care of properly?

I rubbed my temples. If only I could stop thinking. Less than twenty-four hours, and this torment would be over.

When I walked back into the dining room, Levi stood by the cash register, waiting to pay his bill.

Strange. Usually, he'd leave the money on the table with a note.

He pulled out his wallet and handed me a twenty.

I opened the till to make change for him.

"Keep it," Levi said.

Did he just say to keep it? That was a little over an eleven-dollar tip. I looked up at him.

His eyes held mine for a long moment, and his expression seemed beseeching. "Keep it, Tamara."

There was that bizarre feeling again—like somehow, he knew.

"Miss." A man across the room held up his coffee cup and pointed at it.

"Be right there." I turned my attention back to Levi, but he was already walking out the door. After making the rounds with the coffeepot, I went to clear Levi's table.

His small leather-bound journal was still there.

I snatched it and ran to the door, but he was gone. I gently tucked the journal into my apron pocket.

He would be back in a few days, and I'd return it then.

Back at the table, I flipped over the ticket.

The number at the top of the ticket was 2399, and he had underlined the *99*. Then written, *Jeremiah 29:11—Have hope.*

My stomach turned. I shoved the ticket in my pocket, bolted to the bathroom, and barely made it to the toilet before throwing up.

When I came out, Joe stood by the entrance of the women's restroom, eyebrows creased. "Are you okay?"

"Yeah, fine. Just one of the many joys of pregnancy," I said under my breath.

"Are you sure you can do this today? I can call someone in to work for you."

"I can't afford to take any more time off. I'll be fine."

He sighed. "Okay, but you need to take care of yourself. I'll make you some breakfast, and I want you to sit down for a few minutes."

I shook my head. "I couldn't eat right now if I wanted to."

"All right, then, it's break time. Go take a load off." He pointed to the back of the restaurant.

"I just took a break."

His look became stern.

"Fine." Even though I was being a brat about it, his concern affected me deeply. I loved the way he always looked out for me. It made me wish that he would leave Susan, so I could have him all to myself.

That would never happen, though. Joe had made it abundantly clear he fully intended to make Susan his wife, regardless of what I thought.

The other day at my house there was a moment where it seemed like he had wanted to kiss me. I'd replayed it in my head repeatedly after he left my house that day. The chemistry, the electricity passing through his hand as it touched my face, the quickening of my heart as his lips crept toward mine ... My face heated at the memory.

He was just trying to comfort me. How senseless of me to obsess about a fantasy.

Levi's journal jabbed me in the stomach as I sat down in the break room.

Why—today, of all days—would Levi underline the number 99?

I pulled the ticket from my apron and studied it.

A thick, dark line underlined the number as if he had run the pen several times.

I took out Levi's journal and stared at it. Who was this guy? And why did it seem like he knew things only I should know? All his eerily perceptive notes, the weird scribbled-out list, and even the song incident.

The mystery of Levi Taylor gnawed at me. I needed answers, and I could possibly have them here at my disposal.

It would be wrong to read his journal, but he seemed to have gotten into my head without my permission. Wasn't it only fair to take a peek into his?

I let the journal fall open to a random page.

As I look back, I wish I could say I didn't ask for this, but perhaps in some ways I did. However, with deep conviction I can say when I asked God to deepen my relationship with Him, I had no idea this is what it would look like. And when I asked Him for unshakeable faith, I didn't realize the shaking that would take place in my life. But if I could take it all back, I wouldn't. Despite the hardship and the trials, I am more convinced than ever of His love for me. I see the fruit of Him working in my life and hear His voice more clearly than ever.

So, Levi was religious. That explained the Bible verse. But why did he have to be so cryptic about it? He could have just written out what it said. It would've made things easier for me. I didn't even own a Bible.

> *Yet in this one area, where my dreams are shattered and I am undone, He remains silent. Through much prayer and many tears, my wife and I have decided to trust God no matter what the doctors say. Life is a miracle, and today we will embrace it. We choose to be thankful for what we have and not grow bitter for what has been taken from us.*

I shut the journal abruptly. Of all the pages I could have turned to. Life was a miracle? Really? Like I needed any more guilt heaped on me for my decision. I already had my mother's voice and the images of the aborted fetus screaming at me every night when I closed my eyes.

I shoved the ticket Levi had written on into his journal and put it into my purse. Break time was over as far as I was concerned.

CHAPTER 25

February 17, 9:00 a.m.

JOE

The guy in the car behind me honked. The light turned green, and I hadn't noticed. I threw an apologetic wave and pressed on the gas pedal. Nothing in me wanted to take Tamara to her appointment this morning.

It didn't help that I had to lie to Susan in order to leave the house. How could I ever expect her to trust me if I wasn't trustworthy? But I couldn't tell her the truth. Not since she'd finally relaxed her suspicions and given me my freedom back.

More than that, though, this whole thing was stirring up all those old feelings of guilt. And all the wonderings of how my life would be different if I'd acted otherwise. Tamara may think that this decision was what was best for her in the long term, but what she couldn't understand is that her pain wouldn't end today.

I prayed the serenity prayer as I pulled up in front of Tamara's apartment complex. If nothing else, at least I'd be there to comfort her.

She waited out front, head down, arms wrapped around her stomach.

My heart constricted. No matter that I was dead set against her having an abortion, she was counting on me to be strong for her today. Over the last few days she had put on a brave face, but it was obviously eating at her. Now, looking at her, I could tell it had been more than just eating at her.

It was killing her.

She slid onto the seat next to me, keeping her eyes forward.

I put my hand on hers. "Are you sure about this?"

She nodded, the corners of her lips turning down.

I pulled away from her apartment, praying for some sort of divine intervention.

We drove in silence all the way to the clinic.

"Do you want me to come in with you?"

"No." She unbuckled her seatbelt and reached for the door handle. "I need to do this part alone."

I gave her hand a reassuring squeeze. "I'll be here, waiting." Though I put on a strong front, inwardly my heart was breaking.

The time painfully dragged on. What I thought would take twenty minutes took almost double that. It seemed like I looked at the clock every ten seconds. What if somebody saw me here? What if Susan somehow found out? Hopefully this didn't take much longer.

Man, if my mom were able to see me now, she'd be so ashamed.

I flipped on the radio to distract from the noise in my head.

A guy droned on about some political scandal I wasn't interested in.

My phone rang, and I glanced at the clock. 9:47. I checked the caller ID before I answered.

Susan.

My heart jackhammered against my ribcage. She was supposed to be in a meeting today. Why would she be calling me? Don't trip. She didn't know anything. Just act normal. I hit the green icon. "Hey, bab—"

"Don't 'hey, baby' me! I'm going to ask you once. Where. Are. You?"

"What do you mean? I told—"

"Don't give me that junk about how you had some extra stuff to do at the diner, Joe. I just stopped by there looking for you, and they said they hadn't seen you. Oh yeah, and I noticed your little floozy girlfriend isn't working today, either."

Closing my eyes, I rocked back and forth, hitting my head rhythmically on the seat. How could I make her understand without betraying Tamara's confidence? Deflection might work. "Why do you always assume the worst of me, Susan?"

Silence.

Had I disarmed her?

"You wanna know why, Joe? It's because you're a liar." She spoke in sharp clipped words. "Something is going on. I can feel it. I've been through this before with you. And I won't do it again."

"It's not what you're thinking. Just let me expla—"

"You know what? I can't do this. Good-bye, Joe."

The line went silent.

"Susan! Susan!" I shouted into the phone.

Nothing.

I threw the cell across the car and took in three deep breaths. This would be okay. All the other fights Susan and I had indulged in had blown over, and this one would as well.

Tamara approached the car, looking worse than when she went in.

God, help me to help her.

She opened the car door and climbed in, tears streaming down her face.

I gently drew her into my arms. "It's going to be okay," I whispered as she became emotionally unraveled. "I'll be here for you every step of the way. You don't have to walk through this alone."

Her sobs grew even more intense.

Stroking her hair, I wished there was something I could do to take her pain away, but this was the path she had chosen.

She eventually pulled back and looked at me through glossy eyes. "I couldn't do it."

"What?"

"I couldn't go through with it. I couldn't kill it." Her words cut through the air.

"Tamara, that's amazing." I fought back the overwhelming urge to kiss her. "And courageous."

"No, it was that stupid number again."

"99?"

Eyes wild, she nodded. "I swear to you I'm going crazy, but it's just like before. That number is everywhere. When I got in there, they gave me a number to protect 'patient's privacy.'"

"And you got 99?"

"No. I got 107."

"Then ... what am I missing?"

"The girl next to me was having a real hard time." Tamara looked down and wiped her face with her hand. "She kept crying and talking to herself. She had to do it, she kept saying. There was no other way. I wanted to comfort her, knowing exactly what she was going through."

I pulled a napkin out of my glove box and handed it to her.

She wiped her face again and blew her nose. "She was only seventeen years old. Her boyfriend dumped her when she told him she was pregnant, her home situation is unstable, and she couldn't fathom bringing another life into the world."

A car alarm sounded across the street. A door slammed, and someone shouted.

"She became more and more tense as our numbers crept closer to being called, as if being stuck between two impossible decisions caused her physical pain. Then she bolted out the door. Her empty chair had a single piece of paper left behind. Her ticket."

"Let me guess."

Tamara nodded. "The second I saw it, a voice read it over the speakers. I dropped my ticket and ran out."

When she had first told me about the whole 99 thing, it seemed like a weird coincidence, but this was getting kind of spooky. "You're doing the right thing. You'll see. I'm proud of you."

"Proud of me?" She seemed to retreat into herself, unable to handle our conversation any longer.

"Yes, proud."

Her eyes grew more vacant.

It was time to get her out of this dark place. I reached over and buckled her seatbelt, then pulled out onto the road.

Halfway back to Tamara's apartment, she seemed to come back to herself. "Hey, Joe?"

"Yeah?" I glanced toward her.

"Can I ask you a favor?"

"Absolutely." Hadn't I just proven I'd do almost anything for her?

"I'm not ready to go home yet, and I don't know if it's healthy for me to be alone right now."

In all reality, I should have gone back to my place and faced the music with Susan, but I couldn't leave Tamara like this. "Where do you want to go? Are you hungry?"

"I'm not really hungry, but I should probably eat."

"I know the perfect place." I signaled and made a right-hand turn toward the Tin Shed Garden Café, a place known for healthy food and good coffee. Plus, it was far enough out of the way that we wouldn't run into anyone we knew.

Color returned to Tamara's face once she got some food in her. "What am I supposed to do?" She stuffed the last bite of her omelet into her mouth.

"I thought you already made up your mind."

She fidgeted with her napkin. "I guess, but that doesn't make it any easier. I can't do this by myself. Sure, women become single mothers all the time, but I am not like most women. I'm a mess."

"You don't give yourself enough credit. Yes, parts of your life are messy, but life is messy."

The waitress came by and filled my coffee cup. She tried to fill Tamara's cup too, but she covered it with her hand.

"If I could only get ahold of Kyle." She waited before the waitress walked away and leaned closer. "I mean, now that I've decided to have his baby, doesn't he have a right to know?"

My stomach clenched, and my face grew hot. If I was to ever come clean about the whole phone number thing, I should right now. I tried to speak, but the words became trapped in my constricting throat. I coughed.

"Are you okay?"

I took a drink of water. "Yeah. I'm fine." I coughed again. "Got something stuck in my throat."

"I hate it when that happens."

"Me too." I took another drink. Please, let the Kyle subject drop.

"Do you think I should try to track Kyle down?"

My palms began to sweat. "How would you go about it?" A jerk thing to say, but I had destroyed the number over a month ago. It would only upset her if I told her now.

She blanched. "I don't even know his last name."

"Maybe it's better this way. He might be a real scumbag."

"I don't know ... Maybe you're right." She pushed a stray piece of hash browns around with her fork. "But he didn't seem like a bad guy. He was actually kinda sweet." An emotion crossed her face, as if she were remembering something pleasant about him.

Why did she have to defend the guy? "How could you tell? Weren't you drunk most of the time you hung out with him?"

She dropped her fork, cheeks flushing. "Yeah."

"Tamara, I'm sorry. I shouldn't have said that. It came out all wrong. I'm just saying, sometimes it's better to leave well enough alone."

"Wouldn't you want to know if you had gotten someone pregnant?"

"Yes, but not all guys think like I do."

"You're probably right. There isn't anything I can do to find him, anyway."

I reached across the table and touched her hand, shame burning a hole in my guts. "Tamara, I'm so sorry." Susan was right earlier. I was a liar.

Confusion settled over her face. "For what?"

"For all of this. I don't have any right to give you advice." *And I'm sorry for not telling you the truth.*

"It's not your fault." She shook her head. "I did this to myself. I have to live with the consequences of my actions. There's really no way I can run from this one."

"I want to be there for you as much as possible. Every step of the way. As much as you let me." So much for distancing myself from her.

A slight smile, something I hadn't seen for the last few days. "I appreciate that. Thank you."

"You don't have to thank me. I'm here because I want to be."

She smiled again, a little brighter this time. "We should get out of here."

"I'll pay, and we can head out."

"I can pay." She opened her purse.

"No, I got this." I headed to the register.

"I'll get the tip."

CHAPTER 26

February 17, 4:39 p.m.

JOE

Forgetting about Susan and our argument was easy when I was with Tamara, but in the car on the way home all the images of Susan's burning fury blazed through my head. What was I going to tell her? How was I going to make her understand? Should I come clean and apologize yet again? If I did come clean, would that make things better between us? Or would it just add to our problems?

The more I thought about it, the more anxiety built inside me. By the time I pulled into the driveway, I was having a full-blown panic attack.

I breathed easier when I noticed all the lights were off, and Susan's car wasn't in the driveway. But where was she?

I hadn't heard from her since our fight.

I pulled the car into the garage and headed inside. Something felt different, but everything looked the same at first glance. I ran upstairs, but slowed in the hallway, swallowing back the apprehension building in my throat. After switching on the light, I crept toward her closet.

Completely empty.

I blinked, uncomprehending.

Was she gone? *Gone*, gone?

I walked back into the bedroom and found a small folded paper lying on my pillow.

Joe, I'm sorry it has to end this way, but I can't do this anymore. I will be back with some movers later in the week to get the rest of my stuff. ~ Susan

II fell onto the bed and gasped as if the air had been knocked out of me. She broke up with me with a measly three-lined note, without even giving me a chance to explain myself? Was what we had that cheap to her?

I studied the note, reading the three lines over and over again. Did she expect me to come after her? To grovel at her feet and beg her to take me back? I couldn't keep fighting for this broken relationship.

Did it hurt that she left me? Yes, but that wasn't the main emotion rushing through me. Emptiness maybe? Something had been ripped from me, leaving me feeling ... exposed? Vulnerable? Relieved ...

For the last three years, my whole world had been about trying to make things up to her, to prove I had changed, but it was never good enough. The breakup hurt right now, but it made everything else far less complicated.

I ripped up the worthless note, threw the pieces in the wastebasket, and left to get a refund on the ring I had just bought.

CHAPTER 27

February 18, 6:14 a.m.

TAMARA

I checked three times that I had Levi's journal before heading out the door. He probably came in looking for it yesterday, while I'd selfishly skipped work. I should have left it with Claire, just in case he came in, but I felt strangely possessive of it. *I* wanted to be the one to give it back to him. But more than that, I wanted to ask him about the last note he'd left me. Why had he underlined my number? His journal was my hostage to secure his answer.

When I arrived at work, Joe was leaning on the back of his Jeep Cherokee, wearing a black pea coat and blue jeans, arms crossed in front of him. His face brightened when he saw me. "Hey!"

"Good morning. You're awfully chipper."

Joe tilted his head, grin widening. "Just have a new lease on life. That's all." He popped open the back of his SUV. "I got you something."

"Yeah?"

"It's nothing, really. I thought of you when I was out shopping last night." He pulled out two gift bags and held them toward me.

"Shopping? Really?" Joe didn't seem like a big shopper to me.

"Yes." He laughed. "I had a little spare time and some extra money."

"Spare time? You? And who has extra money?" Where was Susan while he did his shopping? Did he tell her about the baby or my appointment?

"Here, open them."

I took hold of one, set it on the back of my car, and rummaged through the bag.

It contained three books: *What to Expect When You're Expecting, Motherhood,* and *Chicken Soup for the Mother's Soul.*

"I figured it would be less stressful if you knew what to expect."

"*Chicken Soup for the Mother's Soul*?" I tossed him a playful look.

"Threw it in for good measure." He shrugged. "Everyone needs some good soul food now and again."

"Thanks, Joe. That's very sweet."

"There's more." He handed me the other bag.

It contained a baby rattle, a couple of binkies, a scrapbook, and a Precious Moments Bible.

His gesture calmed a place inside of me that had been shaking relentlessly since I'd found out I was pregnant. My throat felt thick. Though I tried to fight back the tears, a few spilled from my eyes.

"This is too much too soon, isn't it? I'm such an idiot sometimes."

I shook my head. "No, that's not it. It's just so ... sweet and ... and thoughtful and kind."

"Come here." He pulled me into his embrace, folding his arms around me like a cozy blanket. "I'm here for you."

His words warmed me almost as much as his embrace. For a long moment, I rested my head on his chest, thankful to have a guy like him in my life, even if we would always only be friends. I pulled away and dried my eyes on the back of my sleeve.

"We better get in there." Joe helped me put the gifts back into the bags.

The restaurant was surprisingly busy when I walked through the door. Nine tables were occupied, with one to two customers per table, but no Levi. Maybe he'd be in later.

Trisha looked completely frazzled as she bustled from table to table, filling coffee cups and clearing dishes.

I chided myself for taking so long in the parking lot with Joe.

"Thank God you're here," Trisha exclaimed as soon as she spotted me.

I walked around the counter and grabbed an apron off the hook. "Quite the rush this morning."

Trisha leaned in close and quietly gave me a rundown of the night of endless patrons. "They were hitting on me all night." She grimaced. "Most of them dirty old truck drivers."

"Gross." A little chuckle escaped my lips. My thoughts drifted to Kyle. How often, if ever, did he come through Vancouver? There had to be a way to get ahold of him. "I got it from here."

"Thanks." Trisha threw me a wry smile and headed to the time clock.

The diner stayed busy, and the day went by quickly. Levi and his journal were on my mind my whole shift. Every time the bells clanged, I expected Levi to walk through the door. His little leather-bound book felt as if it were burning a hole in my purse. It was horrible of me to have read part of it, but I couldn't deny I wanted to read more. The quicker I could get it back to him, the sooner I could be free of the temptation.

But the whole shift passed, and he never came in.

CHAPTER 28

February 21, 2:00 p.m.

TAMARA

The week passed in a blur. Before I knew it, it was Saturday, and my work week was over. At the end of my shift, I stood rolling silverware, my mind on Levi Taylor. He still hadn't come in. His journal, along with his ticket where he'd underlined the number 99, were a perpetual puzzle in my mind. Did he know that I hated that number? That I couldn't escape it? That it reminded me of all my failures? There was absolutely no way he could, yet he *had* underlined the number, like somehow it meant something to him too. There had to be a way to track him down. Reading his journal could provide some answers ... But why hadn't he come in to retrieve it? What if he was dead? What if he'd been hit by a bus or something? How awful.

Joe came from the kitchen and took a spot beside me and grabbed a napkin from the pile and began to roll silverware with me.

A familiar humming sensation opened inside of me at his closeness. "You know what's been bugging me? I haven't seen Levi Taylor all week."

Joe stopped mid-roll and turned toward me. "Why would that bug you?"

A part of me wanted to tell Joe about the notes and the

journal, but it was hard enough to convince myself I wasn't crazy. "He's one of my favorite regulars. It feels weird that he's not come in for so long."

"I could see that. Levi is a great guy."

His words brought me up short. I'd never even seen him talk to Levi. "You say that like you know him."

"Yeah, Levi and I go way back." Joe picked up a knife and twirled it through his fingers.

"Really?" I watched the silver object flash round and round in Joe's hand. "He's here all the time, and I've never seen you even say hi."

"Let's just say it's not that kind of a relationship."

"Okay ..." I snatched the knife from his hand. "How do you know him, then?" The words came out more demanding than I meant.

"You know what they say." He smirked and slowly raised an eyebrow. "Curiosity killed the cat."

"Yeah, well." My eyes burrowed into his. "Satisfaction brought him back."

He folded his arms in front of him, smiling. "It's killing you, isn't it?"

Face hot, I turned back to the silverware. Why did he have to be so adorable? Why did he have to be so taken? I grabbed another fork and knife, laid them in the middle of the napkin, and rolled.

"Okay." He let out a dramatic sigh. "We had a therapeutic relationship."

"He's a counselor?" This could be my big break. If Joe knew where he worked, I could find him easily.

"Yup."

"I guess I could see how that would be awkward."

"Ya think?" He teased with a chuckle.

"Where does he practice?"

Lines appeared in Joe's forehead. "You want to go get counseling?"

"No, I—"

The bells rattled against the door.

My head jerked toward the noise.

Still no Levi. Instead, a woman dressed in black slacks and a fitted coat came in. Her dark hair was cut in a short style that framed her face. She adjusted her jacket and read the sign that said Please Seat Yourself, but she remained standing there, looking out of place.

I walked toward her. "May I help you?"

"I'm just waiting for Claire. I guess she got called in to work and couldn't find a babysitter. She said she'd be here soon. I'm her sister, Emma." She smiled, and tiny crow's feet outlined her brown eyes. There was definitely a family resemblance. They had the same eyes and nose, but Claire's face was narrower than Emma's.

"Would you like some coffee or something?"

"No, thanks." She pulled out her cell phone and typed away.

I again took my place next to Joe, who'd dutifully continued rolling the silverware.

"So, what are you doing on your days off?" Joe asked before I had a chance to inquire about Levi again.

I shrugged. "Nothing, really. Why do you ask?"

He looked down at the floor.

"What's up?" My stomach fluttered.

"I've been meaning to talk to you about this for the last few days, but I just—"

The bells jangled again.

Levi?

No. Claire hurried through the door, a little tow-headed boy resting on her hip. She wore large sunglasses and had several bags slung over her shoulder.

The young boy's eyes lit up when he saw his aunt. "Auntie Em," he squealed.

Claire set him down.

He waddled his chubby frame over to Emma and threw his arms around her legs.

She scooped him up. "Hey, Sammy. I missed you."

"I mithed you too." He hugged her neck and giggled.

"Thank you for watching him at such short notice." Claire handed her sister the bags.

"No problem. I love hanging with Sammy. He's my favorite nephew." She tousled his blond hair and kissed his cheek.

Claire laughed. "We won't tell him he's your only nephew."

I turned my attention back to Joe. "Was there something you wanted to tell me?"

"Oh, um, yeah—"

The bells interrupted Joe's sentence.

This time Trudy struggled through the door, carrying a large file folder box.

Joe hurried to Trudy's aide. "Here, let me help you."

I guess I'd have to ask him about it later, along with asking about Levi.

Trudy handed off the box. "Thanks, Joe." She looked back and forth between us and smiled weakly. "Well, if it's not my two favorite employees." Dark circles shaded her eyes, and her face sunk in around her cheekbones.

This normally vibrant woman looked as if she'd aged ten years since the last time I saw her. Which was maybe a week ago. "Trudy, are you okay?"

She waved me off with her hand. "Oh, yeah. Just tired." She yawned. "I was up half the night trying to figure this tax stuff out." She stepped toward the coffeepot. "Joe, I was hoping you would be able to help me with it."

"I'll try, but I don't know." Joe's eyebrows pinched together. "You might have to bite the bullet and hire a tax guy."

Trudy picked up a cup and flipped it over. "I can't afford it right now." She lifted the coffeepot with noticeably shaky hands.

Joe and I exchanged a concerned glance.

"Is there anything I can do to help?" I asked.

"You could help me sort through this mess. Joe, can you take that box into my office?"

"Sure thing." Joe pushed through the double doors.

"Now that's a good man right there, honey." Trudy winked.

"Yes, and a good friend." I stressed the word friend. "Susan's lucky to have him."

"Didn't you hear? They broke up."

My heart skipped a beat. "What? When?" Why did it affect me like this? They had broken up before.

She raised a knowing eyebrow. "Pretty interested for someone who's just a friend."

I smiled awkwardly, my face growing hotter by the moment. Embarrassed as I was, this was the best news I had heard all day.

"That's what I thought." She winked again. "Don't worry, Tammy girl, your secret is safe with me."

"Enough teasing. What's this mess you want us to look at?"

Trudy's face drooped, and she sighed. "It's about the diner. I just don't know what to do. Things have gotten pretty bad."

Hours later, Joe, Trudy, and I were gathered around Trudy's desk. When Trudy had lifted the lid off the file folder box, I expected to see what one would normally see—file folders neatly arranged side by side. Instead, there was a massive pile of invoices, receipts, and who-knew-what-else mixed together in a huge, chaotic mess.

Trudy leaned back in her seat and breathed out a deep breath. "I'm sorry, you guys, for letting it get this bad."

"Don't apologize. I think we're making some good headway here." Joe rubbed his forehead and shuffled a few receipts to a different pile.

"You're too kind, Joe. I've made a mess of everything. If things don't turn around soon, I might have to shut the place down."

"Hey, that's not going to happen." Joe pulled out the company laptop and opened Microsoft Excel. "Check this out."

He explained that he'd been working with the diner's books and realized we turned a profit during morning and evening shifts, but graveyard had become a liability. "Trudy, it's in your best interest to shut down the restaurant during that time. Open from seven in the morning to eleven at night and split up the shifts accordingly. Some employees would lose hours, but that's preferable to losing their jobs."

Lines deepened in Trudy's forehead.

I didn't like the thought of losing hours, but Joe's suggestion did make sense.

"What about the truck drivers we serve in the middle of the night?" Trudy asked.

Kyle could be one of those truck drivers that came through during the graveyard shift. Did he ever think of me? Maybe one day he'd stop by the diner, and I'd be able to tell him about the baby. But if we closed the place down at night, it would lessen the chances by a third.

"Let them go down the street to Denny's."

Trudy curled her upper lip in a snarl.

Joe laughed. "Just a suggestion. Calm down."

"No, you actually have a valid point. I'll think about it." She turned toward me. "Tammy girl, will you be a dear and go get us some coffee? I think we could all use a little break right about now."

"Sure."

The coffeepot in the kitchen was empty, so I started a fresh one. Anthony was working that evening, but he was nowhere to be seen.

Not wanting to wait, I walked into the dining room to check that pot. Anthony was at the other end of the counter standing close to Claire. Was she going to be his next victim? She probably had the good sense to stay away from him, but just in case, I made a mental note to warn her about him next time we were alone. For the time being, I ignored them and walked straight to the coffeepot. I grabbed three coffee cups and filled mine with decaf.

One of the books Joe gave me said caffeine caused low birth weight, so I'd been doing my best to cut back.

I filled the other two cups with regular coffee. Trudy's, black; Joe's, sweet and creamy.

A loud crash came from the back of the restaurant.

"Call 911!" Joe shouted, voice panicked.

I ran to the office as I pulled my phone from my pocket.

Trudy lay on the floor, unconscious, blood trickling from a gash in her forehead. Joe hovered over her, checking her pulse.

CHAPTER 29

February 21, 9:11 p.m.

TAMARA

Joe and I sat in the waiting room for hours, desperate for an update. Joe's knee bounced up and down with the rhythm of the second hand on the clock.

Finally, my nerves couldn't take it any longer. "I'm going to go for a walk."

"What?" Joe looked half-dazed. He hadn't said much since we'd been here. Hospitals probably weren't the easiest place to be for him because of what happened to his mom.

"I can't sit here and stare at the clock for one more moment."

He rubbed his hands on the front of his jeans. "Do you want company?"

"No. I just need to be alone for a few. Text me if you hear anything." Once outside, I smoked half a cigarette. All that did was make me nauseous and put me more on edge. Plus, I felt terrible for smoking. Ever since I had decided to keep the baby, I'd been trying to quit. This had been my second one all day, but the stress of everything made quitting hard. After three laps around the parking lot, I went back inside, but not to the waiting room. I wandered aimlessly around the hospital, reading the signs to the different departments.

Maternity. An arrow pointed to the left.

I took a deep breath and walked down the long corridor. Turning the corner, I faced a large viewing window.

Seven tiny newborns, most of them asleep, lay wrapped in white baby blankets with either a blue or pink beanie on their tiny heads. The sight of them caused a motherly instinct to bring my hand to my stomach, even though it was still flat. I stood there, mesmerized by these tiny people. A little one that profound was growing inside of me.

And I had almost extinguished its budding life.

Shame washed over me. "I'm so sorry," I whispered down at my belly.

"Pretty amazing, aren't they?" A female's voice cut through my one-way conversation. A pretty blonde woman dressed in pink scrubs stood beside me, looking just as mesmerized.

"Yes, they are."

"It's my favorite part of the job."

I smiled at her and looked back at the babies.

"Do you have children?"

I patted my stomach. "My first is on the way."

"Oh yeah?" Her voice pitched changed. "When's your due date?"

"October eleventh."

"Congratulations! You and your husband must be so excited."

I lifted my left hand. "No husband. Just me."

"Oh, I'm so sorry." She twisted her wedding ring. "It's just I was thinking about my husband just now and ..."

Silence hung between us for a few awkward moments.

"There are a ton of resources for single mothers," the woman said. "I could get you some information if you're interested."

"That would be great. It's kind of scary thinking of doing this all by myself."

"I'll be right back." She briskly walked away and returned minutes later with several brochures. "I hope you find these helpful."

Another nurse tapped the woman on the shoulder. "Doctor Franklin needs you in room nine eighteen."

"Guess I better get back to work." She scribbled something on the back of one of the pamphlets and handed them to me.

"Thank you." I shoved the pamphlets into my purse and headed back to the ER's waiting room.

Joe looked relieved when I walked through the door. "Where have you been? I've texted you, like, three times."

"What?" I pulled out my cell. "Shoot. My phone died. Have you heard anything?"

"Yeah. Trudy's stable. They're running some tests. The doctor said he thought it was extreme exhaustion. Her electrolytes were off. She's severely dehydrated and hypotensive."

"What does that mean?"

"Her blood pressure is really low. Basically, she's a mess. She's going to be in here for at least a few days."

"Can we see her?"

"They're not allowing any visitors, only family."

"But we *are* her family. She needs us."

"I know it's awful, but there is nothing we can do. I'll stay here and push to see her. You get some rest."

"What about the diner, though? As much as I hate working with Anthony, one of us needs to go back."

"Maybe we should close down the diner for tonight. Put a sign up that there was a medical emergency."

"That seems like the best thing for now. Do you want me to go let everyone know and put up a sign?"

"I can take care of it. You should go get some rest."

As much as I hated the thought of leaving without seeing Trudy, I wasn't going to be good for anything or anyone if I didn't get some sleep.

Forty-five minutes later, I tried to relax at home, but everything with Trudy made it impossible. I put on some Norah Jones, chewed a piece of Nicorette, and cleaned my already spotless apartment. Finally, I sat down and sorted the contents of my purse. I pulled out the brochures the nurse had given me at the hospital.

One explained how to sign up for state-paid medical insurance. Another talked about different support groups for single mothers. The third discussed adoption. I threw that one in the trash. Abandoning your child with a random set of parents seemed worse than abortion.

The next thing I pulled out was Levi's journal. I ran my fingers over the smooth, leather book and conjured up an image of his face. A lion's share of curiosity welled inside of me. Flipping through the journal—not reading, just looking, I glanced at the entries. Almost every page had been written on.

It made no sense.

If I had left my journal somewhere, I would've searched for it immediately.

Where are you, Levi, and why haven't you come to reclaim what's yours?

Maybe he wanted me to read it.

But why? My eyes flitted to the top of the page.

January 18

I haven't been able to sleep lately. Today is the fourth day in a month that I was woken up by the same nightmare. It's so vivid and surreal. Each time there's only a few subtle differences.

I'm in a barren valley, lined with ashes, overcast by dark shadows. All around me a cold wind blows. Suddenly a man shrouded in darkness appears in front of me. He lifts his head, his eyes sear into mine, and bloodcurdling cries flood the air.

That's when I usually wake up, heart racing, but this time the nightmare continued. I turned to run, fear coursing through my limbs, but the man was in front of me again. The darkness that surrounded him pierced through me, weakening me from the inside out.

Even now as I write about it, the fear remains.

David told me once that sometimes dreams can be a warning of something to come. I hope he's wrong about that.

God, if this dream means something, please protect me and my family.

An eerie sensation tingled at the nape of my neck, sending an icy shiver down my spine. There was something creepy and familiar about his dream. Sure, the backdrop didn't match my dream, but the dark figure felt the same.

I closed Levi's journal, picked up my own, and found the entry when I'd had the dream about the dark figure.

The exact same date, January eighteenth.

Goosebumps prickled up my arms as I read my entry. I'd always felt a connection with Levi, but to find out we'd had similar nightmares on the same day was unnerving. That, along with the other oddities with him, left a gnawing uneasiness in my core. I tried to shake the feeling as I got ready for bed.

I splashed water on my face, then stared at myself in the broken mirror, taking in my distorted image. Circles were forming under my eyes.

I took a deep breath, retreated to bed, and took the last items out of my bag, intentionally turning my attention to the biggest thing on my mind, something I hadn't even had the chance to process.

Joe.

I held the Bible and the motherhood book, while I thought of him. His warm hazel eyes, and the upward curve of his beautiful smile. My heart expanded with fondness then plummeted back into sadness.

Why hadn't he told me he and Susan had broken up? I thought he trusted me enough to let me know what was happening in his life. He'd been there for me through so much. Why wouldn't he let me be there for him?

Setting the books aside, I turned out the light and settled into bed. Maybe he didn't want to burden me. I punched my pillow and rolled over.

Or maybe he just didn't trust me with his problems.

CHAPTER 30

February 22, 5:45 a.m.

JOE

"Better make that a quad shot." I told the excessively tanned woman in the small coffee stand I had stopped by on the way to work. I was going to need as much caffeine as possible after last night. I was at the hospital till almost midnight, and now it was up to me to make sure everything was running smoothly at the diner.

"Here ya go, hun. Quad white chocolate mocha." Her voice was too cheerful for this early in the morning. "That will be five fifty."

"Thanks." I handed her seven dollars. "Keep the change." Making a right out of the coffee shop parking lot, I made a mental list of everything that needed to be done today before I could head back to the hospital.

What would work look like if Trudy couldn't come back for an extended period? There was no way I could manage full time and cook. We would either have to hire someone else for my cooking shift or close the place down for the graveyard shift permanently, like I had suggested last night. I took a sip of coffee and turned onto 99th Street. Hopefully Trudy would be awake a little later, so I could ask her what she wanted me to do. Because even if we did close the diner down from eleven p.m. to seven a.m., I would still need someone to help me manage the place. The job was too big for one person alone.

I pulled into the diner and parked, stomach churning. Resting my head on the steering wheel, I prayed the serenity prayer. I could do this, just like sobriety. One thing at a time, one foot in front of the next. Moment by moment, that's how I'd conquer the day. I climbed out of my car and walked toward the front door.

There was a piece of paper, folded in half, taped to the glass.

What in the world? It was still dark out, which made it hard to read.

I pulled out my phone and turned on the flashlight app. Thank goodness for smartphones.

It had Tamara's name on the outside. Who would leave a note for Tamara? Everyone at work had her number, and if they needed something, they could text her. Should I read it?

It wasn't like someone would put a personal note on the front door of a diner.

Leaving it taped to the door, I flipped it open.

Tamara,

I was just passing through town and was hoping we could pick up where we left off. Give me a call if you're available within the next 24 hours. I believe I still have a few articles of clothing that may be yours.

Kyle

Acid turned in my guts. He wanted to pick up with her where they left off? They had left off in the back of his semi! What a scumbag. To leave a note like this at her place of employment was more than wrong. It was disgraceful.

Anyone could have found it. Might as well shout it from the rooftops—Tamara had sex with some random guy, and now he had her clothes.

I ripped down the note and looked at the back. There was his number.

For a second, everything seemed darker as I let my imagination run wild. I could call him. Tell him Tamara would be in later. Have him show up. Then, I could beat the living snot out of him.

I crumbled the note in my hand. *I believe I still have a few articles of clothing that may be yours?*

I would never treat her with such disrespect. And no one else would either if I could help it. But was it even my place to be her protector?

Everything in me wanted to destroy the wrinkled note. But wasn't it wrong to withhold the number from her again? Especially now? Before, I didn't know about the baby, so at least I had that excuse if she ever found out. Odds were, Kyle wouldn't even show his face here again. I'd seen his kind many times. If she didn't call, maybe he'd lose interest.

But if I gave her the note, who knew how much pain it would cause her in the long run? Tamara wanted the father of her child in her life, but sometimes having a father in one's life didn't help the situation.

My life would have turned out much worse if my mom hadn't kept me away from my dad. Look how much pain Tamara's father had caused her.

I pressed my clenched fist to my forehead. Why did I care so much? Didn't her baby deserve a father? Why was I so against her contacting him?

The answer hit me the way the moon eclipses the sun. In that moment, all I could see was Tamara. She overshadowed every thought, every place inside of me. The reason I didn't want Kyle to be with Tamara was because I was in love with her. As I stood there, holding the note—this little piece of paper that could change everything—I realized I was beyond-reason in love with Tamara. If I could, I would do anything to keep her safe. She had already experienced enough pain to last ten lifetimes. It was time for her to have the happiness she deserved. And maybe, if I was lucky, if I was careful with her, she would eventually let me be the one to make her happy.

I unlocked the door and walked straight to the office. I smoothed out the note and shoved it into the paper shredder, where it belonged.

CHAPTER 31

February 22, 10:30 a.m.

TAMARA

The shrill ring of my phone woke me up from a dead sleep.

"Hello," I said groggily.

"Aw, man, I didn't wake you, did I?" Joe's voice came across the other end of the line.

"No," I said through a deep yawn. "Okay, I'm lying. You totally did."

He chuckled. "I waited as long as I could."

I yawned again. "You could have waited another two hours, and I'd probably still be sleeping."

"Yeah, I read it was like that in the first trimester."

He read about it? I must have heard him wrong. "How could you have read that?"

"I kind of bought my own copy of *What to Expect When You're Expecting*, just in case you didn't do your homework. It's actually fascinating stuff."

I burst into laughter. Where had this guy come from?

"I'm glad that I amuse you, but I called for a reason."

"Is it Trudy?"

"She's better than last night, but she still has a long road ahead of her. I just left her room."

"Oh, good. I'm glad you were able to see her."

161

Joe was quiet for a beat too long.

"Joe?"

"I'm still here. Just gathering my thoughts."

My pulse sped up. Was there bad news he was scared to tell me?

"She wanted me to talk to you about something."

Anxiety bounced around inside my stomach. What if Trudy found out about my being pregnant and wanted me to quit? "What about?"

"She wanted me to ask you if you would be willing to train for the assistant manager position that just opened up."

Of course, Joe would be the one to run the restaurant while Trudy recovered. That part was obvious. But he wanted my help? I couldn't manage a restaurant. I hadn't even graduated from high school. "Really? Why me?"

"Trudy said you're the best waitress she has. You know your stuff and are very reliable."

"I wouldn't know the first thing about managing a restaurant."

"You'd have my help. And just to let you know, we both agreed that you're the best person for the job. It will mean less hours on your feet and more pay, both things you need right now." His tone was thoroughly convincing.

"I don't know what to say."

"Say you'll do it."

I took in a deep breath. "Okay, I'll do it."

"Awesome. Since that's out of the way, training starts immediately. I know it's normally your day off, but can you meet me at the diner in an hour?"

"You're such a tyrant. Making a poor pregnant girl come in on her day off."

He chuckled. "See you in a few."

"Can we make that an hour and a half? I'd like to see Trudy before I come in."

"Sure, that's fine."

"What room is she in?"

"Room three sixteen. But make it a short visit. I've called everyone in for an employee meeting at two, and I want to go over some things with you before that."

I sighed dramatically. "Okay, Mister Boss Man, I'll hurry."

His smile seemed to come through the phone. "Hey, you're the boss now too."

"That'll take a little getting used to, but I like it."

I bought a bouquet of orchids and a get-well card at the hospital gift store before finding Trudy's room. Since her eyes were closed, I tiptoed to her bed and quietly set the flowers on the table, which was already half-full of elegant bouquets, abounding with numerous types of colorful flowers.

Trudy's eyes popped open. "Well, hello there, Tammy girl," she rasped through a slight smile.

"Hi. I'm sorry. I didn't mean to wake you up."

"Don't apologize. I'm glad to see you. Besides, I was just resting my eyes."

I took a seat next to her bed. "How are you feeling?" So dumb. Probably not good.

She winced through a chuckle. "Well, I feel horrible, but they say I'm going to be okay."

I fidgeted with the keys hanging on my purse. "You scared us last night."

"Sorry about that. I guess all the stress finally caught up with me. There's going to be a lot of changes from here on out. I trust Joe has already talked to you about a promotion?"

I nodded.

"Good, good. I know you two will run that place real nicely. You both have good heads on your shoulders. I couldn't think of two better people for the job."

It touched me that she thought so highly of me. "Thank you. I appreciate the opportunity, Trudy, but are you sure you can afford to promote me? Last night the books seemed pretty bad."

"Well, I'm taking Joe's suggestion about closing the diner at night. With fewer shifts to cover, it will even out. Besides it feels right to have you two running the place." She grabbed hold of my hand. "You may not know this, but you and Joe are like the kids I never had. I care about you guys. And I think you have a lot of potential."

A thick lump knotted up in my throat. No one had ever believed in me like that. I swallowed and looked down at the ground. "I need to tell you something."

"I'm listening."

"I'm pregnant." I glanced up to see her reaction.

Her face was hard to read.

"I don't plan on telling everyone right away. You know, just in case. But you deserve to know before you offer me a management position."

Trudy took a moment before she spoke. "Is Joe the father?"

"What? No!" Blood rushed to my cheeks. Was that what people at the diner would assume? "Why would you think that?"

She tilted her head, expression softening. "Have you seen the way he looks at you?"

Heat flooded my cheeks. This was *not* the direction this conversation was supposed to go. "We're really good friends, but Joe's an honorable man. He would have never cheated on Susan."

"I know, honey. Joe is a wonderful young man."

Then why was she questioning his integrity because of my mistakes? "I wish I could say the same thing about me. I don't really know the father." Saying the words out loud was much harder than I realized it would be. There was no way she could believe in me after I'd admitted to such a massive mistake. "It's stupid, I know. But it's one of those things I couldn't take back."

"Oh goodness, honey, don't beat yourself up. Whoever really plans life, anyway? It just happens. My mother used to always tell me, 'If you want to make God laugh, tell Him your plans.'"

"So, you still want me to train for the position?" I held my breath.

"Of course, I do. If anything, it gives me one more reason to offer you the job. You're going to need more time off your feet."

"That's what Joe said."

A voluptuous woman wearing blue scrubs entered the room, pushing a cart. "Time to check your vitals." False enthusiasm filled her voice.

"That's my cue. Joe said we have a lot to cover before the employee meeting."

"Employee meeting, huh? Those are always a barrel of laughs."

"My favorite part of the job. Almost as fun as getting your vital signs taken."

She chuckled and started coughing.

I leaned over and gave her a hug. "Get better," I whispered in her ear.

"I'm working on it."

CHAPTER 32

February 22, 12:15 p.m.

TAMARA

Joe sat behind Trudy's desk, studying a piece of lined paper.

"Hard at work, I see." I walked into the office. He smiled, and my heart threw an irregular beat. Could he tell he had this sort of effect on me?

"Hey, you. Glad you're here. I was just trying to work out the new schedule. Any change in Trudy?"

"Nope, she's still looking pretty rough. She seems to be in good hands, though."

"Did she tell you about the changes we decided on?"

"Yes, and I told her about the baby. She deserved to know."

His eyes lit up. "How did she react?"

"Surprisingly well." Except for the part where she thought Joe was the father. What would he say if I told him about that? I was way too much of a coward to find out. "She still wanted to give me the job, and she didn't seem to think less of me for it. So that's good, right?"

"I didn't expect any less from her." He glanced at his watch. "We better get down to business."

"Where do we start?"

We spent a few minutes discussing the changes, then the next hour and a half going over scheduling and preparing for the upcoming meeting.

Before we knew it, it was one forty-five, and the other employees began arriving. Frank and Claire were already working, so they would have to be filled in later.

Everyone was speaking in hushed whispers when Joe and I walked out of the office and into the break room, then they fell silent and gathered around the large table.

I sat where I could see everyone, while Joe made his way to the front of the room.

"Good afternoon. Thank you for coming at such short notice. I'm sure you've heard about what happened with Trudy last night." He seemed so natural when he spoke in front of people. "She won't be able to return to work for quite some time. Because of this, she has appointed me as manager, for the time being. Also, she has asked Tamara to step into the role of assistant manager."

Anthony exchanged a loaded glance with Tommy.

Irritation rose inside of me for a brief moment before I forced my attention back to Joe.

"There are going to be some major changes that will take effect immediately. After much consideration, Trudy and I have decided it best that we shut down the diner from eleven p.m. to seven a.m."

"What? What about us? What is going to happen to us?" Betty piped in angrily.

"I know it sounds alarming, but there's no need to get upset. Because of the changes, Tamara and I will no longer be working our normal shifts. Those will be wide open for the taking. If you have some reason that only night shifts work, we'll gladly write you a letter of recommendation while you seek employment elsewhere. As for now, Tamara and I have worked out a tentative schedule, but it is open to suggestion. Just talk to either of us about it, and we will see what we can do. Does anyone have any other questions?"

Over the next fifteen minutes, Joe fielded questions ranging from the changes to the schedule to Trudy's condition. I stepped in whenever needed, but Joe handled the questions well.

Everyone seemed to be on board with the new changes after hearing it would help out Trudy. Betty made a few more complaints when she found out her new hours, but it looked as if she was going to stick around.

When everyone was finished, Joe turned to me. "Tamara. Do you have anything to add?"

"I think you covered it."

"Okay, then. I don't want to keep you guys any longer than needed. Thanks for coming."

As Anthony and Tommy left the room, Anthony said, "I can't believe Trudy made Tamara assistant manager. What a joke."

Joe didn't seem to catch the comment, as he was talking to Trisha about the schedule.

Why did Anthony hate me so much? I wished he would quit, so I wouldn't have to deal with his bad attitude. Maybe Joe would let me fire him. I grinned at the thought.

"What are you smiling about?" Joe asked as he walked up to me.

"Just thinking about using my new-found authority to clean up some of the garbage around this place."

His eyebrows shot up. "Can't wait to hear the details on that one."

"Believe me, you really don't want to know."

He rolled up the schedule and tapped my arm with the paper. "Actually, I do, but I'm sure you probably won't tell me, so I shouldn't drive myself crazy about it."

"Pretty much."

"Anyway, I think the meeting went well. How about you?"

"For the most part, it was good." I looked around the empty room. "Except for Anthony being a jerk, as usual."

Understanding washed over his face. "Oh, that's what you meant?"

I tilted my chin and flashed an innocent smile. "I have no idea what you're talking about."

"Uh-huh. I'm sure you don't. Come on. Let's go get some lunch and then we'll start training."

CHAPTER 33

March 7, 4:30 p.m.

TAMARA

On the last day of training, Joe invited me to his house for a home-cooked meal. He said we had worked hard, and it was time to celebrate.

My nerves danced with excitement as I readied myself. With my hair still wet, I applied an ample amount of hair product and blew dried my hair. I brushed on smoky eye shadow and ran eyeliner on my lids.

I pulled on my favorite skinny jeans and tried to button them up. They fit perfectly everywhere except my waist. The stupid button wouldn't get in the hole, where it belonged. I grabbed a hair tie, wound it around the button, pulled it through the hole, and it looped around it. I threw on a deep-red sweater dress and brown boots that hit my mid-calf. I touched up my lip gloss and headed for the door.

A surge of anticipation flitted through me as I pulled up in front of Joe's house. Why was I so nervous? It was just dinner with a friend. Climbing out of my car, I adjusted my sweater and made my way to the door and rang the bell. Butterflies bounced off the sides of my stomach as I waited.

Joe answered the door wearing a gray Oxford and blue jeans. His smile faded as he took in my appearance.

"What?" I brought my hand to my face. Had my lipstick smeared? Did I have something in my teeth? "Do I look bad?"

"Not at all. You're just ..." He swallowed hard. "You're beautiful." He fell over his words. "I mean ... you're always pretty ... very pretty, but you're kind of ... breathtaking right now."

Biting my lip, I looked away. Butterflies banged furiously against my insides.

"What am I doing?" Joe stepped aside to make room for me to enter. "Don't mind me. I'm an idiot. Why don't you come in?" He followed behind me as we made our way toward the kitchen.

In the living room, the stylish white couch had been replaced by a bluish-gray love seat. The only other object in the room was a flat screen TV.

"I hope you're hungry," Joe said as we entered the kitchen.

"Starved. I knew my favorite cook was making dinner, so I skipped lunch, and I can never eat breakfast these days." I looked around.

The place was emptier but felt homier.

"Tamara." His voice changed as he scolded me. "You've got to take better care of yourself. You're eating for two now."

"Hey, I have gained, like, five pounds in the last two weeks. I think I'm eating plenty, thank you very much."

"That's only because I've been force-feeding you."

"You do have a point there." I set my purse on the island. "But it might also be because I am pregnant, as if you couldn't tell." I pointed at my stomach.

"Not at all. You're perfect."

"Thanks, Joe. But speaking of food, what's for dinner?"

"Chicken stir-fry."

"Sounds delicious."

"Everything is prepped. I just have to throw it together." Joe pulled a tall chair over next to the island. "Have a seat while I cook." He turned on a burner on the stove, set a wok over the flame, and adjusted the heat.

I sat down and let my eyes wander. Off to the side of the sink sat a small ice bucket with what looked like a bottle of champagne chilling. "What's that?" I pointed at the bucket.

With a slight grin, he lifted the bottle so I could read the label. Sparkling apple cider.

"I told you, we're celebrating."

But today had been our last shift together. The best part of my job had been working with him. "What if I told you I don't feel like celebrating?"

"What? Why not?" His eyebrows pinched together. "I thought you liked your new job."

"I do, but it feels like the end of an era. We're going to be working opposite shifts, and I'm going to miss working with you."

"We'll still be working together." He turned back toward the wok and added some ingredients. "It just won't be every day, like it has been."

"But I really liked the way things were."

He came over and leaned on the island. "I did too, but sometimes the end of something signifies the beginning of something better." His gaze caught mine and held it for a moment. "So, we'll just have to spend time together outside of work."

"Yeah?" My heart sped up, and I averted my eyes. "I guess we will."

He went back to the wok and stirred the chicken and veggies.

Looking around his kitchen, noticing all the subtle changes I could no longer contain my curiosity about Susan. "So ... um." Why was I so nervous about asking him? I guess a part of me was afraid of the truth. What if somehow, I was the cause of their break-up? "What happened with Susan?" I finally blurted out. "I mean, one day you're telling me you're going to ask her to marry you, and the next thing I know, Trudy is telling me you guys broke up."

He shut the burner off and turned toward me. "There isn't much to tell. She left me."

"I'm sorry." As much as I didn't like Susan, rejection was always painful.

"Don't be. I'm not. And Tamara, please don't think I was avoiding telling you. I was going to, but then with everything with Trudy and the changes at the diner, there never seemed to be a good time. It's for the better, anyway." Joe brought a wooden spoon with some sauce on it to my mouth. "Here try this."

"Mmmm. That is really good." The garlic and cilantro flavors mingling together was almost enough to distract me. "But what is for the better?"

Joe returned to the stove. "It's difficult to explain. I did love Susan. We'd built a life together, and I did want to make her happy. Toward the end, though, it got really hard. When she left me, I felt more relief than anything."

That was hard for me to wrap my mind around. The two relationships I'd been in ended badly and left me reeling for months afterward.

"Also, I didn't want to add to your stress."

So like Joe, always considerate. "It doesn't look like she left you with much."

"Most of the stuff was hers. I own the house. It was the one smart thing I did with the settlement from Mom's death. I didn't like most of Susan's stuff, anyway. It wasn't really me, you know?"

Yeah, I did know.

"Enough about all that. Dinner's ready. You got a lighter?"

"Just a second." I dug through my purse. It had been weeks since my last cigarette but there might still be one in here somewhere.

"Never mind, I found one." Joe grabbed a lighter from a drawer and led me into the dining room.

The table was different, smaller and wooden. On it were two place settings, champagne glasses, and a tapered candle in the middle.

He lit the candle and pulled out the chair for me. "Be right back." He strode into the kitchen and returned carrying the sparkling cider in one hand and our plates loaded with chicken stir-fry in the other. He put down the bottle, then placed the food in front of me.

The aroma wafted up, making my stomach growl.

"There's plenty more where that came from." Joe said and poured us each a glass of sparkling cider.

"I might actually take you up on that." I winked. "Eating for two, right?"

He lifted his glass toward me. "To new beginnings."

I clicked my glass against his and lifted it to my lips.

After we were finished eating, Joe cleared the table.

I stood to help him, but he insisted I relax.

When he came back, he was carrying two DVD cases. "I got a couple movies if you're up to watching."

"Sure, what are they?"

He fanned the boxes out like a poker hand. "*When Harry Met Sally* and *A Lot Like Love*."

I smiled to myself. Was it a coincidence that both were about close friends that eventually fell in love? "Nice. Let's do both."

He pumped his fist in victory. "Which one first?"

Looking back and forth, I pretended to seriously consider the order. "Hmmm, that's a tough call, but let's go with *A Lot Like Love*. Ashton Kutcher has a way nicer butt than Billy Crystal."

He stuck his hip out and put his hand on it. "I know, right? Ashton Kutcher has such a nice butt."

I burst into laughter, and Joe joined me. "Oh, my goodness," I said between fits of giggles, "you do that way too well."

Still grinning, he offered me a hand and pulled me up. I followed him into the living room. In the middle of the room there was an Xbox on the floor that I hadn't noticed earlier.

"Get comfortable. I'll get this going." He knelt down and pressed a button on the Xbox. "Good thing these are multipurpose."

"She took everything, didn't she?"

"Pretty much. I put my foot down about the flat-screen TV,

though, and she didn't want this amazing machine." He popped in the DVD.

I shivered as a cold chill ran through me.

"Sorry. I've been keeping the heat turned down. Trying to save on the electric bill. I'll turn it up." Joe walked out of the room.

I could think of other ways he could heat me up. I sniggered. *Calm your hormones.* "He just broke up with his girlfriend," I berated myself quietly.

Joe returned carrying a blanket. "What was that?"

I pasted on the most innocent smile I could muster. "Nothing. Just talking to myself."

He spread the blanket out delicately over my lap. Leaning over, he gently tucked the edges around the outline of my body. "There, that should help until the heat kicks on."

I smiled up at him, my heart skipping a beat. "Thanks."

"You're welcome." He pressed play and sat next to me on the love seat.

I stole glances frequently, watching Joe's reaction to Ashton taking pictures of a pretty woman he didn't know before they boarded the plane.

He caught my gaze and grinned.

I redirected my focus onto the television, but it was hard to ignore the way my body reacted to his nearness. I wanted to reach out and touch him—to run my hand over his strong arm and weave my fingers through his. Could he sense the tension I felt? Did he feel the pull like I did?

Eventually, I relaxed and focused on the movie. Somewhere around its midpoint, I nodded off.

The next thing I was aware of was waking up in the crook of Joe's arm. I opened my eyes to the credits rolling on the screen and lifted my head off his chest. "What happened?" I asked groggily.

"You fell asleep."

I yawned deeply. "I guess I was more tired than I thought. I didn't snore, did I?" Self-consciousness tightened my loose muscles.

His lips arched at the edges. "Just a little. It was cute."

"Man, how embarrassing." I worked myself into a sitting position.

He chuckled. "Wanna try the second movie?"

Disoriented, I looked around. "I should head home. I'd probably just fall asleep again."

"Want me to give you a ride? You could always get your car tomorrow."

I took in another yawn. "That's okay. I'm awake enough now to drive home."

"All right. I'll walk you out." Joe stood, took hold of my hand, and pulled me up. He didn't let go of it as he led me through the door and out to my car. A nervousness radiated from him.

Once we reached my car, I gave him a goodnight hug. "I had fun tonight."

Joe wrapped his arms around my shoulders and put his lips to my forehead. He pulled away, took a few steps back, and sighed.

Did I miss something? What had him so keyed up?

"Ah, forget it," he muttered, pacing back and forth. He looked toward me and raised his hand. "Have you ever had something build up inside of you so much that if you didn't say it out loud you might explode? Because that's how I feel right now. I know this might be the selfish thing to do, but I can't take it any longer."

I inhaled sharply. Was he actually going where I thought he was?

He ran his fingers through his hair, then stepped closer to me, locking me into his gaze.

My heart beat wildly.

"Tamara," he whispered, swallowing hard. "How do I even say this?"

"Just say it."

His eyes filled with intensity. "I think about you all the time. When you're not with me, I miss you. When you *are* with me, I want more of you."

Inwardly, I began to freak out. This was what I had wanted. But this could change everything.

"I don't know. Maybe it's just that I want it so badly, but it seems like there's been something building between us."

I drew in a long, steadying breath, determining within myself not to get carried away with the heat of the moment. There was more to think about than just me. "Joe, I feel it too, but it's complicated."

He brought his hand to my stomach, gingerly spreading his fingers over it as if trying to protect what was inside. "I know ... It doesn't matter, though." He leaned down and brushed his lips softly across mine, as if testing the waters.

A fiery heat spread through me.

"Tamara." He intertwined his fingers through my hair. Then his lips were touching my lips, hungrily. He brought his hand around the small of my back, pulling me closer.

I slid my arms around his neck and lost myself in the blazing fire of his embrace.

Eventually, Joe pulled away, breathless, and rested his forehead on mine. His hands gently caressed the sides of my arms.

We stood there for a moment, quietly soaking each other in.

A big part of me wanted to grab him by the hand and lead him back into his house, the way he had led me out, but that probably wasn't the best idea. Besides, I was pretty sure Joe wouldn't have allowed that, anyway, being the gentleman that he was. Was he fighting the same battle? "What are you thinking about?"

"Not thinking. Just feeling."

I pulled myself tightly against him. "Yeah ... me too."

He wrapped both arms around me. "This is all your fault, you know."

I laughed softly. "How so?"

"It's been hard keeping myself in check the last few weeks, but when you showed up at my house looking like that—I mean, what's a guy to do? I can only handle so much."

"Oh, I see how it is. Just like a guy to blame it all on the woman."

He chuckled. "I know. So typical."

We were quiet for another few minutes as we embraced. How quickly things had changed, yet in many ways they remained the same. We were still just Tamara and Joe, best friends, but now we were so much more.

"You know, I'm wide awake now. We could watch the other movie."

He shook his head. "I don't think that would be wise."

I looked up at him.

He leaned in and kissed me again. "Not that I don't want you to stay." He pulled back. "But we both know if you come back in we won't be watching a movie."

He was right, and it meant saying goodnight. And that he cared enough about me to take things slow.

Joe reluctantly withdrew from our embrace and opened my car door.

Following his cue, I climbed in.

He made sure I was completely inside before he shut the door.

I rolled down my window.

He hit his head on the top of the window frame as he leaned in to give me another quick kiss. "I'll talk to you tomorrow."

"'Kay, good-night." I rolled up the window, trying not to laugh at his adorable sweetness.

As I drove away, my phone buzzed in my pocket. I pulled it out.

A text from Joe:

I miss you already :)

The moment washed over me again and lingered all the way home.

CHAPTER 34
March 8, 11:18 a.m.
TAMARA

That next morning, I stood at the sink, washing dishes trying to distract myself from my inner turmoil. Last night had been wonderful—like a beautiful dream. But like most dreams, it faded under the shadows of my past hurts and memories of the last time I had trusted someone with my heart.

Thoughts of Danny lounging around in his sweatpants, plucking at the twelve-string guitar I'd bought him for his birthday, filled my mind. He was always picking away, forming chord progressions for the lyrics he came up with. That last day as I got ready for work, he looked up at me, his chin-length dark hair falling over his sapphire eyes. "I'm writing this one for you, beautiful girl." I wanted to believe him, but his words felt false. A foreboding sensation had snaked its way along my spine as I leaned in to kiss him goodbye.

Work ended up being slow, so my boss sent me home after only a few hours.

I walked into our bungalow, and immediately something seemed off. I quietly latched the door behind me and inched my way toward the bedroom. I opened the door, and there was Danny on top of Shelby Turner, who I'd thought was my best friend.

At first, I couldn't breathe. I just stood there watching everything I had built over the last year crumble into pieces. Then I freaked out. I don't even know what I said. I just remember Shelby snatching up her clothes and darting out of the room.

I grabbed my duffle bag and tore around the apartment, packing everything I could think of to take with me as Danny followed after me, going on and on about how sorry he was and that he hadn't meant for it to happen and how it just happened.

How did something like that 'just happen' is what I want to know.

I had run out to my car, thrown the bag in the backseat, and sped out of there, my tires spinning out in the gravel driveway. In the rearview mirror, I'd seen Danny staring after me, looking bewildered.

Stop it, Tamara. Joe was nothing like Danny.

The coffee cup I'd been washing slipped out of my hand and crashed into the sink.

At least I hoped he wasn't. Somehow Joe had snuck past every barrier I had placed around myself. If he did end up hurting me like Danny, I didn't think I could recover.

Did Joe even realize what he was getting into with me? And what about Susan? Was I the rebound girl? I wanted to call him. Hearing his voice had a way of silencing these old demons. I glanced at the clock. His workday had only started a little over an hour ago. And if I stopped by work, I would be coming across as way too forward. I thought back to the way he'd kissed me last night and the way he'd held me. It wasn't a dream. Joe really did care about me.

I dried off my hands, grabbed a pen and paper and sat down at the table to start a to-do list.

1. *Do paperwork for medical insurance.*
  2. *Schedule an appointment with doctor.*

I doodled on the paper, not really paying attention. Before I realized what I was doing, I'd sketched out Joe's full name in bubble letters, with a large valentine heart around it.

Ridiculous.

I threw the pencil down on the table. I couldn't even stop thinking about him for five minutes. I had to see him. I would go do my errands, then think of some excuse to stop by the diner.

Tap, tap, tap. A light knocking at my door.

"Just a second," I called.

No one ever came by at this time of the day that I was aware of.

I opened the door.

Joe leaned on the doorway, holding a single, red, long-stemmed rose. "Hey, beautiful."

"Joe! What are you doing here? Why aren't you at work?"

"I couldn't sleep, so I went in early and finished all the managerial stuff. I asked Frank to come in and help just in case it got crazy and then headed over here to surprise you." He handed me the rose and kissed me on the cheek. "Is that okay?"

I stepped back, smiling from the inside out. "It's more than okay. I've been doing everything I could to distract myself from calling you or heading over to the diner."

"Why would you do that? You can call me anytime you want to."

I walked into my kitchenette to find something to put the flower in. "I wasn't quite sure where we stood after last night, and I didn't want to make any assumptions." I filled a tall glass with water and put the rose in it.

Joe came behind me, put his arms gently around my waist and rested his chin on my shoulder. "Tamara, I thought I made myself extremely clear last night. I want to be with you."

"It did seem pretty clear, until I got home, and I got inside my own head." I closed my eyes and placed my hand on his. "You're not like the other guys I've been with, but those experiences still make me uneasy. It's hard for me to believe that you would want to be with me with all my baggage."

He gently pulled me around, so I was facing him. His eyes searched mine.

What could this wonderful man possibly see in me?

"Tamara, I know you've been through a lot." He traced the outline of my cheek. "But when I look at you, I don't see your past. I see our future."

I rested my head on his chest, listening to the rhythm of his heartbeat. Being in his arms felt almost like the past didn't even matter. But what about our future? How would our being together affect him? "So you don't care if people know we're together?"

Joe took hold of my arms and gently pushed me away from him, forehead creased. "Why would I care if anyone knows we're together?"

"You're telling me you haven't thought about how it's going to look to the people we work with? They'll probably think this is your baby. Trudy even asked me straight out if you were the father. Which would look like you cheated on Susan. I don't want you to take the fall for my mistake."

Joe took a moment to process my words, as if he really hadn't thought about it. "Let them think what they want to think." He pulled me close to him again. "It doesn't matter. I don't want to hide in fear of somebody assuming a lie. What matters is we are together now."

"You would take on that burden for me?"

"Tamara, I want you. The whole package, baby and all. I know what I'm getting into." His arms tightened around me. "We need to stop worrying about everybody else and just enjoy ourselves, because I haven't been this happy in a long time."

"Me neither." I whispered.

"All right. Then it's settled. I think it's time for our first official date. It's a beautiful day out. I was thinking we could go for a drive to Cannon Beach."

Longing and joy blossomed in my stomach. It had been so long since I'd seen the ocean. Ever since I'd left Ocean Shores, to be exact. Being there with Joe would be even more incredible. "That sounds amazing. Let me get ready." I moved across the room to my dresser, pulled out a pair of jeggings, an undershirt and a heather-gray sweater, and headed to the bathroom to change.

"Whose vehicle do you want to take?"

I pulled on my jeggings and threw on my undershirt and sweater.

"Let's take mine," I said through the door. "We can drive there with the top down." Joe's car was nicer than mine, but if I could drive with the top down every day, I would. I loved the wind on my face, and my hair dancing every which way it wanted to.

"You're nuts. It's way too cold for that."

"No such thing." I ran a little bronzer over my face and brushed on some mascara.

"Um, yes, there is."

"You're such a wimp sometimes."

Joe laughed, his baritone echoing through the door. "We should take mine. It has a better system and co-pilot gets control of the radio."

"Sold. I'm all over that." I flung the bathroom door open and made my way toward him. "But I still think you're a wimp."

He chuckled. "And I still think you're certifiably nuts, so we're even." He took hold of my hand and led me out the door toward his SUV.

The sun hung bright in the cloudless blue sky. Joe was right, though. A chill hung in the air.

He opened the door for me, rounded the Jeep, and climbed in. "There are some CDs in here." Joe lifted the lid to the center console. "Or we could listen to the radio. Your choice." He started the Jeep and backed out of the parking spot.

"CDs? Going old school on me, huh?"

"It's how music like this was made to be heard."

I chuckled and scanned through his collection. Joe pretty

much had the same taste in music that I did. We had always agreed on the same radio station at work. Cold Play, Ed Sheeran, Toby Keith, Merle Haggard—

Merle Haggard?

Grimacing, I picked up the CD as if I were holding something contaminated. "What the?"

"You got a problem with some good country music?"

"I don't mind country music, but Merle Haggard? So hick."

"Whatever, I likes me a little Merle Haggard twang every once in a while," he said with an exaggerated southern drawl.

I dropped the CD. "As long as I'm not in the car." I pulled out a Monster Ballads CD. "Now this is my kind of music."

"Yeah, eighties butt rock. So much classier than Merle."

"Totally." As I put the CD back in the console, my hand brushed against a brochure stuck in between the cases. Pulling it out, I studied its contents.

An advertisement for an upcoming community class on business.

"What's this?"

Joe kept his eyes on the road as he weaved through traffic. "Just something I've been thinking about." He shrugged.

"Thinking about for how long?"

"Off and on over the years, I've dreamt of opening my own restaurant. Working with you over the last couple of weeks got me dreaming again. I think I'd like us to have our own little diner someday." Even though we had been together for less than twenty-four hours, he spoke in the plural—as if we'd been together forever.

"Tell me more."

"My mom dreamed of having her own restaurant. So, it would be more like resurrecting her vision. I'd use a lot of her recipes, and we could call it Emily's Rose Garden Café, after her. It could be this elegant little eatery with all sorts of gourmet entrees."

I knotted my fingers through his. "I think we should definitely do it."

Joe was quiet, seeming thoughtful.

Had I overstepped? "What's wrong?"

"Absolutely nothing." He smiled. "I was just thinking how easy it is to be with you like this. Whenever I brought up the dream of owning a restaurant to Susan, she would roll her eyes and call it a pipe dream. But you—you're ready to jump on board."

"Well, I believe in you. I've seen the way you stepped up to the plate at the diner. You're really turning that place around," I said. Joe seemed to be a natural at managing a restaurant. Why shouldn't he have a place of his own?

"I couldn't have done it without you."

"I don't know if I believe that, but I like the sound of it."

Everything in me wished that we weren't driving. I wanted to be closer to him.

Joe abruptly pulled to the side of the road and turned toward me. "Do you have any idea what you do to me?" His eyes were full of vulnerability.

More Than Words by Extreme played in the background.

He pulled on my arm, inviting me to come closer. I crawled over the center console and wedged myself in his lap. His embrace was so sweet, so gentle—like he was holding something delicate and valuable. I could have stayed in this spot all day and been perfectly happy.

After a few minutes, Joe ran his fingers through the ends of my hair. "We should probably get back on the road if we're ever going to make it to the beach."

I wrapped my arms tighter around his neck, not ready to let go.

"Or not," he said, a smile in his voice.

I brought my lips to his, kissing him softly before making my way back into the passenger seat.

CHAPTER 35

March 8, 1:10 p.m.

JOE

It took great restraint not to pull the car over a hundred times and draw Tamara close to me again.

As we parked next to the beach, Tamara unbuckled her seatbelt and threw open the door. "You have no idea how much I love the ocean."

I grabbed the cooler from the back, along with a couple of blankets. By the time I closed the trunk, Tamara was running barefoot toward the crashing waves.

"Come on!" she called out, twirling around and laughing, throwing her sweater to the ground.

Though I had known it was there, I'd never witnessed such freedom in her spirit. I picked up her shoes from the side of the road and followed her.

I set our things next to her sweater. Running into the frigid Pacific Ocean was not normally in my plans this time of the year, but Tamara was hard to resist, so happy and fun-loving, almost childlike. In that way she reminded me of my mother, so full of life and wonder. With a huge grin on my face, I kicked off my shoes, sloughed off my coat, and chased after her. Icy waves chilled my body as my feet touched the water.

Each step into the water was like walking across a bed of nails.

I'd heard one should remove one's mind from one's body, so that's what I did, putting my attention on Tamara. The sun radiated off her skin, and the water glistened around her.

In the distance, a wave crested and rushed toward us.

Tamara changed direction, splashing near me.

"Now you've angered it." I reached out and took ahold of her as the wave hit and soaked both of us.

She pressed her face into my chest.

I wrapped my arms around her. "You happy now?"

"It was totally worth it." She giggled, teeth chattering.

"Let's get you warmed up." I rubbed my hands up and down on her goose bump-covered arms. "How 'bout we watch the coast from the Jeep."

"Yes, let's do that."

I gathered our things, while she shivered on the way back to my Jeep.

After starting the Jeep, I pulled Tamara onto my lap, and we cuddled in the passenger seat, hot air blowing on us from the heater. Having her this close to me, feeling her breath on my face made it hard to resist the urge to kiss her.

But I didn't have to resist. She was mine.

I ran my fingers up through her hair and pulled her face closer, gently pressing my lips to hers. She tasted sweet, like mint gum and vanilla.

Her breath hitched as she brought her hand up to my face. When she touched me, it felt as if someone lit a match over dry wood drenched with gasoline.

Her hand trembled as she moved her mouth softly against mine.

I leaned back, eyes closed, completely overwhelmed by the insane fire that burned between us.

Her lips touched mine again.

I brought my hands to her face and gently drew it away from mine. Though her closeness weakened me, I wanted to take things slow, to never hurt her. I kissed her cheek and then her forehead, and brought her head to my chest, wrapping my arms around her. How had it taken me so long to see what was right in front of me?

She brought her hand to my chest and outlined small circles. "I like the way you warm me up."

Laughing, I tightened my arms more securely around her. "I'll gladly warm you up anytime."

She played with a button on my shirt, her face seeming troubled, maybe even sad. "You warm me on the inside too." She hesitated, seeming to struggle for the right words. "It scares me. I don't trust it."

I put my hand under her chin and made her look at me. "I understand. It scares me too, but you can trust me."

"I know, but I don't trust the feelings."

I folded my arms back around her. That trust couldn't be spoken. It would have to be shown.

Her stomach gurgled.

We both looked toward the noise. "Sounds like somebody is hungry." I placed my hand on her stomach.

She laughed and rested her hand on top of mine. "Guess so."

"I got some sandwiches in the cooler. Let's get you two fed."

After lunch, we made our way north to Seaside and walked along the promenade for hours, eating ice cream, and strolling in and out of different shops.

As we walked, I told her about my childhood and how my mom had raised me.

"How did your mom die?"

Most of the time I didn't like to talk about it. When she died, the foundation of my life was shaken to its center, making large crevasses that seemed impossible to overcome. "A commercial vehicle struck her head-on."

Tamara gasped and clenched my hand a little firmer. "Oh, Joe, I'm so sorry."

"It was ruled the driver's fault, and I received a large settlement from a wrongful death lawsuit. There I was, with a ton of money, but no one to guide me through the pain. The only thing I wanted was my mom back."

She nodded, an emotion crossing her face. Was she thinking about her family?

"Have you ever thought about tracking down your parents?" There, I said the words before I could think better of it. Her parents both caused her pain, but I couldn't understand her shutting them out forever.

She was quiet for a long time, and tears welled in her eyes. She swallowed hard before answering. "For the first year or so after leaving home, when I got really lonely, I'd call home, hoping my mother would answer, just so I could hear her voice. I'd always hang up if anyone else picked up. Every once in a while, my mom would answer, and a part of me wondered if she somehow knew it was me." She looked down at her feet. "She probably wouldn't even care if she knew, though."

I was pretty sure she was wrong, but who said she was ready to face those old demons? I gazed at the horizon.

There was no way to change the past. All I could do was love her now.

I hooked my arm around her waist and pulled her in front of me, so we were both facing the ocean.

The sun set, and wide strokes of pinks and purples colored the sky. Smells from the surrounding restaurants wafted through the air, a mixture of charbroiled steak and scampi.

"Beautiful," I whispered in her ear. "You hungry?"

"A little."

"Me too." I took her hand and guided her toward a restaurant.

"Do we have to go here?" she asked. "It seems like a popular place. With that long of a line, we'll have to wait to be seated."

"Doesn't hurt to check." I opened the door for her.

The hostess greeted us. "Dinner for two?"

"Yes, we have a reservation at six thirty for Phillips."

Tamara threw me a questioning look.

"What? I called first thing this morning." I winked at her.

The hostess led us toward a quiet table near the fireplace and placed menus in front of us. "Your server will be right with you."

Tamara pursed her lips and placed a hand on her chin. "And how did you know I would come with you, Mister Phillips?"

"Psychic powers."

Her eyebrows shot up. "Oh really? So, tell me how it works, then. Do you see visions or consult a crystal ball?"

"I can't reveal my secrets. Haven't you heard the story of Samson? He lost his powers because he told a woman."

She smacked me playfully on the arm.

I grabbed hold of her hand, flipped it up, and studied her palm. "Interesting." I said after a long moment.

"What do you see?"

I dropped her hand abruptly. "You couldn't handle it if I told you."

Her mouth fell open. "You're such a stinker sometimes."

A gentleman walked up and filled our glasses with water. To his side, a slender woman holding a bottle of red wine came. "Good evening! My name is Cynthia, and I'll be your server this evening. Can I offer you a bottle of our house Merlot? It goes well with our stuffed rib eye, the special tonight."

Tamara and I exchanged a playful glance.

Nice. Offering a recovering alcoholic and a pregnant woman alcohol? I looked up at the waitress. "No, thank you, but we will take an order of crab-stuffed mushrooms."

The waitress scribbled on her notepad and walked away.

"That was funny, wasn't it?"

Tamara held back a muffled laugh. "Like either one of us will be drinking anytime soon." Her eyes widened as she scanned the menu.

"What?"

"Joe, the mushrooms you just ordered are sixteen ninety-five for six. That's kinda spendy."

"Yeah, that should be enough for us, right? Six mushrooms? I mean, I can only eat two, two and a half, max." I tried to keep a straight face.

Tamara's face turned a lovely shade of pink. "Is that some sort of joke about me eating so much? 'Cause you're hilarious." She patted her tummy. "There are three of us on this date, you know. Things could get expensive fast."

"Tamara," I said, my eyes softening toward her. "Please, order anything you want. Let me spoil you."

"Now I know you're too good to be true."

The waitress delivered the mushrooms and took the rest of our order. I convinced Tamara to order the filet mignon and prawns while I went with the special.

Our conversation shifted to more serious topics after our dinner arrived.

"You know how we were talking earlier about my dream to open a diner?"

Her eyes brightened. "Yeah?"

"I'd like to hear about your dreams." I put a dollop of A.1. Sauce on the steak before slicing into it.

She dabbed her mouth with a napkin and took a sip of water. "Dreams?"

"You know, what makes you come alive?"

Her eyes darkened and shifted to the table. "I've been surviving for so long that I'm not sure if I still know how to dream."

Reaching across the table, I took her hand in mine. "Tamara, you of all people deserve to dream."

"I don't even know where to start."

"Okay, what are you passionate about?"

"Besides ...?" She smirked playfully.

"Not like that." I laughed. "What do you enjoy doing?"

"I like to write."

"Really? I didn't know you were a writer."

"I'm not a writer. I just journal and write a little poetry."

"Poetry? Would you feel comfortable sharing?"

She squirmed in her seat. "I don't know. I've never shown anyone my writing before."

"Please." I begged.

"The one I'd be most comfortable sharing isn't finished, and it's kind of dark."

"Every poem needs some sort of emotion tied to it to be good. I would be honored to hear it."

She riffled through her purse, pulled out a small journal, and flipped through the pages. She cleared her throat and began reading. "I am walking, but I know not where I go. I look around this forsaken place without a care in the world." She looked up, her gaze meeting mine.

The fire flickered across her face, making her green eyes more intense.

"Wandering the lonely streets, without a purpose. A man stands in front of me, and all around me at the same time. I look at him, but only darkness surrounds my vision. I know this man, I know this place, I have been here before, but I do not want to stay. So I run."

The emotion in her voice was palpable. I didn't know if I should smile or frown. I wanted to do both.

"I turn away, but he calls out. I try to run, but my head is filled with tormenting cries. Deception consumes me; his lies, my bread. I have no face to show the world. The glow of my life burns out. So I hide." She closed the journal. "That's all I have so far. It's not quite finished."

"That's powerful and ..." My mind fumbled, searching for the right thing to say. "and somewhat melancholy, I guess. It really captures the sentiment I assume you were going for."

"I don't know if I was trying to capture anything. I just write about the things I feel. It was inspired by a dream I had a while ago. Or more of a nightmare."

"I'm sorry that you feel like that."

"I don't feel that way anymore."

"Oh yeah? How do you feel now?"

"It's hard to explain." She placed her journal back in her purse. "Do you recall when I told you about my number?"

"Ninety-nine?" What did that have to do with what we were talking about now?

"When I first had my experience with the number, I thought things had changed. Like my past could no longer hurt me." Her eyes held mine. "And things did get better. I met you, got my job, and settled into Vancouver"

"I feel like there's a 'but' coming." I leaned in closer, caressing her arm.

"There is." She smiled a sad smile. "That number became a false promise after a while. The hope that I felt at the beginning turned into more pain because I couldn't outrun myself. I couldn't escape my past, since it was locked up inside of me."

Everything in me longed to take all the pain from her, to go back in time and right every wrong ever done to her.

"Then I just kept making stupid choices that made everything worse." Her lips trembled as she spoke. "I began to wonder if maybe I was the darkness I had been trying to escape. And that crazy number kept taunting me."

I pulled my chair around the table, so I could put my arm around her. There had to be a way to make her see herself the way I saw her—beautiful and resilient. Nothing about her spoke of darkness.

"But now, with you." She rested her head against my shoulder. "I feel hope again."

"And that frightens you?"

"It terrifies me."

"I think I understand."

"Do you? Because I'm freaking out right now. You're too wonderful to be real."

Was she putting me on some sort of unrealistic pedestal? "Tamara, I'm not. I'm really not."

She glanced away from me and took in a deep breath. "Have you ever seen that movie *Rent*?"

"Sure, five hundred, twenty-five thousand, six hundred minutes and all." No clue where she was going with the question.

"Yeah, so you remember when they sing that song about everyone having baggage, and how we just need to find ones that match our own? I think that's us."

"Our baggage does seem to match." I hadn't really believed in soul mates, but perhaps she was mine.

"But that's the thing. This is too perfect. We're too perfect. It makes me afraid because ... good things don't happen to me."

"I'm scared too, but this could be the beginning of something amazing."

She snuggled into my neck.

The waitress brought us our check and removed our plates.

The damage was only eighty-one ninety-eight.

"How much?" Tamara asked, cringing.

"Don't worry about it." I put a hundred-dollar bill in the check folder and when the waitress returned, I told her to keep the change.

The ride home was peaceful. Tamara popped one of my Jack Johnson CDs into the player and curled herself up around my arm. Soon after, her breathing changed as she drifted into slumber.

It had been a long day. A long, perfect day. The sound of her cute little snore made me smile. Before I knew it, I was pulling into her apartment complex. "Tamara, honey," I whispered, shaking her slightly. "We're home."

"Already?" Her grip on my arm tightened. "I'm not ready to say good-night."

"Come on, you." I gently removed my arm from her hold.

She let out a protesting moan.

I walked around the Jeep and opened her door.

She slowly stepped out.

When we reached her doorstep, I pulled her into an embrace. "Thank you."

"No, thank you." She looked up at me. "Today was hands-down the best first date I have ever been on."

"I'd have to agree with you on that."

She locked her arms around my neck and stood on the tip of her toes to reach my lips. My hands rested on her waist. We lost ourselves in each other for a while before I pulled back, knowing I needed to stop. "I better go."

"I don't want you to go," she whined in this adorable, pouty voice that made me want to kiss her again.

I laughed. "I am trying to be a decent guy here. Do you have any idea how hard you make that?"

"What if I don't want you to be a decent guy right now?" She reached up for another quick kiss.

"It's best to take things slow."

Her eyebrows lifted skeptically. "How slow?"

"Wedding night." I kept a straight face.

"You're joking, right?"

"Maybe not that slow, but we need to get to know each other before we take it to that level. I don't want to do anything to hurt this."

Her expression was hard to see under the dim streetlight. Finally, she smiled and wrapped her arms around my waist. "I can do slow."

I wanted to tell her right then that I loved her, but instead I held her for another few minutes. "Want to do breakfast tomorrow?"

"At the diner?"

"No, I can come over and cook you breakfast before I go to work."

A huge smile broke across her face. "I'd love that."

CHAPTER 36

April 8, 8:53 a.m.

TAMARA

On our one-month anniversary, Joe made me breakfast at my studio, like he often did.

After letting him inside, I had crawled back into bed and listened to the sounds of him humming his favorite songs as he cooked. Today was our split shift at the diner. He worked this morning, and I would come in this afternoon and work till around eight. Then we'd be off to celebrate our first month together.

Joe came over and knelt down beside me. "Okay, sleeping beauty, the soufflé is in the oven. It will be done soon. Are you going to get up and hang out with me before I have to leave for work?" He gave me a quick, soft kiss.

"Actually, I was hoping you would crawl in bed with me and snuggle for a few minutes." I patted the spot on the bed next to me.

He climbed into the small bed and wrapped his strong arms around me. "Like this?"

"Yes. This is exactly where I want you." I lay quietly, soaking in his embrace. He hadn't told me yet that he loved me, but the way he held me now said he did.

My lips caressed along the line of his jaw and down his neck.

Joe's hand tightened on my back.

"What?"

"You are drivin' me crazy."

"You mean this?" I kissed his neck again.

He took a deep breath and pulled me on top of him.

I leaned over and kissed his soft lips. My hands found his chest, and I unbuttoned the top of his shirt.

His hands came up, abruptly taking hold of each of my wrists. "You're playing with fire," he warned playfully.

"Maybe I like the heat." I worked one of my wrists out of his grasp.

"Tamara." He said my name with a quiet pleading. His voice was soft and gentle, but for some reason it stung.

I slumped off him and turned away, putting my face against the wall. Why did he always have to put the brakes on? Maybe he didn't care about me as much as I thought he did. Wasn't it natural to want to be intimate with the person he loved?

His hand touched my shoulder. "Tamara?"

"Maybe you should go to work now." I held my growing stomach. Was this the reason he didn't want to touch me? Did he think I was gross?

His hand grazed the line of my neck as he pulled my hair away from it. He came closer, brushing his lips up and down my neck. "Please," he whispered. "Please talk to me." His warm breath in my ear sent shivers down my spine.

I let out a muffled sigh and turned toward him, nuzzling my face into his shoulder.

"What did I do?"

Though the question really was more about what he didn't do. What he wouldn't do. "It just seems like ..." It was so embarrassing saying the words out loud. "Like you don't want me."

"Are you serious?" A laugh crept into his voice.

"It's not funny."

His eyes deepened with emotion. "Do you have any idea how beautiful you are?"

My face flushed hotter.

"I don't think I ever wanted somebody so much. Every time you touch me, it's like wildfire."

"Then why do you always shut me down?"

"You know why, Tamara. You and I both had horrible relationships that just held on because of sex, and I want things to be different with us. I want us to get to know each other before we get physical."

"I understand and appreciate that, but we *do* know each other."

He rested his hand on my hip and slid it under my shirt, around to the small of my back, leaving a trail of warmth. "I guess we do, don't we?"

In the background, an alarm shrilled, and the smell of smoke filled the air. Joe jumped off the bed and ran to the oven. A thick cloud of blackish-gray smoke wafted out of the oven as he opened it. Joe grabbed the nearest hot pad and took the burning soufflé out of the oven.

I opened the window next to my bed, grabbed a towel, and waved it at the smoke alarm.

Joe put the pan in the sink and ran water over it. Then he hurried across the room, reached up and took the battery out of the smoke detector, cursing under his breath.

Was he angry with me? All that cooking wasted because I couldn't control my hormones?

Our eyes met, a huge smile spread across Joe's face, and he burst into laughter. Putting his arms around me, he leaned down to kiss me. "I hate to say this, but I need to get to work."

"But things were just getting interesting."

"Hey," he leaned in for another quick kiss. "We've got the rest of our lives for that. But if I don't get out of here, I'm going to be late."

I locked my arms around his neck. "Fine. But we *will* finish this later."

CHAPTER 37

April 8, 7:48 p.m.

TAMARA

At the end of my shift, I stood behind the counter, taking money out of the till to go make change for Trisha before I left. Soon I would be off the clock and onto my date with Joe.

The diner had settled into the after-dinner lull. There were still a few full tables of people eating dessert and several single patrons sitting at the bar, drinking coffee.

The bells clanged against the glass door, announcing someone had come in, but I focused on the till. Trisha could take care of whoever it was.

"Hey, beautiful."

"Joe, you're here earl—" I raised my head.

Kyle stood in front of me.

The blood rushed from my face. "Kyle! What are you doing here?" I dropped the money into the drawer and shoved it closed.

He flashed a flirty grin. "I was in your neck of the woods. Figured I'd stop by and drop off an item I have that belongs to you."

My stomach twisted and my heart felt as if it would pound out of my chest. I had finally come to terms with never seeing this man again, but there he was, standing in front of me like an apparition.

Kyle furrowed his eyebrows. "You okay?"

"I wasn't expecting to see you, but I'm glad you're here."

His mouth twisted into a self-assured smile. "Cool. I was thinking maybe we could go get a drink and catch up when you get off." He stepped in closer and brushed a stray piece of hair away from my face.

Was he trying to pick me up again? I needed to tell him about the baby, but I had no interest in hooking up with him. My life was with Joe, and nothing was going to change that. "I don't think that's a good idea."

"Why do you always have to play hard to get?"

"Look, Kyle, a lot of things have changed in my life since we hung out that night. I'm with someone now."

"Oh." His smile faded. "Well, I guess that changes things. Sorry for bugging you. For some reason, I've thought about you a lot since our night together. Looks like I'm too little too late."

A twinge of sadness pricked at the edges of my conscious. If I wouldn't have freaked out like that when I woke up in the back of his truck, would things have turned out differently? "I've thought about you too. We actually really need to talk."

Confusion settled over his face. "What's left to talk about?"

I looked around the diner. There were still customers here. Joe could show up at any time, and my place of employment was not the best place to have this discussion, but what choice did I have? "Can I get you a beer? You may need one."

"You're kind of freaking me out. Just say what you need to say."

I leaned on the counter for support. "I just want you to know, I don't make it a practice of getting drunk and sleeping around." I spoke quietly.

Unless it was my imagination, one guy at the bar leaned closer.

"I didn't get that impression from you. If anything, I thought you were overly cautious."

"You are the only person that I have slept with for over a year."

He rolled his eyes and folded his arms. "Could you get to your point, please?"

"What I'm ... um ... what I'm trying to say is ..."

"Spit it out."

"I'm pregnant!" I blurted out and walked around the counter.

His eyes widened and his mouth dropped open. "And it's mine?"

"I just told you that I hadn't slept with anyone else."

"Then why didn't you get ahold of me?"

"Well, at first I was going to get an abortion, bu—"

"Without even talking to me?" He clenched his teeth and a muscle pulsed in his jaw.

Who did he think he was? "You know what? You have no right to talk to me like that. When I found out, I was all by myself. I was alone and scared and had no way to contact you."

"What do you mean? I gave that guy my phone number when I came into the restaurant the next morning, and I left a note last month when I was in town, asking for you to contact me."

What? Joe immediately came to mind, but he had been at my house that morning. "What guy?"

"I don't know his name. He snatched the number from me and said he was on the way to your house. I really wanted to see you again."

The room closed in around me. It didn't make any sense. If Joe had Kyle's number, why wouldn't he have given it to me? He knew I wanted to tell Kyle about the baby. Why would Joe do that? Why would he have lied to me?

What an idiot I'd been. I had given him my heart. I had trusted him completely, and he had been lying to me this whole time. What else had he lied to me about?

"Tamara?"

"I never got your number," I whispered.

"What? You're kidding me! What kind of person does that? You're pregnant with my child!"

The question echoed through my mind like a broken record. What kind of person does that? What kind of person does that?! What kind of person does that?!! Fury built with each rotation of the words. Danny, Ryan, my dad ... and Joe.

It had all been a lie? Joe was just like the rest of them? Joe was a liar!

The pieces of my fragile heart came undone.

I looked around. All eyes in the diner were on me. I couldn't stand there and fall apart in front of everyone. I had to go.

I had to run.

CHAPTER 38
April 8, 7:51 p.m.
JOE

I pulled into the diner parking lot and turned off my Jeep. Anticipation buzzed through me at the thought of the night I had planned for us. I walked toward the building and paused at the door. Tamara leaned against the bar, as if to balance herself, looking bewildered, and panicked.

A vaguely familiar guy paced back and forth, face etched with anger.

I froze and the ground gave way beneath me.

Kyle!

By the look on Tamara's face and his angry stance, things weren't going well.

I threw the door open.

She pushed herself off the bar and bounded toward me.

Was she running to me so I could comfort her?

She rushed past me, almost knocking me over.

I grabbed her. "Tamara, what's going on?"

"Let go of me, you liar!" She struggled against my hold. "I can't believe you lied to me about Kyle." Tears streamed down her face.

This couldn't be happening. What could I say to make her understand I only wanted to protect her? He probably made himself out to sound all innocent. "Tamara, yes, I lied, but he's a creep."

"He's the father of my baby, Joe," Tamara struggled to get free, but I couldn't let her go. Not like this. She was too angry. She could hurt someone. Or worse yet, she could hurt herself.

"Let me go!" She yanked away from my hold.

How had I suddenly become the bad guy? I followed as she ran to her car.

She backed up, practically hitting me, and floored it so hard her tires screeched as she sped away.

I forced my way back to the diner and through the door.

Kyle paced back and forth, hands balled into fists.

"What did you do to my girlfriend?" I stalked toward him.

He lifted his livid gaze to me. "Your girlfriend? Is that why you didn't give her my number? Because you were trying to get her into bed?" He scowled. "From what she said, you didn't get very far on that mission."

"You're disgusting! That's all guys like you think about."

"Guys like me? You've got a lot of nerve. She's carrying my child. You're the one that's been lying to her for the last few months. And now she's taken off without my number again."

I looked him dead in the eye, tightened my hands, and visualized punching him square in the jaw.

A strong hand clamped around my wrist. "Time to break things up, boys," Frank said.

I glanced around. Several people were wide-eyed on the edge of their seats.

Why was I wasting my time here when I needed to go make things right with Tamara? Without giving Kyle another glance, I turned away and walked out the door. I sped toward her apartment, praying that I wouldn't get pulled over.

Things would be okay between us. Things had to be okay between us. Now that I had her, I couldn't lose her. If she wouldn't forgive me, I would never forgive myself. Less than fifteen minutes later, I pulled up in front of her apartment.

Her car was in her normal spot, but still running, and the trunk was wide open.

She struggled to carry a large box from her apartment.

Was she leaving town?

Of course, she was.

When the going gets tough ...

I got out of my Jeep, slamming the door to emphasize the fact I was here. I wouldn't let her do this.

Her face turned toward me for a quick second, then she stuffed the box in the trunk.

My heart dropped into my stomach at the pain in her eyes. Pain I had put there. I took hold of her arm. "What are you doing?"

She flinched and pulled away from my grasp. "Don't touch me."

"Tamara don't do this," I pleaded, coming unraveled at the seams. "Please don't do this."

She glared up at me through hate-filled eyes. How could she hate me so much? When she looked at me, it was as if she wasn't just seeing me, but every person that had ever hurt her. "Why shouldn't I leave?"

"Because I'm in love with you. I'm in love with you." I said the words with such conviction that there wasn't any way she couldn't know they were true.

Her face softened for a moment. "I wish I could believe you, Joe, but when you love someone, you don't lie to them like this. This was not a white lie. I could forgive that. You had his number this whole time. You had his number!" She slammed her trunk closed. "Do you know how much anguish it would have saved me if I had been able to get ahold of the father of my child?"

"Let me explain."

"Why, so you can lie to me some more? I don't think so."

"It's not what you think, okay?"

"It's exactly what I think. But what I don't get is why you didn't leave me alone? You had Susan. Kyle's a decent guy. If you would've given me his number, we would be together. He came looking for me. Doesn't that count for something? What gave you the right to take that choice from me?"

How could I have hurt her so deeply when all I had ever wanted to do was protect her? My mother's voice shot through my mind like a flaming arrow. *The way to hell is paved with good intentions.*

Tamara pushed past me. "You're not the man I thought you were." She got in her car and slammed the door.

My heart felt like it was being violently extracted from my chest as this woman I loved with everything in me drove out of my life.

CHAPTER 39

April 8, 8:30 p.m.

TAMARA

I sped north on I-5, tears streaming down my face. Why did history have such a sick way of repeating itself? Once again, I'd lost my best friend and boyfriend in the same day. This time it happened to be the same person, which somehow hurt worse.

Much worse.

The paper-thin line between love and hate had become transparent. I hated Joe for making me love him. I hated him for giving me hope. The last month had been one of the best times of my life. I was finally daring to dream again. I should've known it was all too amazing to be true. I should've known there was no such thing as a happy ending for me.

Just before I hit the Woodland exit, it occurred to me I was driving in the wrong direction. Washington State was the last place I wanted to be. I dug through the center console to find some smokes. It had been over a month since I lit up, but I remembered stashing an emergency pack there. As I lifted the pack, the number 99 jumped out at me from the box. Anger welled within me.

That number had led me to this miserable place. To this land filled with false promises, dead ends, and my shattered heart. I wouldn't let it lead me anywhere again. I furiously tore and ripped at the pack until it lay in hundreds of little pieces all over my car.

Flashing blue and red lights lit up my rearview mirror.

"You gotta be kidding me. Could this night get any worse?" Memories of my last run-in with the law assailed me as I pulled over.

The officer made his way to the side of my vehicle and shined his flashlight in my eyes. "Have you had anything to drink tonight, miss?"

"No, sir. I haven't. I'm pregnant."

"Well, you were swerving all over the place back there."

"I'm sorry, sir," I said. "I'll be more careful."

"I'm going to need your license, registration, and proof of insurance."

I looked around the car for my purse, but it wasn't there. Where was it? Had I left it at the house? I grabbed the registration and insurance card out of the glove box and handed them to the officer.

"I can't find my purse. My name is Tamara Jensen."

He studied the registration for a moment. "All right, Miss, I'm going to go run your information through our system, but just so you know, it's illegal to drive without your license on you."

"Yes, sir." Tears stung my eyes. Where had I left my purse? Hopefully it was at my house and not the diner.

My phone vibrated as the officer walked away.

I thought about ignoring it. It was probably Joe, and as far as I was concerned, I was never going to speak to him again.

But it was a number I didn't recognize.

"Hello?"

"Hey."

"Are you serious, Joe? I made it clear earlier that I don't want to talk to you!" I yelled into the receiver.

"This isn't Joe. It's Kyle."

"Oh, you sound a lot like him. How did you get my number?"

"Some guy named Frank gave it to me before I left the diner."

"I see. I wasn't expecting to hear from you after what happened back there."

"That's why I'm calling. I'm sorry about how I reacted. It had caught me off guard. I was hoping we could get together and talk."

The cop approached my vehicle again.

"Hey, Kyle, hold on a sec."

"What's going on?"

I thought about lying, but my mind went blank. "I got pulled over, and the cop is back."

He chuckled.

"Not funny!" I lowered the phone and looked up at the policeman.

"Miss, I'm going to have to ask you to step out of your vehicle," the officer said.

Another police car pulled in behind us.

Not this again. "Officer, is that really necessary?"

"Ma'am, there is a bench warrant out for your arrest."

"For what?" This could *not* be happening.

"An unpaid speeding ticket issued on January nineteenth."

"But I paid—" No! I sucked in a sharp breath as I racked by brain, searching my memory. How could I have forgotten about the ticket? "How about I pay it right now? I have money." Then again, I didn't know where my purse had gone.

"Sorry, ma'am, it doesn't work like that. I'm going to have to bring you in."

Bring me in? I glanced down at the phone in my hands. "Could you give me a minute?"

He crossed his arms. "Ten seconds."

I lifted the phone back to my mouth. "Did you hear any of that?"

"No. What's up?"

"They're going to arrest me."

It sounded as if Kyle was choking on something.

"Miss, time's up."

"I have to go." I hung up the phone and stepped out of the car, bracing myself for the most humiliating moment of my life.

CHAPTER 40

April 8, 9:05 p.m.

JOE

For the longest time, I sat in my Jeep in front of Tamara's empty apartment, staring at my phone. She wasn't answering my calls or returning my texts. She was gone, and from what I knew of Tamara, she wasn't coming back.

My whole body ached for her. How could I have lost her like this? All I had ever wanted was to keep her safe—to shield her from more pain. Somehow, in doing so, I'd hurt her more deeply than I could have imagined. But why couldn't she have at least tried to hear me out?

I turned the key in the ignition. Obviously, my reasoning didn't matter to her. This whole time, I had been so careful with her heart. Why should one mistake cost me everything?

The hole where my heart used to be burned at the edges. There had to be something to numb the pain—the overwhelming pang of remorse.

I could only think of one thing.

I shifted into gear and stomped on the accelerator. Within minutes, I pulled into the parking lot of the Ice House. I stepped out of my Jeep and slammed the door before heading inside.

The place hadn't changed in the three years since I'd been here. It still smelled like malt liquor and sweat, with a hint of stale cigarette smoke from years ago, when smoking inside had been legal.

Behind the bar stood the same guy who'd worked here before. Bill, maybe?

I took a seat at the bar. "What's the strongest drink you've got?"

"Rough day, huh?" Recognition seemed to dawn. "Joe? Good to see you, man. It's been a while."

"Yeah, good to see you too. Now how 'bout that drink?"

He chuckled. "I can see you haven't changed much."

I laughed a humorless laugh. Three years and, yeah, I guess I hadn't changed much at all. "Listen, it's been one of the worst days of my life. I'm not trying to be pushy, but I need something strong."

"You got it." He whirled around. "Now where did I put it?" He muttered as he searched through the assorted liquors. "Here it is." He turned around, a silver bottle in hand, holding it proudly like a trophy. "It's a 99-proof tequila, hardest stuff I have. Just got it in today."

"You're kidding me." I did a double take of the label.

Tequila marketed by a company called Agave 99?

"Yeah, it's heavy. The company wanted to wait and launch it for Cinco de Mayo next month, but because it's kosher, the producer released a limited amount for Passover tomorrow."

"Pour me up a double shot."

"All right." Bill opened the bottle and free-poured the clear contents into a large shot glass.

I lifted the glass to my lips.

A familiar laugh rang out behind me.

I turned.

Susan, across the room, played pool with some guy. She wore a black miniskirt, a sparkly red top, and stilettos. On a date, no doubt.

Just another reminder of how screwed up and rejectable I was. And of how quickly Tamara would get over me.

Relationships. They really did need to have a more descriptive name for them. Like "torture land" or "rip-out-my-heart-and-drive-all-over-it-ville."

I tipped the glass and let the contents slide down my throat.

It was strong, but not strong enough to reach my heart.

"Another one." I slammed the glass down.

"I don't know, Joe," Bill said. "I only have a limited amount. How about a beer?"

I stared at the empty glass. A beer wasn't going to cut it. "I'll take a double shot of Fireball?"

Bill eyed me warily. He hadn't seen me for years, and now I show up, demanding multiple shots in a row. He poured a double shot of Fireball in the same glass. Classy.

I downed it quickly, hoping for the numbness to take over. I just felt worse.

"Joe, I trust you and all, but you gonna open up a tab?"

"Yeah, of course." I patted myself for my wallet. I pulled out my card and handed it to him. "Keep it open and give me another shot."

"All right, my friend. But a couple more shots this fast, and I'm taking your keys."

"I hear ya." I didn't really care. I was on a mission, and I was going to see it through.

When I closed up my wallet, a business card fell from it onto the bar. I picked it up and studied it.

Levi Taylor.

Shame burned inside me stronger than the whisky. All the internal work I'd done with him and still this is where I ended up tonight. I thought I was stronger than this.

Looking up, I caught Susan staring at me, dark eyes full of empathy.

Why did she have to be here? I didn't want her pity.

Her date slid his arm around her shoulder and whispered something in her ear.

Had he noticed her watching me?

He seemed more Susan's style than I ever had been. If I'd seen her a week ago with him, I might have actually been happy for her.

I looked back at the card. "Hey Bill, go ahead and cash me out." I pulled out my phone and typed out a message to Levi.

Hello. I know it's late, but are you available?

I hit send, but instantly regretted it. Levi was my counselor, not my friend. Messaging him this late on a Wednesday was out of line.

I'm just wrapping up a card game with some friends. What's up?

I stared at the text message, my heart heavy. Thoughts of Tamara's angry words poured through my mind. *You're not the man I thought you were.* She, just like Susan, hadn't even given me a chance to explain. My chest burned like rubbing alcohol being poured into a fresh wound. I looked up at the rack of booze behind the bar. How much would I have to drink to take this pain away? I took in a deep breath and typed out another message. I had to get out of here before I made everything worse.

Sorry, I didn't mean to interrupt. I'm just in a bad spot.

Bill gave me my card back, and I tucked it into my wallet. Behind me, Susan laughed again. The sound grated on my raw nerves.

No worries. How can I help?

I wasn't exactly sure ...

I don't know. I need to get out of here, and I need someone to talk to.

I slid off the bar stool. My wobbly legs sat me right back down. I hadn't drank that much, but it had been a long time since I'd had any alcohol. A really long time.

You are welcome to come by, unless you would like to talk one-on-one?

What was I thinking, texting Levi?

It would be one thing confessing in his office that I had fallen off the wagon but showing up to his house after all this drama with Tamara was another story. I racked my brain. Who else could I call?

Caleb.

Why hadn't I thought of calling him before? Probably because we had grown distant since I started dating Tamara. Not that I meant it to be like that. I had just given all my time to her.

"Joe," Caleb answered after the first ring, the excitement in his voice apparent. "How have you been, man? It's been forever."

"I know, I'm sorry." Could he hear the slur in my speech? "Hey, listen, I could use some help right now."

There was a long silence. "Sure, what's up?"

"Tamara just broke up with me." I was being mild with the term "broke up." It was more like she ripped my heart out and crushed it with her rear tires. "I'm at a bar. I don't want to go home, but I don't want to stay here either. Could I crash at your place tonight?"

Another long silence.

He must've thought I was a complete idiot, giving up three years of sobriety over a girl I dated for a month.

"Wow, Joe, I'm sorry to hear that."

"Yeah, it's stupid. I don't know what to say. I really cared about her." Again, I was being careful with my words. I loved Tamara more than anything.

"I hear you. You know I'd be there for you, but I'm out of town."

I looked over at the bartender. Maybe I should get one more shot of Fireball.

"Is there anyone else you could call? It's not good for you to be alone. What about your sponsor, Nick?"

"Nick is the last person I want to call. He'd be worse than Levi."

"Who's Levi?"

I cringed. Why had I said his name out loud? "Nobody, Forget I mentioned it."

"Dude, who is he?" Caleb's tone implied that I had already said too much.

"He's just a counselor. Someone I went to a few years back. I texted him in desperation a couple of minutes ago. He said I could come to his house, but I don't want him to see me like this."

"Listen, I always give it to you straight, right?"

I let out an exasperated sigh. "Yesssss."

"You need to get out of there, stat. If Levi is your only way out, you need to take it."

"Levi's married, and it's too late on a weeknight for him to be talking to me. Could you imagine his wife's reaction to a drunk guy showing up on their porch at this hour?"

"Sounds like you're just making excuses. He wouldn't have told you to come over if it was going to be an issue."

As much as I didn't want to hear it, Caleb was right. I needed to swallow my pride. After hanging up with Caleb, I texted Levi.

What's your address?

CHAPTER 41

April 8, 10:06 p.m.

LEVI

David stood and helped Clay gather the poker chips, while I texted Joe my address.

"I had a great time. Let's do this again." Clay waved and headed out the door.

David and I said good-bye to him and walked into the living room.

"Thanks for staying," I said. "He sounded like he was in rough shape. It will be good to have some back-up."

"Of course, Levi, anyway to help. What's his name?"

"Joe Phillips. He works at the diner I took you to that one time."

His eyes widened. "Joe Phillips?"

"Yeah, you know him?"

"Actually, I think I do. If it's the same Joe Phillips I'm thinking of, he used to come to my youth group back when I was still the youth pastor at Hope Chapel. His mother died in a terrible car accident. Devastated the poor kid. We never saw him after that."

"Yeah, that's definitely him," I said. "Crazy."

David brought his hand to his chin and narrowed his eyes. "I wonder what God's up to."

I chuckled, but something in me stirred at the notion that perhaps God was at work.

Twenty-five minutes later, there was a light tapping at my door. I opened up to let Joe in. His eyes were slightly red, and he smelled of mint and alcohol. Not good. What had spurred him to break his sobriety streak? "Hey, Joe."

"Thanks for letting me come over."

"Of course." I invited him in. "You might remember David."

Joe came forward a few feet and spotted David. A look of confusion settled over his face. "Pastor David?"

David spread his arms open wide. "In the flesh." David embraced him as if he was his long-lost son returning home.

"It's so good to see you, Joe."

"It's good to see you too." Joe seemed a bit uncomfortable. "But I wish it was under different circumstances." He broke away from David and was quiet for a long moment, seeming to be fighting an internal battle. "Three years clean and sober down the drain." Regret weighed down Joe's words. "All over a crazy woman."

"Did you break up with Susan?" I asked.

Joe looked at me, his expression questioning. "Susan? Susan and I broke up a while ago. I'm talking about Tamara."

"Tamara?" Maybe David was right about God being up to something. I hadn't seen Tamara for a few months. I'd been praying for her this whole time and often wondered how she was doing.

"Do you want to talk about it?" David asked.

Joe's eyes welled with tears. "I don't even know where to begin."

CHAPTER 42
April 8, 11:00 p.m.
TAMARA

Over the last two and a half hours, I'd gone through the process of being stripped of all my belongings, booked, dressed in a ghastly orange suit, and then escorted into a small cell with an eaten-up crack addict.

Tears streamed down my face, as I lay on the small uncomfortable jail mattress, replaying the events of how I got there. So much failure. I'd once again failed at picking an honest man, failed at making life better for myself, and now, I'd even failed at running. Only this morning, it seemed like I knew exactly where my life was headed. It all seemed amazing, like a dream ...

But, as always, my dreams turned into ridiculously cruel nightmares.

When everything happened with Danny, I'd had a feeling things were off, so I was somewhat prepared for it, but tonight's events had completely blindsided me. I actually believed Joe was different. Tonight, I was supposed to be safely wrapped in his arms. Instead, I was alone in one of the scariest places I had ever been in.

There was no one I could call to bail me out. Joe would, but no way would I let him play the rescuer in my life again.

Maybe I could call Trudy.

No, she couldn't handle this kind of stress in her condition.

I was stuck. This was my lot for making so many bad decisions. I cursed God for abandoning me and Joe for not telling me the truth.

"Tamara Jensen," an officer called.

Rising cautiously from my bed, I wiped away my tears. What now? What else could they possibly do to me?

"You made bail." The guard opened the cell door and motioned for me to follow him. "Come this way, and I'll get you your things."

Stunned, I trailed him through several locked doors. At the end of the hall there was a small empty room.

"Knock on the door when you're done changing." He let me in and closed the door behind me. At the other side of the room there was a window, where a woman stood. She made me sign for my belongings and then handed me my clothes. I quickly changed and then tapped on the door. The guard took me through a few more doors. I turned the corner and spotted Kyle, sitting on a bench, foot tapping against the concrete floor.

"Kyle?" I walked toward him.

"Hey." He stood and hugged me.

"Thank you so much. I thought I was going to be stuck here all night."

"Of course. Let's get out of here." He put his arm around my shoulders and led me outside to the parking lot.

A sick feeling wormed its way around my stomach. I was glad he bailed me out, but what did he expect in return?

We stopped in front of a black semi that read Fletcher and Sons on the side. There wasn't a trailer on the back. He must have dropped his load before he swung by the diner earlier.

How strange all this must be for him. Did he regret coming in to the diner?

A wave of déjà vu hit me as I climbed into the semi and looked around the cab at all the levers and buttons.

Kyle stepped up into the cab and sat down.

"Thanks, again. Sorry about all this craziness."

He ran his hand along the steering wheel. "Don't worry about it. I'm sure there's some way you can make it up to me." Turning the key, He kept his gaze on me. The engine rumbled to life.

Uneasiness pricked my stomach again. He obviously hadn't changed. "I mean it. Thank you for bailing me out. I'll pay you back."

"Don't worry about it." He shrugged.

I gave him directions, and we started driving. All this meant I was trapped in Vancouver, once again. I'd been saving money ever since I decided to keep the baby, hoping to move to a nicer place. I had enough to leave town and live on until I found another job, but with paying off the fines, retrieving my car out of the impound lot, and getting my license reinstated, most of the money would be gone. I was back to square one.

As soon as I had this mess sorted out, I'd be looking for a new job. I might be stranded in town, but I wasn't going to be stuck working with Joe.

"Can we stop at a store? I really need some smokes."

"You're still smoking?" Judgment laced his words.

It struck a raw nerve. One cigarette wouldn't hurt the baby, and I deserved one after the day I'd had. "I am today. And I don't want to hear about it, okay? If you haven't noticed, I've had a rough night."

"Calm down. I'll take the next exit. We'll get you your nicotine fix." His tone made it clear that he was offended.

"I'm sorry, you didn't deserve that." I should treat him better after everything he'd just done for me.

"Quit apologizing. I get it. You're stressed." He maneuvered his way into a Chevron station and parked. "Listen, Tamara. I understand why you're on edge but remember we're in this together. I'm not the bad guy."

No, he wasn't. Joe was. Where would Kyle and I be right now if Joe had given me Kyle's number in the first place? Or if I'd never left the semi? Would Kyle and I have hit it off in the morning? Would we be in love? He was certainly attractive, with his blue-green eyes, sturdy jaw, and flirty smile. But was there more to us than that one night together—a night I couldn't even remember? I didn't know.

"Why don't you just sit tight? I'll go buy you a pack of smokes."

"You don't have to do that."

"I want to. What kind?"

"Marlboro Red 100s." After tonight, I was definitely switching brands.

"You got it. I'll be right back."

Once he exited the truck, I pulled down the visor and looked in the vanity mirror. I didn't look as bad as I thought I would, but still not great. I adjusted my ponytail and pinched my pale cheeks. It didn't help.

A few minutes later, Kyle entered the cab, carrying the cigarettes and a six-pack of Miller Genuine Draft. "You have your vices, I have mine." He handed me the smokes and a book of matches.

I gave the box a few quick slams on the palm of my hand and then tore off the cellophane. "Do you mind?" I tapped out a cigarette.

"Go right ahead. Just crack the window." He started the truck and drove out of the parking lot toward my apartment.

I lowered the automatic window and lit up.

"So, are you going to tell me why you got arrested?"

I inhaled another drag and coughed. "It's stupid really. My life has been a whirlwind over the last few months. Somehow, I forgot to pay a speeding ticket, and they put out a bench warrant for my arrest."

"That sucks." He turned on his blinker and made a right turn.

"No kidding." I took another drag. It made me nauseous, so I threw the rest of the cigarette out the window. The baby apparently did *not* want me smoking. "Now my license is suspended, and my car is impounded."

"I'm in the area for a few days. I can help you get your car out of impound tomorrow."

"Kyle, you don't have to do that."

"I can't have you going car-less. You're carrying around some precious cargo. Why wouldn't I help you?"

"This is my apartment, up on the left." I pointed quickly, and he pulled in.

He somehow fit the large truck into one of the parking spots and then turned toward me with a smug grin.

"Impressive."

"One of my many talents." He wiggled his eyebrows.

I laughed weakly. At least he was keeping things light. "I have to warn you, it's kind of a dump. I was trying to save up to get out of here before the baby was born, but now, with everything, I guess it's good I have another five months or so."

Kyle grabbed my hand and squeezed it. "You're not alone in this anymore. I'll help you."

My stomach tensed and I pulled my hand away. Before tonight I had never felt alone because Joe had always been there. But having Kyle step into that role so soon was terrifying. I didn't even know him. Not to mention he was a man, and none of them could be trusted.

Kyle exited the truck and walked toward the building before glancing back. I was still in the passenger seat, unable to move.

Being alone with Kyle in my apartment didn't seem like a good plan. He had been dropping innuendos sense rescuing me from jail. What if he expected something I wasn't ready to give?

He turned toward me, lifting his hands in the air, giving me a "what gives" look.

Hesitantly, I climbed out of the truck. "Kyle, I don't know if it's a good idea for you to come in."

He seemed caught off guard by my statement. "You've been through a lot tonight, and I don't think you should be alone. I promise to be a gentleman."

"Pshaw! That's what you said last time and look where that got us."

His lips curled around a carnal smile. "I think I said something more along the lines of, 'I won't do anything you don't want me to do.' I can't help it if I'm so irresistible."

I couldn't help but laugh. "Someone's got quite the ego." Despite my misgivings, I led him to my apartment, unlocked the door, and pushed it open.

The inside looked like someone had ransacked it. Things were strung in all directions. The drawers hung open and the nightstand lamp lay on its side.

Kyle took a step back, his eyes wide and mouth agape.

"It's nothing, don't worry about it." I shoved a drawer shut and righted the lamp. The problem was, it did mean something. It meant all this was real and that Joe had lied to me. Why had I let Kyle in? He'd probably hurt me too.

Kyle wrapped his arm around my shoulders. "Go get in the shower. I can straighten up out here."

I settled into him, suddenly feeling exhausted. "I made this mess. I should clean it up."

"Go take care of yourself." He pushed me toward the bathroom.

I closed the door, turned on the shower and waited for the water to heat up. I slid down onto the floor and let myself break down all over again.

Somehow Joe had snuck past every wall, every barrier, straight to the core of who I was and now, I was in shambles. I hated him, yet I ached for him.

Was it possible that I had overreacted? Should I have let him explain? But there wasn't a good enough explanation to change the way I was feeling.

My mind scanned over the last few months, trying to make sense of the situation. All I could think of was the day Joe had taken me to that appointment and our conversation at the restaurant. I had poured out my heart to him about how much I'd wanted to get ahold of Kyle. And he'd had the audacity to tell me that Kyle would probably be a jerk about it.

Joe had been dead wrong. Kyle had been a bit thrown off when he'd first found out about the baby, but who wouldn't be? Besides the time in the diner, he'd been completely sweet. He'd bailed me out of jail, for goodness' sake. Joe had absolutely no right to withhold Kyle's number from me.

I peeled myself off the floor, unwilling to shed another tear over the situation. I undressed, stepped into the tub, and furiously lathered myself up with mango body wash. Closing my eyes, I stood in the stream of hot water, letting it wash away the tension from my body and the filth from the jail.

I turned off the water, grabbed a towel, and wrapped it around me. As I stepped out of the tub, my foot slipped on some water. Before I could find my balance, I toppled over, hitting my arm on the bathtub faucet.

Kyle flung the door open. "Tamara! Are you okay?"

I groaned and tried to pull myself up. "Could someone just shoot me now and put me out of my misery?"

Kyle crept toward me.

"Just give me a minute." I raised my hand in protest. "I can do this." I made another feeble attempt to get up.

A half-smile tugged at Kyle's lips.

I secured the towel around me.

He raised an inquisitive eyebrow, appraised me for a moment, then stooped over, scooped me into his arms, and carried me to my bed. "What am I going to do with you? You're seriously falling into the damsel in distress category."

I smiled ruefully. "Does that mean you're my knight in shining armor?"

He leaned his face closer to mine. "Do you want me to be?"

I didn't say anything but lost myself in the steadiness of his gaze. Could he save me? Could he take away this pain inside my chest? Could he put the fractured pieces of me back together? It didn't seem possible.

He swept his finger across my brow line, brushing away strands of wet hair. "You're so pretty," he whispered, his lips dangerously close to mine.

My heart skidded to a halt. This was the exact thing I was afraid of. "Kyle, don't," I said, softly.

His eyes shifted from mine, and darkness settled over his face.

"I'm broken." I said.

"No, darlin'. You just slipped." Kyle slid into bed next to me. His eyes landed on my stomach.

It was wrong for him to be there. Just this morning, Joe was right in the exact spot, and I was open and ready to give him my whole world. How could I even recover from something like that?

"Don't you feel cheated? Because I do. Who knows where we would be right now if Joe would have just given you my number? We could be a family, Tamara. Instead, we're both completely blindsided." His eyes locked with mine. There was something in them that was hard to read. Anger? Desire? A mixture of both?

"I can make you forget about him. Let me help you heal. He did all this to keep us apart. Are you going to let him get away with that? Are you going to let him win?"

Confusion swirled around my mind. Something inside of me felt Kyle was wrong for me, even if I was carrying his child, but I no longer trusted my judgment—not after being completely wrong about every boyfriend I'd ever had. Tears stung my eyes again, flooding over before I could fight them off.

"Don't cry. You're too pretty to be this sad." He wiped the tear away and kissed my cheek.

My broken heart threw a jagged beat. I was not ready for this.

Kyle brought his lips to mine.

They felt wrong.

Foreign.

Grief gripped my heart again, because whether I wanted to admit it to myself or not, they felt wrong because they were not Joe's lips. Fury flooded me, and I moved my lips angrily against Kyle's.

His hands were suddenly everywhere. Again, they felt wrong, but I forced myself not to care. Anger morphed into passion, and I gave myself completely over to it.

When it was over, he pulled me in close. My bare back fit snug against his stomach, and he rested his hand across my slightly swollen belly. "This is how it's supposed to be."

In the darkness, a tear slid down my face. *I wish I could believe that.* The raw edges of my empty heart flared in pain. *I really wish I could believe that.*

CHAPTER 43

April 8, 11:30 p.m.

JOE

I was a gaping wound, a compound fracture, oozing and spilling out all over Levi's living room. "The worst part is that I don't think I'm ever going to see her again." I looked back and forth between Levi and David. Their expressions mirrored each other's —compassion mixed with sympathy. I hated it. I wished for something to ease the torturous ache in my chest. The alcohol had worn off, along with the slight numbness it brought.

For what felt like hours, I had poured out my heart. I told them all about Tamara and about blindly protecting her by throwing away Kyle's notes. And how none of it mattered because now she was gone

"Joe, I hear the pain in your voice," Levi said, "and I understand it. When these things happen, sometimes all we can do is pray and trust God."

I fidgeted in the hard, leather chair. Why did people give pat answers to such significant problems? Pray and trust God? That's it? Almost nine years ago, I had done that very thing after my mom's accident. She had been in the ICU for three days. I'd cried and pleaded with God to heal her and bring her back to me, but she still died. Why would I ever trust in my mother's Christian God after that?

"Have you tried giving your life to him?" David asked.

"Why would I want to live for a God who let my mom die? My mother was the most faithful person I've ever met, and yet he chose to take her away."

Tension filled the room. Or my heart. I couldn't really tell.

David cleared his throat. "Joe, I can't give you answers to why your mom died or why Tamara left, but I do know that if you're willing to open yourself up to him, God can work all this together for your good."

I wanted to lash out at his words. How could God make my mom dying good? How could Tamara leaving me be anything but misery?

"Look at me, Joe." David said.

I didn't want to, but I needed answers and respected David enough to trust him. I brought my gaze reluctantly to his.

The expression on his face was sincere and earnest—one that reminded me of a less complicated time.

In my mind's eye, I could see a seventeen-year-old version of myself sitting in youth group, listening to Pastor David preach. I was so full of life and faith back then.

"It is more than a coincidence that you called Levi the same night I'm here. You feel like God abandoned you when you needed him the most, but Joe, he's never left you."

"If he never left, then why is he allowing all these awful things to happen?"

"He's not," Levi said. "It's the enemy's strategy to bring misunderstanding to us about God's character."

"Exactly." David nodded. "Just think about tonight with Tamara. You love Tamara, right?"

"More than anything."

"And the only reason you got rid of Kyle's number is because you wanted the best for her, yet since she didn't understand your intentions, she ran away from you."

"Yes." I massaged my temples. My head ached—an echo of the

internal agony. Hopefully David would make his point soon. I was over this conversation, and I was done with this night.

"Her wounds and baggage caused her to have a wrong idea of who you are." David leaned forward. "She viewed your act of love through her lens of hurt and ran. In that same way, some difficult circumstances in your life have given you a misconception of who God is, and you're running. But you've been running long enough, Joe."

He was right. Just like Tamara had been running from her past, I'd been running from God. And just like Tamara's choices, mine were only causing more pain. The barrier inside me started to crumble. "I hate running."

"God isn't a big fan of it, either. He wants to heal you, if you'll allow him. Believe me, if you just open your heart, he'll give you the answers you've been looking for."

"I wish I could." I whispered.

"Can we pray for you?" David asked.

I nodded.

Levi put his hand on my shoulder and closed his eyes. "God, we ask that you bring healing to your son."

That old, familiar presence settled inside my heart. The same presence I used to feel during a worship service or when my mom would pray with me. I blocked out Levi's words and focused on that sense of peace.

An image of my mom came into my mind. She was luminous, vibrant, and smiling. As much as I missed her, I knew in that moment that she was in a good place, full of love and peace.

I was pulled out of the vision when Levi said Tamara's name. "Lord, please have mercy on Tamara, wherever she is. Protect her and show her your love."

CHAPTER 44
April 9, 9:24 a.m.
TAMARA

As I slept in Kyle's arms, I dreamt I was a little girl back in the living room of the old trailer my family used to live in. I sat on the same ugly, brown couch where I had cowered with my siblings as our parents had fought, but this time I was alone. The TV blared as my parents yelled at each other in the background.

Loneliness and fear wrapped around me like a tattered blanket. The feelings intensified as I snuck down the hall toward my parents' room.

The shouting escalated as I crept closer.

A loud thud and then a crash thundered through the air.

The bedroom door was cracked slightly, so I put my eye up to it to see what was going on, heart thrashing around in my chest.

My mother was holding her face as if she was in pain.

Had my father hit her?

I accidentally made a noise, and they both turned toward me. All the air sucked sharply out of my lungs. It was not my mother and father fighting, but me and Kyle.

Then the scene shifted, and I became myself, looking at a little girl in the doorway. One who looked almost exactly like me. My daughter.

I jolted awake and shot up in bed, adrenaline coursing

through me. The room spun as I scanned the area. Kyle was no longer next to me, and that realization made it easier to breathe. What had I been thinking last night? I knew it was a mistake to let Kyle come inside. Was this dream trying to warn me about him? Something niggled at my brain. I scanned the room. It was still somewhat a mess from the previous night's failed getaway.

My subconscious threw another image through my brain from a dream I'd had months ago. Me running down a dark corridor, trying to escape a man cloaked in darkness. Was Kyle that man?

Had Joe been right about Kyle?

Knock it off, Tamara. Kyle wasn't the bad guy.

Then why were my dreams telling me he was? And why was my body longing for Joe's comforting arms?

I threw off the blankets and dressed in the same clothes I'd had on the night before. Shame caused my face to warm. How could I have allowed myself to sleep with Kyle again? I was so stupid. There was no end to my list of mistakes.

And where was Kyle, anyway? Had he decided he couldn't handle all of this and left? I couldn't blame him. I would leave me too if it was possible.

I ran my fingers through my hair, to brush out the tangles, and threw it up into a ponytail.

Kyle burst through the door, carrying a couple of McDonald's bags.

Anxiety whirred in my stomach at the sight of him.

"Got us breakfast." He set the bags on the table and motioned for me to join him. "I didn't know what you liked, so I bought a bunch of stuff." He pulled out a breakfast sandwich and unwrapped it.

"Uh, thank you." I should have been starved, but I didn't think I could eat with the earthquake going on inside my guts. "Do you think we could eat on the road? We've got a ton of ground to cover to get my license and car taken care of."

"Sure," He said, around a bite.

"Gimme a minute, would ya?" I ran to the bathroom. After relieving myself, I washed my hands and then did a quick rinse with mouthwash. It would be nice to get my car out of impound, so I could have my clothes and toothbrush back. I splashed water on my face and patted it dry before returning to the living area.

Kyle stood by the door, bags of food in his hand. "Ready?"

"Yeah, just need to grab my purse." I scanned the apartment. "It has to be here." I walked back into the bathroom.

It wasn't there. It wasn't in my car last night, either. That left only one place it could be.

A wave of nausea rippled through me.

"I need some air." I walked outside and sucked in a deep breath.

Kyle followed me. "What's going on?"

"My purse is at the diner."

"The diner?"

"Yes." I groaned. How could I get it without having to go back there? If I called Claire, she could bring it to me after work, but she didn't get off until two thirty. That would be too late to get everything done. "What time is it?" Maybe we could make it in and out of the diner before Joe showed up.

Kyle looked at his cell phone. "Just past ten."

I groaned again. "He'll be there already."

"Who will?"

"Joe!" Pain radiated out from the middle of my chest. "I'm not ready to see him."

Kyle grabbed ahold of each of my arms. "Calm down. I'll be there with you. It will only take a minute. You know where your purse is, right? You just gotta walk in like you own the place and grab it. No big deal."

"You make it sound so easy."

He flashed an arrogant smile and dread overtook me.

"Why are you smiling like that?"

"Looking forward to seeing the expression on Joe's face when you walk in the door with me."

His words gouged a fresh wound through my soul. I'd never faced the people that had hurt me but facing Joe in this way might be unbearable. "Don't be like that."

"Like what? I mean, come on. That pompous jerk seriously messed with both of our lives. I don't think I'm being unreasonable if I want to cause him a little agony. Look what he did to you."

He had a point, but I wasn't that cruel. I took in a deep breath and composed myself. There was no way to avoid Joe.

CHAPTER 45

April 9, 10:04 a.m.

JOE

I entered the diner parking lot at 10:04 a.m. Only a few minutes late. Not bad, considering the night I'd had. As I walked toward the diner, my phone rang.

Trudy.

I hadn't had a chance to tell her Tamara had left town, and I wasn't looking forward to it. Trudy loved Tamara almost as much as I did. How was I supposed to tell her she was gone?

I answered after the second ring.

"Hey, Joe. I heard there was a little drama last night. Are you okay?"

"The gossip around this place is ridiculous."

"I'll take that as a no. I'm pretty close. I'll head over right away."

"Yeah, it's pretty bad. I'll explain when you get here."

"I'll be there in less than five minutes."

I hung up my phone and prayed for strength before walking through the door.

Claire's eyes brightened when she saw me. "I'm glad you're here. I need some change from the back. Tamara didn't make change before she left last night."

Of course, she didn't. She was in too big of a hurry leaving me. Man, it hurt that she was gone. But as excruciating as it was, somehow I could bear it. Something happened last night that made it possible. Because, in spite of everything, deep down I knew God would work everything out. It didn't look like it now, but that was how faith worked—believing despite what I saw. "Sure, I'll go take care of it." I took four fifties from the register and headed to the back.

It was difficult walking into the office. Tamara's scent still lingered there, a mixture of her vanilla body spray and mint gum.

I closed my eyes, overwhelmed by the ache of her being gone. It's crazy how emotional pain could actually hurt physically. Standing there, feeling her absence, it literally felt as if someone had punched a hole straight through my stomach.

"Joe." Trudy walked in behind me.

I slowly turned around.

She came to me and put her arms around me. "What happened?"

"I messed up. And now Tamara is gone."

"What do you mean 'gone?'"

I sat down and explained to her the whole story about Kyle, the number, the note, and Tamara taking off.

Worry and confusion lined her face. "But why would she leave town?"

"She's been hurt before. The only coping device she knows is to run away."

She was quiet for a few moments. "Maybe you should take a few days off. I'm not really cleared for work, but I can cover for today."

I picked up a few random papers from the desk. "No, Trudy. I can do this. I need to stay busy."

"Are you sure?"

Tap, tap, tap.

Claire stuck her head in. "Hey, sorry to bug you, but I really need that change."

"I got distracted."

She threw me a sad smile. "It happens."

I put in the combination on the safe and pulled out a bag full of change. The three of us walked out to the dining room.

Four people entered the restaurant and sat down at a booth. Claire made her way toward them, while Trudy followed me to the cash register.

A loud clanging filled the air as the door opened again. Instinctively, I turned toward the noise.

Tamara?

For a brief moment, hope rose. Had God brought her back to me? Kyle trailed in right behind her and put his arm possessively around her. The physical pain in my stomach returned with such force I actually looked down to make sure my insides weren't spilling out onto the ground.

Tamara pushed herself closer to Kyle.

I had already lost her but this? I was wrong before—the hurt was unbearable. The room seemed to swirl for a moment, so I focused on the cash bag in my hands. Anything to distract me from Tamara in Kyle's arms. Suddenly, every part of my body was aware of Tamara approaching the counter.

She blew past me.

It took all the restraint I had not to grab hold of her, just to make sure she was real. Kyle was still by the door and Claire waited on her tables. Where had Trudy gone?

I looked down at my cash bag. Change. Claire needed change. Somehow, I pulled out some ones and started counting, ignoring Kyle's insolent glare. I couldn't think about him. If I did, I wouldn't be able to control myself from walking across the room, dragging him outside, and beating the smug expression off his face. So, I went through the motions of counting, blocking out everything else around me. For a minute, it worked.

Kyle's phone rang.

"Hey, Jimmy. I guess you got my message. Yeah, I need at least a week. Ten days would be better." Kyle said. He seemed to be talking louder than necessary, like he wanted me to know he was sticking around for a while—like he was staking his claim.

"Yeah, man. I'm sorry. It's just something has come up." He paused. "Have Wilson do it." His voice escalated. "I've covered for him plenty of times." He was quiet again. "All right, I guess that will have to work, but please try to get me more time if you can."

I couldn't take it anymore. I put the rest of the change in the drawer without counting it and headed out back to get some fresh air.

CHAPTER 46
April 9, 10:12 a.m.
TAMARA

I barely held my emotions together as I walked down the hall to the office. It had been much, much harder than I'd thought it would be to see Joe. I'd expected it to hurt to see him, but I didn't expect that seeing his pain would affect me so deeply. When I saw the anguished look in his eyes, it took everything within me not to run to him. But I couldn't make myself vulnerable to him like that again.

As I entered the office, I sensed someone following me. *Not Joe, please not Joe.* It would only take a second to grab my purse, then I could bolt.

"Tamara." Trudy's voice came from behind me. "Why would you do such a thing?"

I turned toward her. "What do you mean?"

"Bringing that guy in here. Are you trying to kill Joe? I know you're angry with him, but that's uncalled for."

I spun and entered the office. Was she actually putting this on me? Unbelievable.

"Did you hear me?"

"Of course, I heard you. I didn't come here to hurt Joe, but I couldn't face him alone, either. I needed this." I snagged my purse off the back of the office chair and held it up.

Trudy narrowed her eyes. "I guess not having access to funds makes it hard to leave town."

"Who told you I was leaving town?"

"Joe. Who else? I can't believe you're going to do that to me. I need you right now. The doctor hasn't released me to go back to work."

Guilt sharply twisted my insides. I hadn't even considered how this would affect Trudy. "Listen, I'm not leaving town. But I *am* giving my notice."

Sadness washed over her features. She took three steps toward me and got right in my face. "You listen to me, Tammy girl. This job is the best thing you've got going for you. Believe me, you don't want to be looking for a job in this economy. You have more than just yourself to think about."

I backed up. "I can't work with him, Trudy."

"You won't have to. You guys already work opposite shifts. I can be the middleman. If there's something you need to communicate, you can go through me."

Why couldn't she just let me go? Other people could do the job just as well as me, if not better. "Why do you want me to stay so badly?"

She looked down at the floor. "I've already told you why. You and Joe are like my kids. I care about you."

She wasn't fighting fair. It was hard to deny her when she put it like that. It was wrong to leave her in a lurch. And it *would* be hard to find a job, especially in my circumstances. I drew in a deep breath. "Fine. I'll stay, but you have to keep your word."

She raised an eyebrow. "You ever heard of a thing called forgiveness, Tammy girl? It does wonders for the soul."

"You're one to talk. I've seen you hold a grudge or two."

"True, but they actually deserved it."

Irritation surged through me. "Do you even know what Joe did?"

She nodded. "Things aren't always what they seem, though.

The only thing that man is guilty of is loving you. He was just trying to protect you."

Protect me? Seriously? "Kyle is the father of my child, and Joe knew that I wanted to get ahold of him."

"It was wrong of him to withhold the truth from you, but how much do you even know about this Kyle character, anyhow? Joe loves you. His intentions were pure."

My heart softened a little. "Maybe so, but everything between Joe and me has been built on a lie. He should've told me before we got together. He should've told me as soon as he found out I was pregnant. If Joe hadn't messed with fate, Kyle and I would have been together three months ago."

"But you love Joe. I know you do. You guys are perfect as a couple."

Her words hung between us for a moment. Before all this, Joe and I were perfect, but now everything was all twisted up and convoluted.

It was over.

Tears gathered in my eyes. I needed to get out of this room and away from this conversation.

"Just promise me you won't be taking off anytime soon."

"I promise. But I gotta go. I'll talk to you soon." I hurried down the hall toward the back door to sneak out. Just in case Kyle was still in the diner, I lifted my phone to text him before pushing the door open.

Joe sat in my normal break spot, his body hunched over, head buried in his hands.

My heart lurched, and I froze, paralyzed by the sight of his brokenness. My defenses came crashing down. And this time Kyle wasn't there to strengthen my resolve.

Joe looked up, his tortured gaze meeting mine. "Tamara," he breathed. And then he was out of the chair and moving toward me.

Before I could react, his arms enclosed me, and for some reason I didn't stop him.

"Tamara, I'm so sorry. Please forgive me."

I stood there with my arms at my sides, not embracing him back, but not resisting him, either. Tears spilled from my eyes.

He brought his hands to my face, taking hold of it on each side. He rested his forehead on mine, his tears mingling with mine.

All my anger melted away as I breathed him in and felt his touch. As always, it felt so tender, so honest, and so right.

Was there any way to undo what had already been done?

My mind flashed to Kyle. I stiffened, thinking of last night.

There was no way to undo his mistake—or mine.

I pushed against his chest.

His arms fell to his sides. "Please listen to me. Just hear me out."

I averted my eyes. "Joe, there's nothing you can say. You can't turn back the clock. What's done is done."

"I should have told you."

"You're right. You should have."

He took hold of my hand. "I know I can't take it back, but what we have is bigger than this. I love you." He put his hand under my chin, pulling it up, looking me in the eye. "I love you."

Anger burned inside of me again, but this time it was directed inward. Standing there, hearing the sincerity behind his words, I hated myself. If I would have believed in him just a little, if I would have slowed down and let him explain, we might have made it through.

But I slept with Kyle.

Joe wouldn't forgive me for that, and I certainly wouldn't forgive myself.

"If you can forgive me," he said, "I believe we could make it through anything." His eyes were pleading and hopeful.

"Anything?" Dare I hope?

"Yes." He spoke with such conviction, it was hard not to believe him. "Anything."

Every cell in me wished I could lie and pretend last night never happened. How hypocritical would that be? There was no choice, I had to tell him. "I slept with Kyle last night." The words left a bad taste in my mouth.

His hands abruptly dropped, and he took a few steps back from me. "What?" he demanded. "Why would you do that?"

"I don't know. I was confused and angry."

"And Kyle took advantage of the situation again." He paced. "You know, Tamara, I never treated you like that. I've always treated you with honor and respect. I make one mistake, and you run off and jump in some other guy's bed?" His words came out like acid, stinging and bitter.

My icy heart absorbed the severe words, causing it to crack and splinter.

He kicked the garbage can beside him. "I was ready to give you my whole world, and you threw it away like it was worthless."

"You're unbelievable! When it's your mistake, you expect me to forgive and forget, but when it's my mistake, you have nothing but judgment. 'Oh, Tamara, we can make it through anything,'" I mocked him.

"You slept with another guy! Do you have any idea how much that kills me?"

"And you lied to me for the last three months. I don't know if I can trust a word you say."

He snorted. "Well, I guess that makes both of us."

I searched for the words I knew would wound him the most. "You know what, Joe, it doesn't even matter anymore. I'm with Kyle now, the way it's supposed to be. The way it would have been if you hadn't interfered. So just stay away from me!"

The expression on his face shifted back to grief.

A sharp ache twisted my stomach. I hardened my heart once more and turned from him. I stormed back toward the dining room and darted past Kyle. Once outside, I ran straight to the truck, climbed over the seat, and headed for the bed. I lay down, and curled myself up in a tight ball, wishing I could disappear.

The sobs were excruciating as they made their way from my chest, up my throat, and through my mouth.

What had I done?

What had I done?

I had ruined everything!

The truck door opened and closed.

"Tamara."

I curled myself more tightly. I didn't want him to see me like this.

"Tamara," he said again and then his hand was on my back.

A part of me wanted to flinch away from his touch. It was the mistake I had made with Kyle that cost my relationship with Joe. But I couldn't bring myself to push him away.

He lay down on the bed next to me and wrapped himself securely around me.

Try as I might, I couldn't hold back the sobs, which came in waves. When I thought it was finally over, another wave hit.

Kyle didn't say much. He just held me and let me cry it out.

Eventually, I pulled myself together and turned toward him. "Kyle, I understand if you don't want to stick around for me. I'd never keep the baby from you."

He tucked a lock of hair behind my ear. "Tamara, I'm not going anywhere. I understand that you're brokenhearted right now, and I can be patient with that, but could you please stop pushing me away?"

"I'm trying to give you a way out, if you want it."

"Look, I'm not the kind of guy that gets a girl pregnant and then bails. Yes, this situation is screwed up, but we can try to make the best of it. I admit I've been somewhat of a player over the last few years, but this has been a wake-up call for me. I think I'm ready to settle down. It gets lonely out there on the road." He held up his cell phone. "When you were taking care of things in the diner, I was on the phone taking care of things too. I've got the next five days off, and I'm hoping to get more. I'm calling in favors because I want to be here with you."

"I want you to be here too." I said, and it almost felt like the truth.

"We better get this show on the road." He got up quickly and made his way to the front.

I lay there for a moment, still not ready to face the world.

He looked back, throwing me a longing glance. "You coming?"

I pulled myself into a sitting position. "Yeah." I climbed into the passenger seat and buckled up.

Forty-five minutes later, as I stood next to Kyle in line at the DMV, the conversation I'd had with Joe replayed in my mind. Could my life get any worse?

Finally, the lady behind the counter gave me the total amount to reinstate my license.

I slid my debit card across the counter.

"Ma'am, we don't accept debit cards." She pointed to the Cash or Check sign prominently displayed at the window.

Luckily, I had my checkbook in my purse, so I pulled it out and wrote the check with a pen the worker generously let me borrow. She didn't even charge me for the ink.

Afterward, Kyle ran to the bathroom, and I headed to the truck.

While inside, I hadn't recorded the check in my register because of feeling rushed. If I trusted myself to do it later, it might end up like the speeding ticket. I fished through my purse.

Still no pen.

I looked around the seats and dash.

Nothing.

I popped open the glove box and dug around.

A few CDs—Megadeth and Rob Zombie.

Grimacing, I tossed them aside.

A pile of papers. A couple of small boxes—they looked like samples of drugs from a pharmaceutical company.

I picked up the first box. Flunitrazepam. What was that for? I read the box. A drug that helped with sleeping.

Made sense. He was on the road all the time. It was probably hard to sleep in the back of his truck with new noises everywhere he went.

On the label, a warning jumped out at me. *Do not mix with alcohol—it may cause blackouts, memory loss, or even coma.*

A strange buzzing sensation opened up in me. I picked up the next box.

Rohypnol?

The date rape drug?

Revulsion tore through my stomach. My mind went back to that first night with Kyle. All the missing time, waking with no clue how I'd ended up in the back of his truck, the panicked feeling I'd had.

How could I have missed it before?

Kyle had drugged me!

The words Joe spoke to me earlier that day replayed in my mind.

And Kyle took advantage of the situation again.

Nausea exploded inside of me.

I opened up the door and vomited down the side of the truck.

"Tamara?" Kyle jogged across the parking lot. "Are you okay?"

Was I okay?

Of course, I was not okay.

"You drugged me!" I threw the evidence at him, and it landed in the vomit near his feet.

"Let me explain." He reached toward me.

"Stay away from me." I said through clenched teeth, climbing out of the semi. "You ruined everything!"

"Tamara calm down ... It's not what you think." He said under his breath as he lunged toward me.

"Stay away from me! Help! Somebody call 911."

Kyle grabbed me and slammed me against the truck. "Stop making a scene."

"You're such a snake." I spat at him.

Kyle covered my mouth. "Shut up! I have issues sleeping. That's all."

My eyes scanned the area as I struggled to break free. There was a woman not far from us talking on her cell. Had she heard me? God, please, let her be on the phone with the police.

"What's going on here?" A man in a baseball cap and jersey ran over and grabbed ahold of Kyle's shoulders, pulling him off me.

Rage boiled up in Kyle's eyes. He turned and swung at the man. The guy ducked and punched him in the stomach. Kyle staggered back and swung again, this time connecting with my rescuer's face.

"Kyle, stop!"

Kyle looked at me, gasping for breath.

Just then, the sounds of police sirens filled the air as two cars entered the parking lot.

Kyle darted toward the cab of his truck, but Baseball Cap Guy tackled him to the ground.

A large officer went to his aid.

The woman who was on the phone came over to me and put her hand on my arm. "I saw everything, honey. It's going to be okay."

As Kyle struggled with the large police officer, a scrawnier one moved in on Baseball Cap Guy.

"He didn't do anything wrong. He was defending me." I pointed at Kyle. "He attacked me after I found these in his glove box." I motioned toward the box of pills still lying in the vomit.

The larger officer picked Kyle up by his shirt, shoved him against a police car and forced his hands behind his back.

"You have the right to remain silent—"

"She's a liar," Kyle interrupted the larger officer. "Just ask her about last night."

His words pierced through me, giving my heart its death blow.

He may have drugged me the first time, but last night, I'd willfully given myself to him. And now Joe hated me.

"—anything you say can and will be used against you in the court of law." The officer continued reading Kyle his rights while shoving him into the back of the police car.

"You're gonna pay for this—" The door slammed closed, muting Kyle.

Bewildered, I watch the police car drive away.

CHAPTER 47

April 9, 1:49 p.m.

JOE

I should have beaten the crap out of him while I had the chance, I thought for at least the hundredth time that day. The harder I tried to suppress the anger, the more it fought back, coming up in bursts of rage.

Images of Tamara and Kyle pummeled me relentlessly.

Why had she even told me?

It was so cruel. It seemed like I was getting through to her, but when she told me about Kyle, it all blew up. How was I supposed to react? Did she expect me just to grin and bear the fact that she'd slept with another guy?

No matter how confused she was, how could she do that? Last night was supposed to be our night. My hand tightened into a fist.

I should have beaten the crap out of him when I had the chance. Rage boiled in my veins like hot oil—torrid and painful.

An image of Tamara and Kyle, wrapped in each other's arms, pressed hard against my brain.

Bile rose in my throat.

My other hand curled into a fist. I wanted to hit something. I wanted to hurt something the way I hurt. The peace that had helped me through this morning had vanished as my heart petrified into stone. Did God expect me just to forgive such a thing?

He probably did, but I was in no mood for that.

In my mind's eye, Kyle stood in front of me and my fist connected perfectly with the smooth line of his jaw, my solid uppercut knocking him to the ground.

"Joe." Trudy's voice broke through the vision right before I kicked him in the abdomen.

My head jerked toward her.

"I think that invoice might be kind of important." Her gaze was on my clenched fist, face creased with worry.

"Oh. Um ... yeah, sorry about that." I smoothed out the wrinkled paper.

"Joe." Her mouth opened like she was going to say something, then she snapped it shut.

I glanced at the clock, then stood. 2:30. "I'm gonna get some coffee. You want some?"

"Coffee would be good."

I walked out of the office.

Anthony and Claire stood by the time clock. Anthony picked up his timecard and put it in the slot. The clock made a clicking noise as it stamped his card. "Did you hear about Tamara?" he asked.

My ears tuned in at the sound of her name.

"The stupid tramp got knocked up by a truck driver."

I didn't even think; I just reacted. All the fury I had been struggling to suppress rose up from within me. I took three long strides toward him and let the rage flow out with a right hook.

My fist connected with Anthony's face with a loud cracking sound. It struck with such force that it laid him out cold.

"You're fired!" Not as satisfying as punching Kyle would've been, but it felt good nonetheless. Anthony had disrespected Tamara way too many times. He had gotten what he deserved.

"Oh my—" Claire stood next to me, her mouth hanging open.

A few seconds passed before Anthony raised a hand to his face. "Hey, what the—?"

"I have had enough of you and your big ugly mouth, Anthony. It's time to get your things and get out."

"What is going on out here?" Trudy's voice came from behind me.

"I just fired Anthony," I said, tone flat.

"It looks like you did more than fire him. Sheesh, Joe, you can't go around punching people."

Anthony staggered to his feet, rubbing his jaw.

"Go on," I said. "I don't want to see your face around here again."

Anthony looked to Trudy with questioning eyes.

"You heard him." She shook her head. "You don't work here anymore."

"I was only stating a fact." Anthony sneered. "I don't think I should lose my job over it."

I snarled and lunged toward him.

Anthony flinched and let out a disgusted sigh. "Fine! I'm out. You better watch your back, Phillips." He stalked out of the kitchen.

I rolled my eyes and turned toward Trudy.

She crossed her arms in front of her. "That was not okay," she scolded. "I understand you're having a bad day, but that doesn't excuse this kind of behavior."

"Oh, come on, Trudy. You didn't hear what he said. You would have punched him too."

"Don't give me that. You've wanted to hit something all day." She shook her head. "This is my fault. I knew you couldn't handle working today. It's time for you to go home."

"But, Trudy—"

She put her hand out in front of her. "I don't want to hear it. This could get really ugly for all of us. Anthony could sue me for your little stunt or call the cops on you and charge you with assault. You go sort things out in your own head. I don't want to see you here for the rest of the week."

I sucked in a loud breath. I hadn't thought about any of that. But I couldn't take it back, and in spite of the possible consequences, I didn't want to. How screwed up was that?

Reluctantly, I walked back to the office and grabbed my coat off the back of the chair.

By the time I got in my car, I had reached an all-time low. The anger I'd dwelt on all day had been like a drug, keeping me safe from the emotional devastation, but now that I had released the rage on Anthony's face, I was completely deflated. I sat in my car for who knows how long, reeling from the overwhelming pain.

How had everything gotten so turned upside down? Just yesterday, everything seemed perfect, but it went to crap so quickly. I had lost the woman I loved, and now I was on the verge of losing my job. My life had somehow been reduced to a bad country song. Good thing I didn't own a dog.

A familiar pang gnawed at the back of my throat. I had already thrown away the last three years. Why not go for another drink?

In the distance, storm clouds gathered in the sky.

My phone buzzed in my pocket.

There wasn't anyone I cared to talk to at the moment, but I answered it out of habit. "Hello."

"Joe?"

"Who else?" I probably sounded like a jerk, but who cared? Maybe if I were more of a jerk earlier, I would have ended up with Tamara. It was always the jerk that got the girl.

"Er, you don't really sound like you. You okay?"

"Who is this?"

"Levi. I wanted to check in with you after last night."

"Oh, I'm sorry." Levi didn't deserve my snideness—not after last night. "It's been a rough day."

"Sounds like it."

I didn't want to talk about it, but he would probably ask about Tamara anyway, so I spilled my guts. I didn't leave out a single excruciating detail, from Tamara showing up with Kyle to me punching Anthony in the face.

"Joe, that's awful."

"Even more twisted is that I still want her. I've willed myself all day to hate her, and yes, I am angry with her, but I still love her. Maybe I just like to be tortured." Rain pelted the windshield. Why was I still in the diner parking lot?

"Or human and in love." Levi said.

"This is going to sound completely stupid and totally cheesy, but it kind of feels like we were in the middle of this epic love story that got cut short in the first act." I turned on my jeep and flipped on the windshield wipers.

He chuckled.

"Wow, that sounded way worse when I said it out loud."

"It wasn't that bad. I get it."

"I don't know, Levi. I just can't get over the feeling that we're supposed to be together. I wish I could figure out a way to make things right with us, but I can't see how to get through to her. The last words she said to me was, and I quote, 'Stay away from me.'"

He sighed, but said nothing.

"What?" I asked after a long silence.

"Joe, do you want me to give it to you straight?"

"I don't think lying is going to be very productive at this point in time. I need the truth, as much as it might hurt."

"Just don't shoot the messenger."

"Say what you need to say." I'd already reached my maximum pain level for the day. Nothing he could say could make it any worse.

"All right. There is this scripture that keeps coming to mind, and I feel it directly applies to your situation. I may be paraphrasing a bit, but the Bible says that if you seek to save your life, you will lose it. But if you lose your life for the sake of the Kingdom, you will find it."

How was I supposed to take that? Give up my life? How?

"I'm still pretty new at this. I get the principle, but how exactly does it apply?"

"I don't know for sure if Tamara is God's will for your life. You could try to get her back, but you would probably make the situation worse. If you put your life in God's hands and lose your life to him, you will find peace and fulfillment."

I heard what he was saying, but I didn't like it. Not at all.

"We all have stuff that is painful that we have to trust God with." Levi said.

"Oh yeah? Your life seems pretty perfect to me." The words tumbled out of my mouth before I thought about how sarcastic they sounded.

"Really?"

"Well, yeah. Nice house, good job, beautiful wife."

"There's a lot of things you don't know about me. It's never good to assume."

He was right. "I shouldn't have said that."

Someone spoke to him in the background.

"Hey Joe, David and I are headed out for a late lunch. You should meet up with us."

Moments ago, the addict's voice had been so strong. Being by myself was *not* a good idea. "All right. Where?"

"We were thinking The Skyline. David tells me they have fantastic burgers."

My stomach tightened at the thought of food. Eating sounded awful but being alone in my thoughts sounded worse than force-feeding myself. "Okay. I'll meet you there."

CHAPTER 48

April 9, 3:12 p.m.

TAMARA

"Can this thing go any faster?" I snapped at the taxi driver.

He gave me an annoyed look in the rearview mirror and sped the car up.

When I left Kyle, I had only one mission in mind—get my car out of impound and then get out of town. It didn't matter what I had promised Trudy this morning. If she knew what had happened, she would understand it was time to go. I tried not to think about the people I'd be leaving behind as I rode toward the impound lot.

Despite my efforts, Joe kept forcing his way into my thoughts. The words he'd said to me this morning, the way he'd held me, the weight of his tears as they'd fallen on my face, the pain in his eyes when I'd told him about Kyle.

The words I said to him echoed through my mind. *I'm with Kyle now, so stay away from me.*

Joe had been right to protect me from Kyle. The only thing Joe had ever done was care for me. He loved me. He truly loved me, and I was so damaged that I hadn't believed it was real.

Running would only add to his pain. I had to face him. I needed him to know I was sorry. I needed him to know that, if I could take it all back, I would. I needed him to know that I loved him too.

After the driver dropped me at the impound lot, I quickly filled out the paperwork and paid more fees.

Once I got my car back, I sped toward Joe's house, planning what I might say to him, but nothing seemed quite right. I turned onto his street.

Would he be able to forgive me?

I didn't see how, but I had to tell him, even if he turned me away. He deserved to hear the words from my mouth. I pulled in front of his house and shut off my car. With shaky hands, I reached for the door handle, opened the door and stepped out. Drawing in a deep, steadying breath, I walked up the sidewalk toward his house.

"He's not there," a woman's voice called out from behind me.

I slowly turned around. "Susan? What are you doing here?"

She was parked directly in front of me. How had I not seen her?

She eyed me suspiciously and then smiled curtly, as if she'd just put a puzzle together in her mind. "I stopped by to check on Joe. He looked terrible at the *bar* last night." Her expression turned accusing. "I can't imagine what could have pushed him to drink."

Her words sucked every ounce of air out of my lungs. Joe had been drinking last night? What had I done to him? My gaze fell to the ground, unable to handle the heaviness of her glare.

"I knew you were trouble from the moment I set eyes on you."

I wanted to scream. I wanted to deny it. I never wanted to hurt him.

I glanced back up.

Scorn lined her flawless features. "If you really care about Joe, you'll stay away from him."

It was so selfish of me to be here. What was I expecting,

anyway, for him to forgive me? For him to take me in his arms and tell me it was going to be okay? "I shouldn't have come," I whispered, turning toward my car. Loneliness and despair crashed over me, making every step toward my car feel heavy and forced. This was all my fault. Everything.

I had no one to blame but myself.

April 11, 9:05 p.m.

JOE

The next two days were like that ride I'd gone on once at Six Flags, the Apocalypse. Up and down, spin all around, and in the end you're lucky if you don't throw up.

Opening myself back up to God had been wonderful. I'd gone to a men's group on Thursday night at Hope Chapel, with David and Levi, and it seemed like a homecoming. Being there also made me feel closer to my mom. I could almost imagine her rejoicing with the angels when I walked in the door.

If it hadn't been for the break up with Tamara, I would've been overwhelmed by this love I'd rediscovered. By Saturday night my peace evaporated as the anxiety built, an orchestra of angry butterflies battering my insides with each rise and fall.

I had called Tamara countless times over the last couple days, with no answer. Each time, I told her voicemail how much I loved her, how much I didn't care what had happened between her and Kyle, and how sorry I was.

But she never answered or called back.

I should have let it go, but I couldn't. Not like this. I wanted to fight for her. I would've given in to my impulses Thursday night if it hadn't been for Levi and David advising against it. They both thought it would be best to give her space, but I couldn't take the silence a second longer.

As I drove toward Tamara's apartment, I prayed and then prayed again. Only divine intervention could break past the walls Tamara had built between us.

Pulling into her parking lot, I breathed a sigh of relief that her car was parked in her normal spot.

So she hadn't skipped town.

I stepped up to the doorway and knocked—a quick *rap, rap, rap*—and listened.

Were those subtle movements, possibly steps toward the door?

I waited a few moments before knocking again, this time more forceful. "Tamara!" I called out, fear opening a pit of ice in my stomach.

What if she had taken off with Kyle? What if he had done something to her? Worse yet, what if she had done something to herself?

CHAPTER 50
April 11, 9:23 p.m.
TAMARA

"Tamara, please," Joe pleaded, voice desperate. "Please, if you're in there, just let me know you're okay."

The only thing that had gotten me through the past couple days were Joe's phone calls.

Not in a way that gave me hope. We weren't getting back together. Not after everything. Too much damage had been done.

His calls, in this agonizing way, reminded me that I couldn't hurt him anymore. In those dark moments, when I wanted to slit my wrists or swallow an entire bottle of sleeping pills to make the misery stop, his voice on the recording kept me from it.

He once again was rescuing me, even though I didn't want to be rescued.

There he was, on my doorstep now, voice tender and concerned, begging me to let him in, and I couldn't do it. Letting him in would weaken my resolution, and he deserved better than me.

"Tamara, please."

I swallowed back the tears rising in my throat. I wasn't going to drag him back into this cesspool of a life I'd created for myself. The most loving act I could do was to keep him locked out.

Hearing his voice, though, knowing he was this close, made my chest twist with longing for his arms to be wrapped around me.

More knocking. "Tamara, I'm not leaving till you open this door."

There was silence for a long moment.

My phone hummed.

I just need to see that you're ok.

I stared at the message. I wasn't okay. I didn't know how to be okay after everything that had happened.

The knocking started again, but softer this time.

Tap, tap ... tap, tap, tap. Almost like a Morse code message.

There was a light thud on the door that sounded like he had rested his head against it. "Tamara." The desperation in his voice split me in two.

How could I torture him like this?

"I need to see you."

Ignoring him was only causing him more pain. I unlocked the deadbolt and opened the door.

He was the most beautiful sight I'd seen in days. Looking at him was like staring directly at the brilliant sun after being enclosed in a pitch-black room for months—painful and blinding.

CHAPTER 51
April 11, 9:43 p.m.
JOE

The door creaked open, and Tamara stood in front of me, a ghost of the woman from a couple days ago. She wore an oversized T-shirt and sweatpants, and her hair was pulled back in a loose ponytail, a disarray of flyaways circling her face. She wore no makeup, and dark circles lined her eyes. "Hey." She said, and even that one word seemed a strain for her.

What had happened? What had Kyle done to her?

She was still beautiful, but cloaked in a tangible depression, that made it hard to see. And her eyes—Oh my Lord, her eyes were as vacant as an empty tomb.

"Tamara." I pushed through the door and drew her into my arms.

She stiffened at first, like I was an attacker needing to be fought off.

"Joe ... I can't do this."

"I'm not going anywhere until we talk. I will force you to listen to me this time."

Her body softened then, all the fight leaving her.

How could I make her understand this feeling that had been growing in me for days? This feeling that told me that she wasn't okay, the same way I wasn't okay. We were meant for each other.

Without each other, neither of us would be whole. "I love you. I don't care what happened with Kyle."

All the color drained from her face, as if I were confessing a murder instead of my undying love.

"I'm not good for you. I'm not good for anyone. Do yourself a favor and stay away from me."

"You're wrong."

She shook her head. "I don't think I could live with myself if I hurt you again."

"Tamara," I said her name like a prayer, pleading and earnest. "I want you. I don't feel whole without you."

"Just give yourself time. I believe in you." She said.

"I believe in us." I tightened my arms around her. "You're home to me."

"Joe." She said my name with such a tangible sadness it was hard to breathe. "You're all heart." She put her hand on the left side of my chest. "I know it hurts now, but in the long run you'll thank me."

I buried my head in her neck, unwilling to hear any more of what she was saying.

"You've got to let me go." Her voice quavered.

"I'm not ready to do that."

"You have to, though."

She was running once again—not from someone that had wounded her, but from someone she had hurt. "Please don't push me away. I love you, and I know you love me. I can hear it in your voice."

Her gaze locked on mine, and her expression hardened. "Joe, you're wrong." She pushed herself free of my grasp and turned away. "I don't."

"You can't possibly mean that." Moisture welled up in my eyes. "You love me, Tamara. I know you do."

"If that was true, would I have slept with Kyle?"

Her words struck my heart like a rusty knife, rough edges cutting me open in the most painful way.

She stepped around me to the door, grabbed the handle, opening it wider than it already was.

"No. This isn't right. Something happened. Let me help you."

"You can't save me, Joe."

As much as I wanted to save her, I knew she was right.

CHAPTER 52
April 11, 10:02 p.m.
TAMARA

Everything in me wanted to run after Joe as he left my apartment. Instead, I pressed my body against the door, barricading him out. It was the hardest thing I had ever done, especially with the lingering presence of his embrace on my skin.

I closed my eyes and relived the moment with him over and over, my grief mingling with anger, overtaking every part of my being. I'd already been tainted by the time I first met him. He loved me, and I was so damaged and jaded that I had destroyed it.

I was so sick of the pain. "God!" I cried. "Why did you make me like this? Why am I so messed up?"

The fury twisted and fought within me like a feral animal clawing from the inside out.

"Do you even care?" I screamed. I tore across the room, lifted the glass lamp above my head, and threw it to the floor.

It shattered, and shards of glass flew across the floor.

"Do you even see me, God?" I ripped through my apartment, flipping and hitting things, abusing my stuff like I had been abused.

Exhausted, I slouched to the floor. "Please, God, if you're real, make it stop. Make the pain stop."

An absurd desire to find my journal hit me. I waded through the mess, searching, then found one.

Not mine, but Levi's.

I took a long, hard look at it and set it down. Eventually, I found my journal underneath the overturned nightstand.

I stared blankly at the poem I'd been working on for months. Where was the hope I needed? I found a pen and wrote new lines.

> *I scream for more, but my call is unheard.*
> *My love is lost, my end is near, so I fall.*

Defeated, I looked around my destroyed room. What was left? Was there any light left?

My eyes drifted to Levi's journal.

Something leaped inside of me.

Levi had always exuded hope. And in that moment that was exactly what I needed. I cleared my bed, snatched up the journal and let it fall open to a random page.

October 16

My wife miscarried last night. Though it's happened twice before, she's never been this far along. After the first trimester, she was supposed to be out of danger, but Sarah was seventeen weeks along this time. We had finally let ourselves get excited about it. We were only a few weeks away from finding out if the baby was a girl or a boy. I don't understand why this is happening. We've been faithful, haven't we? It just doesn't make sense.

I swept my hand over my stomach. How awful that must have been for him and his wife. It's senseless how unfair life could be. Here I was, completely unstable, with nothing to give a child, and everything had gone perfectly in my pregnancy so far.

I looked down and began to read the next page.

October 22

As I prayed this morning, I began to read through the Psalms. David stirred himself up in some of the hardest times in his life by putting his hope in God. It's so hard for me to engage with that kind of truth right now. Honestly, a part of me wanted to throw my Bible across the room. I'm so disappointed.

My hope is dashed. I've been going to church for as long as I can remember, but for the last few months I'd felt so strongly that there must be more to this walk that I've chosen. But now, I feel like I'm back to just going through the motions. In this moment though, I have a feeling if I don't grow closer to God, it's possible I'll lose my faith altogether. Is this why this is happening? Is it an attack against me going forward with my relationship with God? Before the miscarriage, I'd felt more alive than I had in years.

Lord, help me grow closer to you in this. Help me to put all my trust in you. And please bring comfort to my wife. All she has ever wanted for as long as I've known her is to be a mother. Don't take that dream from her.

Page after page was filled with Levi's love for his wife, his grief over the death of their unborn child, and his grappling with his faith. Instead of blaming God, Levi did everything he could to deepen his faith.

When I was a little girl, I had tried to find comfort in God, yet he'd abandoned me.

Levi spoke of this same feeling of abandonment, but instead of turning away from God, he chose to run after Him. Had it worked?

Because if it had worked for Levi, maybe—just maybe—it would work for me.

November 7

Sarah and I continue to grieve the loss of our baby, but something has changed inside of me. Every day I dig into the Bible and find nuggets of hope. God is carrying us through. And every day, hunger builds in me to know more about this God I serve.

There is also a longing stirring inside of me to make a difference in the lives of those around me.

Just yesterday, I ran into David Williams at the grocery store, of all places. He's back at Hope Chapel on the pastoral staff as a counselor. We made plans to have coffee next week.

God, thank you for the hope you've been putting in me about the future. I trust that you'll continue to do this as I seek after you. And thank you for the opportunity to reconnect with an old friend like David. He's such a compelling person. The way he talked about you made me feel he knows you like a friend. Father, show me what it means to be your friend.

My heart stung as I read the next page and a half of the journal. November 11th was Sarah and Levi's anniversary. Reading about his love for his wife, made my heart twist with longing for Joe and hurt for Levi and Sarah. This couple, more than anything, deserved a child.

November 12

Sarah is on my heart this morning. Last night she confided in me that she is reluctant to go see a specialist because she's afraid of what they might find. She isn't ready to face them telling her she may never be able to carry a baby to full term.

God, please give me the wisdom on how to be there for her through all of this.

This life could be so messed up sometimes. I conceived because of a date rape and now I even wondered if I could go through with the pregnancy. I swept my hand over my stomach.

They were ready and wanting, yet it was so hard for them.

November 23

Last weekend I attended a conference with David at Hope Chapel. The presence of God was there in a tangible way. People were up at the front, creating beautiful works of art during worship. Some people danced with banners. Others raised their hands in surrender.

When the preacher spoke, my heart came alive. At the end of the service, a crowd of people gathered at the front and repented of complacency, crying out to God to fill them and use them for His glory. I don't completely understand all of it, but I want more.

I scanned through the next few entries, feeling a bit guilty. It hit me suddenly how wrong it was to be reading his journal, but for some reason, I couldn't stop myself. His spiritual journey intrigued me, and I had to know if he and Sarah got the happy ending they deserved.

December 3

Ever since the conference, I've been meeting up with David and a group from Hope Chapel to do what they call "treasure hunts." It's a sort of Holy Spirit-led evangelism. Before we go out, we ask God for visions that lead us to the people He wants us to minister to.

Today I saw a clear vision of the ninety-nine rocks, an image from my recurring dream. I told everyone to be on the lookout for the number 99. We went out walking and found a few people to pray for, but by the end of our time together, no one had seen the number. I left disappointed but on my drive home, exit 5 to NE 99th Street stood out to me. I quickly made a right, praying for God to lead me. I drove for a while, not sensing anything. Finally, I decided to turn around in the 7-Eleven parking lot, which was on the corner of Highway 99 and NE 99th Street. Directly across from me, lit up in green neon, a sign said Highway 99 Diner.

Stunned, I looked up from the journal, frightened to read the next line. The number had followed him too? How was that possible?

As I walked into the diner, I expected to be greeted by an angelic entourage or heavenly chorus, but I stood in a common diner. Nothing special or unique. And I wasn't even hungry. But I couldn't shake the feeling I was supposed to be there. I ordered a cup of coffee, pulled out my journal, and now here I sit.

So, I just saw Joe Phillips, an old client of mine, cooking in the back. I can't go and talk to him, as that would break all sorts of confidentiality laws.

And then there's the waitress. She keeps looking at me with those deep-green eyes.

Lord, help me understand why I am here. When she came over to fill my cup with coffee, I tried to say something, but nothing came out. But I do feel compassion stirred in me.

Is this why I'm here, to make a fool of myself in front of this pretty waitress? Are you trying to humble me? God, if you want me to have a conversation with her or Joe, you have to bring them over to me.

I just found out the waitress, Tamara, is clumsy when she is stressed out. She spilled a cup of water on my lap, but at least that got us started talking. Sounds like she's having a hard day. I tried to make her feel better but got nervous because I've never done anything like this before. I don't even know why I'm here. At least I wrote a little encouragement on the bottom of her ticket. I may not speak well but I can write. My deed is done here. I'm going to change my pants.

So strange to see my name in the pages of his leather-bound book. But the fact that *my* number led him to me was even crazier. Maybe that was why I'd always felt connected to him. Was there a reason we were supposed to meet? If that were true, where was he now? How could I get ahold of him? Perhaps the answers were between the pages of his journal.

CHAPTER 53

April 11, 11:00 p.m.

JOE

I lay in bed that night, haunted by the images of Tamara's vacant eyes. Maybe I shouldn't have gone over there, but I couldn't regret trying.

How would I ever get over this woman?

This woman who wanted nothing to do with me. This woman who didn't care enough about herself to love anyone else. This woman who said herself, she wasn't good for anyone.

And yet she was locked up inside of me. I longed to show her love until she knew beyond a shadow of a doubt that she was lovable and that she was worth fighting for.

I sat up in bed and flipped on the light.

My Bible stared at me from the nightstand, as if to remind me faith and trust were the only answers.

I didn't feel like praying. That's all I had done for the last couple days, and it clearly wasn't working. Tamara had only gotten worse. But prayer was my only option. "God, why does this have to be so hard? Lord, please speak to me about how to let go of her." I picked up the Bible and let it fall open.

Song of Solomon? Great. The one book I always steered clear of, with all those strange analogies.

I slammed the book shut. "God, I'm desperate here. Do you hear me?" I opened the Bible again.

The same page in Song of Solomon, chapter eight. Fine. Here goes. I began reading out loud. "'Oh, that you were like my brother, who nursed at my mother's breast!'" I grimaced. "This is why I don't read this book," I muttered. "It's so weird."

Verse six and seven jumped off the page. "'Set me as a seal upon your heart, as a seal upon your arm; For love is as strong as death, jealousy as cruel as the grave: Its flames are flames of fire, a most vehement flame. Many waters cannot quench love, nor can the floods drown it. If a man would give for love all the wealth of his house, it would be utterly despised.'"

Peace crashed over my heart. In the last few months Tamara had been sealed to my heart. Her name, her face, her everything. Perhaps the way I felt about her wasn't crazy, but supernatural.

My love for Tamara, as impossible as it felt, was a gift that many people went their whole lives without knowing. "God, thank you for letting me know your kind of love."

The prayer resounded in my heart. God's kind of love—one that still loved even if someone rejected him.

"Show Tamara your love. Break through to her. Let her know your peace and joy and give her hope."

I closed my Bible and turned off the light. There in the dark, my mind conjured up an image of Tamara's face again, but not like I'd seen it tonight, nor like I had seen it before. But how it was created to look, full of hope, peace and joy, completely unbridled from the brokenness of her past.

CHAPTER 54
April 12, 9:45 a.m.
TAMARA

When I woke the next morning, I had the briefest moment of clarity—the way someone should feel when they're starting a new day. Then reality struck, imploding my soul until I could barely breathe from the pain. I pulled the covers over my head. Sleep-filled nothingness was the best I could hope for these days. Rolling over, I hit my head on Levi's journal. It was right next to my pillow where I'd left it last night. Longing stirred in me. I had to know if his story had a happy ending.

January 17

The Highway 99 Diner has become my personal sanctuary. Writing in my journal at my little booth helps me sort out life.

My wife goes in for a whole battery of tests this afternoon. Within a couple of weeks, we'll know if anything is physically wrong with her. I just need out of my own head. I'm not the only one on this planet with problems.

Tamara seems sadder than usual today.

How can I brighten her day?

Lord, I pray that you remove the burdens that are weighing Tamara down and show her your love. Also, be with Sarah today and help us bravely face what the tests may find. And please take me outside of myself. I give myself to you. Use me for your glory.

January 18

Right before I walked into the diner today, I saw Tamara stumble out of a semi, looking quite distraught.

She has so much potential yet chooses to sell herself short and give herself away like that. Lord, please protect her. Show her how much you value her. Bring someone to her that values her like I value my wife. Thank you for Sarah. Please help her this week as we wait for the test results.

Shame overshadowed me. Seeing that morning through Levi's eyes made the whole situation seem worse. Yes, I'd been drugged, but he didn't know that. What he must have thought of me.

Trying to shake off the thoughts, I scanned back over what I'd just read. It didn't seem like Levi judged me. His tone was more of a concerned father. Tears stung my eyes as I read what he prayed for me that day.

Had Joe been God's answer to that prayer?

This day is getting stranger by the minute. Joe Phillips came by my table. Once again, he acted like he didn't know me. I guess if I saw my therapist in public, I would do the same thing. He only came out to get my order and let me know the waitress didn't show up. I mentioned seeing Tamara in the parking lot and against my better judgment, I told him what I had witnessed. I kind of feel like I gossiped. On top of that, Joe got mad at me for not helping her. Joe obviously cares deeply for Tamara. Hopefully, he'll find a way to reach out to her.

Regret washed over me. Even before we were together, Joe had been watching out for me.

CHAPTER 55

April 12, 10:45 a.m.

JOE

The next morning when I woke, I immediately began to pray for Tamara. I didn't know what it was going to take to break through all of the walls she had placed around her heart, but I knew the one who was able to demolish the walls of Jericho. I looked over at the clock. 10:45 a.m. Since I was still suspended from my job, I had planned to go to church, but now I was late. Home church sounded pretty good. I turned on a Jeremy Camp CD Levi had loaned me and crawled back into bed with my Bible.

Luke 15 popped in my head, so I looked it up. My eyes settled on verse four.

> *What man of you, having a hundred sheep, if he loses one of them, does not leave the ninety-nine in the wilderness and go after the one which is lost until he finds it?*

Ninety-nine? Was the number spiritual?

> *And when he finds it, he joyfully puts it on his shoulders and goes home. Then he calls his friends and neighbors together and says, 'Rejoice with me; I have found my lost sheep.' I tell you that in the same way there will be more rejoicing in heaven over one sinner*

who repents than over ninety-nine righteous persons who do not need to repent.

Again, the *ninety-nine* jumped off the page like a dancing flame.

As if a veil were lifted, everything became clear. The number was not leading her toward a dead end or hell but was a sign of God following her wherever she ran.

God had been pursuing her, and she had no clue.

I had to tell her. I threw on a hoodie and some jeans and rushed out the door.

CHAPTER 56

April 12, 11:00 a.m.

TAMARA

For a long time after reading that journal entry, I thought about Joe. Life made more sense when I was with him. He was truly the sweetest guy I'd ever met. He'd always treated me with care and tenderness, pouring his heart out to me with such kindness. That kind of love only happened once in a lifetime, if a girl was lucky.

He'd come by last night, practically begging me to give us another chance. I couldn't help but believe that I'd done the right thing, though. One day Joe would thank me for letting him go.

But where did that leave me?

Alone. Bitterly alone.

Depressed, I picked up Levi's journal again.

January 20

On the way to the diner this morning, I listened to a podcast from one of the speakers at the conference. He spoke about the gifts of the Holy Spirit and how they were intended to also be used outside the church, so that the people who didn't believe in God could know his love. It definitely challenged me. It is easy to hear God in the comfort and safety of church, but outside? That's another story.

The speaker claimed hearing the voice of God takes practice.

He encouraged his listeners to be bold, even if what we may hear doesn't make sense. It's freeing to know that it's okay to just "practice" hearing God. The funny part was he was talking about practicing on waitresses, and here I'm at a diner.

God, I pray that you would help me make a positive impact on Tamara's life, to show her you are real.

Strange. I'm seeing an image of a trailer park. A trailer park? Okay, now I see a wooden pew.

God, I'm sorry.

I definitely need more practice. Tamara's going to think I'm nuts. I wrote down "trailer park" and "wooden pew," then crossed them out. I didn't want to categorize her as the trailer park-type. And I didn't want to write anything about the church because I didn't want to seem religious. If that was you, God, forgive me for being disobedient. Please help me hear your voice more clearly.

Goosebumps rose on my arms. Levi had no idea where I'd came from. Not a soul on the planet knew that I used to hide under those pews. Only God Himself knew that.

January 21

Yesterday, I went home feeling bad that I didn't have enough courage to share with Tamara the vision that I'd had. I asked God to use me, but my inhibitions got in the way.

As I sit at this table, I'm getting an image of her with a baby and God picking both of them up and singing a lullaby over them. I hear the song in my mind "Lullaby" from Shawn Mullins. I don't even like that song, but I'm supposed to write down the line about how everything is going to be all right.

God, I'm doing the best I can here. The rest is up to you.

Tears stung my eyes. It was all so surreal. He'd heard from God about that song? And he knew I was pregnant before I even knew? Was he some sort of Christian psychic?

February 10

I haven't been this broken since Sarah last miscarried. The specialist is fairly certain Sarah won't ever carry a baby to term. She was diagnosed with having a unicornuate uterus. Her uterus is smaller than normal, and she has only one functioning fallopian tube. Some women carry to full term—or at least close enough to save the baby—but all our miscarriages make that highly unlikely.

Doesn't the Bible say, delight yourself in God and he'll give you the desires of your heart? This is our deepest desire and it's shattered.

No! It was all wrong. Tears spilled down my cheeks. If things couldn't work out for a man like Levi, clearly there wasn't any hope for me. What kind of sick God would allow this to happen after Levi had been so faithful? I was about to throw the book across the room, but instead, I flipped a few pages ahead, to the last page of the journal with writing on it and read the date. Sadness washed through me. That was the last time I saw Levi.

February 16

It's hard to believe, after everything that's happened, that I can feel such hope. But I do.

Sarah believes she's meant to be a mother, even if it's not in the conventional way. We're looking into adoption. Perhaps that was God's plan this whole time.

I had never liked the idea of adoption because it felt like abandonment but reading Levi's journal and seeing his and his wife's struggle, it was hard not to believe there was something bigger at work bringing us together.

There's a dark cloud looming over Tamara today, a depression wrapping itself around her, holding her captive.

God, whatever is going on with her, please give her hope. My ticket has the number 99. The number from my dreams.

God, is Tamara who my dreams are about? Is she the one who's running from the dark figure that seems to consume her life? Such fear, God, such loneliness. She is why you had me come here, isn't she? Lord, please show me what to do.

God had brought Levi to me? The last ticket on which Levi had written a note to me was still jammed in the pages of the journal. I pulled it out and studied it.

Jeremiah 29:11 beside the words *Have hope.*

I scanned my messed-up room trying to find the Precious Moments Bible Joe had given me. I found the table of contents, got the page number, and flipped to it.

"For I know the thoughts that I think toward you, says the Lord, thoughts of peace and not of evil, to give you a future and hope."

Future and hope? Was that possible for me?

I wished I could talk with Levi about this verse and ask him about his visions of my baby. Wait, it was Sunday morning, and I knew which church he'd be at.

I Googled Hope Chapel and found the address. It was only a couple of miles away. I grabbed Levi's journal and my keys and ran out the door.

CHAPTER 57
April 12, 11:37 a.m.
JOE

Anticipation came over me as I parked in the visitor space in front of Tamara's apartment and made my way to her door.

Would she think I was insane?

I knocked on the door.

It inched open.

"Tamara?"

No answer.

Strange. Tamara never left her door open. Or unlocked, for that matter.

I pushed the door open a little bit farther, revealing a vandalized apartment. "Tamara?" I ran through the living room and almost tripped on the knocked-over bookcase and the cushions from the couch. I checked the bathroom. "Tamara!" I yelled again, heart sinking.

Had she run again? Or had Kyle taken her against her will?

I pulled out my phone and dialed Tamara's number.

As soon as it rang in my ear, a phone rang in the apartment. Not good.

My phone rattled in my hand. A text from Levi.

Where are you?!

Long story. What's up?

Moments later, Levi texted back.

I'm at church and so is Tamara!!!

Tamara?!

Relief, confusion, and excitement—all at the same time—gave me a crazy adrenaline rush.
My phone vibrated again.

Yes, Joe, Tamara!!!! Your Tamara!!!

I ran to my car and peeled out of the parking lot as fast as I could. Everyone seemed to be driving worse than usual. Even the traffic lights were fighting against me.
Five blocks from the church, it seemed like my luck was finally changing. In the distance, the light turned green, and I pressed on the accelerator.

CHAPTER 58

April 12, 12:05 p.m.

TAMARA

I stayed in the back of the sanctuary for a while taking in my surroundings. It was a large room, split up into three separate seating sections. I finally took a seat off to the right on the very back pew, not wanting to disrupt the service that was in full swing. I scanned the crowd.

There were so many people in the room, but Levi was nowhere to be seen. I looked down at the journal grasped tightly in my hand. I opened it up to the last page and noticed writing that I hadn't seen before. At the very top it said my name.

Tamara,

If you are reading this, I want you to know that was my intention in leaving my journal. I believe God led me to leave it with you. I wish I had been more obedient and shared His love with you a long time ago.

God wants you to know that you don't have to live in fear, that the darkness chasing you is no match for the light He offers. He's been pursuing you for a long time now. The Bible says, in Luke 15:4, about how if a Shepherd has 100 sheep and one wanders off, He will leave the 99 and go after the one. He has truly left the 99 to come after you. I won't be coming into the diner anymore because God has told me not to and I'm finally learning to listen to his leading. I've included my phone number so *please, if you finish this and you read this page, feel free to call me. I would love to pray with you.*

Much Love,

Levi Taylor

My mind spun around this last message Levi had written. Could his words be right? Could it be that God led him to me? Could this be the reason I had kept seeing the number 99 over and over? Had God been trying to save me or bring good things in my life through that number?

If it weren't for that number, I would have never met Joe. That number brought Levi to me. It had kept me from having the abortion and from leaving Vancouver.

A melodious riff began to play in the background.

I looked around the room. Everyone's heads were bowed. "If anyone here would like to receive Christ as his or her Savior," the pastor said, "come to the front, and a member of the staff will pray with you."

My heart felt as if it could beat out of my chest, but I was frozen to my seat.

"Also, if there is anyone that just feels hopeless, we would love to pray with you. God wants to give you a future and a hope."

There it was again. A future and hope. It was like the pastor was speaking only to me, but several people from around the room went up front and knelt at the altar.

The scene was too much. The emotions were too much.

I wanted to bolt—

But then a man started singing in a soft, soothing voice. "Who was, and is, and is to come," repeating it over and over again.

I closed my eyes, letting the beautiful words wash over me and blocking out everything else around me.

His voice continued to fill the air. "God, you leave behind the ninety-nine, you cause the sun, the stars, and the moon to shine.

You search the field and every mountain you climb, until you find the one that was left behind, and you restore them like they were there all the time, all the time, all the time. You restore them like they were there all the time."

The words pierced my heart, overwhelming me with love. Tears fell from my eyes.

Someone else spoke into the microphone. "While Joshua was playing that song, I got a vision, and I believe that it's for someone in this room. There is a young woman, possibly in her early twenties, and she's been running for a long time."

Was he speaking about me?

"God wants you to know that he is coming after you. He wants to meet with you this morning to give you hope. I encourage you to come to the altar. When we make one step toward him, he is so faithful to run toward us."

A force propelled me to my feet and then toward the front. With every step, the presence became stronger and heavier.

By the time I reached the front, I could no longer stand. I fell to my knees, weeping. Words sprang up out of my mouth from a deep place within me. "God, forgive me. Jesus, I give myself to you." I cried and I cried, releasing all the pain. While I did, seas of love crashed over my heart.

Two people knelt by me, one on each side.

"Tamara." Levi's voice. "The Bible says that, in order for God to forgive us, we need to forgive. I feel like God wants to give you a clean slate today, but in order to receive it, there are some people he wants you to forgive. Can you do that?"

I nodded, keeping my eyes closed.

"God will bring those people to your mind. As He does, just tell them in your heart that you forgive them."

The first face I saw was my dad's, and the words just poured out.

Dad, I forgive you, for everything. I forgive you for not being there when I needed you. I forgive you for not protecting me. I forgive you for not loving me the way I needed to be loved.

More faces came before me. My mom, my brothers, Ryan, Danny, Shelby, and Kyle. They all came up before me individually. One by one, I set them free.

As I released them from my heart, I became free. Free from the torment, free from the fear. Free to love, free to be loved. For a long time, I knelt there in God's presence, overwhelmed by his love, his amazing love. *I don't deserve this kind of love.*

"Tamara." A woman's voice. "There's one more person you need to forgive, and that's yourself. You need to let yourself off the hook because God is able to redeem your life completely, like the words to that song. 'He restores them like they were there all the time.'"

Could I trust that God could redeem my mistakes?

I believed he could, and even more, that he *would*. I forgave myself for making such a mess of my life. I forgave myself for letting myself be deceived by Kyle. And finally, I forgave myself for what I did to Joe.

Joe. Oh, my goodness, Joe. I needed to talk to Joe! To find him and ask for his forgiveness.

I opened my eyes. Levi was on one side, but on the other was a familiar-looking woman, but I couldn't place her face.

Levi smiled and put his arms around me in a friendly, father-like hug. "It's so good to see you."

There were so many things I wanted to say to him but didn't know where to begin. "Thank you so much, for praying, for watching, for caring."

He pulled back after a moment. "I would like you to meet my lovely wife, Sarah."

This was Sarah? But why would she seem familiar to me? Sure, I had read about her for half the night, but the journal didn't include pictures. She smiled, and I remembered where I knew her from. I had met her at the hospital when Trudy was sick.

"Nice to meet you," I said. "We met once before. You work at the hospital, right? You gave me a couple of brochures for single mothers."

"Oh, yes, I remember. Nice to see you again."

"I have something that belongs to you. It's in the back."

Levi and Sarah followed me toward my seat.

A man sat in the back pew, off to the left.

Joe?

I did a double take.

It *was* Joe. What was he doing here? I didn't think he even went to church. Could God have brought him here for me? I was beginning to think anything was possible. I picked up the pace and snatched up Levi's journal. "There's still so much we need to talk about, but there's something I have to do."

Levi turned his head in Joe's direction. "Completely understandable."

"Thank you." I handed Levi his journal and turned toward Joe.

What if he couldn't forgive me? Would I be able to hold on to the peace I'd just received?

I walked up the aisle and sat down next to him, but not too close. "I'm so glad you're here. I really need to talk to you."

A nervous energy bounced off him, but he didn't make eye contact. "I'm listening."

"I've been awful to you. I can't even begin to tell you how sorry I am. For last night. For everything. I honestly thought you'd be better off without me. I'm so sorry."

Everything in me wanted to touch him. But I'd hurt him so much. How could I ever make it up to him? I would literally do anything to take away the pain I'd caused him. "I know things can never be the way they used to be between us, but I hope we can still be friends."

He lifted his hand and scratched the side of his head. "What if I told you I didn't want to be your friend?"

My heart sank. I had pushed him too far. I had hurt him too much.

"The thing is, Tamara ..."

My mind filled in the blank. *I can't be friends with someone that treats me like this. I can't live with what you did to me.*

His eyes caught mine. "The thing is, Tamara, I want to be so much more than just your friend. I want you to be the first person I see when I wake up in the morning and the last person I see before I go to bed. I want to cook for you and take care of you. I want you, all of you. To have and to hold, till death do us part."

"You still want to be with me after everything?"

He cupped my face in his hands. "For love is as strong as death. Jealousy as cruel as the grave. Many waters cannot quench love. Nor can the floods drown it."

His words intoxicated me. And then his lips were touching mine so tenderly, I almost melted into the pew. I pulled away, smiling. "Joseph Michael Phillips, did you just kiss me in a church? Isn't that, like, a sin or something?"

He chuckled, eyes full of amusement. "God did create kissing, you know."

"Maybe we should finish this conversation somewhere else."

He helped me to my feet, laced his fingers through mine, and pulled me out of the church. Once outside, he wrapped his arms around me, drawing me tenderly into him. "I love you so much," he whispered.

I slid my arms around his neck. "I love you too." I stood on my tiptoes, so I could reach his lips, kissing him the way I had wanted to minutes ago.

We lost ourselves there on the church steps, drinking each other in.

He pulled back after a few moments.

I kept my eyes closed, willing him to kiss me again.

His fingers traced the edges of my face.

I opened my eyes to see him studying me with an expression of wonderment. As if he was seeing me for the first time. "What are you thinking?"

His eyes glazed over with such intense emotion it was hard to stand up under his gaze. "Marry me."

"What?"

"You heard me. Marry me." He spoke the words almost like a challenge.

"You're absolutely crazy, you know that?"

Joe smiled this amazingly radiant smile that made me weak and strong and completely giddy. "Tamara, sweetie, you know as well as I do that, we're never gonna survive unless we get a little crazy."

I laughed. He was so right.

"Marry me!"

"Are you serious right now?"

"Do you need me to get down on my knees? Yes, I'm serious. Of course, I'm serious. I love you. I don't want to spend another second without you by my side."

"Yes!" I exclaimed. "Yes! Of course, I will marry you. I love you!"

He kissed me yet again, another deep, lingering kiss.

It made me dizzy in a very good way.

"Let's go to Vegas."

"Vegas?" I pushed away from him to search his face.

"Absolutely! Vegas!" His eyes were clear and full of hope. "I want to make you mine forever."

I looked down at my stomach and with my hands, cradled the baby that grew within me. There wasn't a doubt in my mind that Joe was the man for me. He had been right last night. He was home to me, as I was to him.

But when I gave myself to him, I wanted to be whole. God had started something in my life this morning, but that didn't mean it was finished. I hadn't even told Joe about Kyle. I didn't want what happened with Kyle to overshadow our wedding night. I couldn't marry Joe while I was still pregnant with Kyle's child.

"It's too quick, isn't it?" Joe asked, his eyes holding concern.

My heart constricted, sadness gripping me momentarily. "It's not that simple. There are still so many things I need to work through." When I said the words, I knew my past problems were far greater than just what had happened with Kyle. If it were possible, I first needed to reconcile with my family.

Joe pulled me into his arms once more. "It's okay," he whispered. "God is in control. We can work through anything with him being the center of us."

He was right. With God leading the way—and Joe at my side —I would find the courage to somehow face the past and be wholly free to run into our future.

Epilogue

"Push!" Doctor Reynolds' voice echoed off the walls as unrelenting pain bore down on my body. I lay there, unresponsive for a moment too long, wondering again why I'd refused the epidural.

The answer was simple, yet in retrospect, totally idiotic. Needles always made me queasy, but a six-inch needle shot straight into my spinal cord was downright terrifying. After what felt like hours of pushing, I would try anything to take the pain away.

Joe stood at my right side, and Sarah at my left.

They tried to coax me into a position to push. I couldn't do it.

"Tamara, sweetie, you're doing great," Joe encouraged. "It's almost over."

I wanted to scream. This agony wasn't almost over. He had no idea how much pain I was in.

"He's right, Tamara," Doctor Reynolds said. "Just a few more good pushes, and it's all over."

Sarah dabbed a cold washcloth on my forehead, and it sounded like she was whispering a prayer over me.

I lay back, wanting to give up.

"Tamara, look at me." Joe brought his face close to mine "You can do this. Just remember to brea—"

My cry filled the air as another contraction ripped through my body.

Joe and Sarah quickly helped me into the sitting position, and somehow I found the strength to bear down.

Only two more pushes later and the baby was out. Screaming and vigorous. Hope Elizabeth Taylor. We'd known from the ultrasound a few months ago the baby was a girl, and Levi and Sarah had come up with the name. To me, it seemed perfect.

I took in a deep breath, relief working its way through me. Not only because it was over, but because Hope sounded healthy. We had all been concerned when my water broke last night, a little over a month before my due date. Doctor Reynolds told us then that, when a baby is born before thirty-seven weeks gestation, there could be complications, most commonly underdeveloped lungs.

The cries that filled the room now gave little doubt her lungs were full and healthy.

I looked up at Joe. His eyes had misted over. Moisture leaked from my eyes as well. He kissed my forehead. "You're amazing," he whispered.

To the side of me, nurses cleaned and swaddled Hope in a blanket.

It was hard to see her around them. Even though she wasn't mine to keep, something in me ached to look at her.

The room eventually calmed down, and Sarah handed Hope to me.

I looked back and forth between Sarah and Joe, my eyes filling with a silent plea for a moment alone with my daughter, so that I could say a private goodbye.

Before Hope was born, I'd asked Levi and Sarah if I could spend a few minutes with her. I wasn't sure if it was customary, but then again, it wasn't a "normal" adoption. Most people didn't have the privilege of knowing the adoptive parents the way I did.

And if that wasn't the case, I didn't know if I would have the strength to follow through with giving up Hope.

Levi and Sarah were a wonderful couple, who had tried for years to conceive, only to be disappointed time and time again. I knew beyond reason that God had brought me into their lives with this purpose in mind.

"I'm going to go tell Levi she's arrived." Sarah smiled fondly and caressed the top of Hope's head. "You want to come with me, Joe?"

Joe's eyes, filled with awe, were still on me. "Yeah, for sure. I wanna see the look on his face when you tell him." He kissed me on the forehead, then turned, and they walked out the door.

For a long moment, I stared at Hope. She was tiny. A mere five pounds, seven ounces, but she was perfect. Her features were small and symmetrical.

I peeled off the pink beanie to find a full head of dark-brown hair. I thought of the one picture I had of me as a baby. She looked like me. But if I looked hard enough, I thought I could see Kyle too. The recognition gouged a fresh wound in my heart, and tears stung my eyes.

This was why I had to give her up. Every time I looked at her, I would see Kyle and remember what he'd done to me. I didn't think I could handle the constant memory. But it wasn't Hope's fault. Her conception was a result of a date rape, but her life would be a result of God's mercy and grace.

I ran my fingers along Hope's forehead and down her tiny nose. Looking at her now, despite everything, I could understand how some women changed their mind at the last moment about adoption. Because regardless of the circumstances and the hurt I knew it would cause me, there was a fierce longing inside of me to hold on to her. I could see clearly that, in letting her go, a part of my heart would go with her. It didn't matter how she was conceived, I loved her. She was part of me. But I had to let go.

I thought back to the scripture God had given me just last week, during a particularly doubtful moment. While writing a letter to Hope, God led me to 1st Samuel. It was the story of Hannah and how she cried out to God for a child, saying if he gave her a son, she would give him back to him. Even though I wasn't like Hannah, I felt like God was saying that my giving the baby to Levi and Sarah was like giving the baby to him. And just like Hannah had received more children, God would give me more children in the future. The idea brought some comfort, but giving her up, felt like it would rip my heart out. I was sure that I'd feel the depth of her absence every day for the rest of my life.

My thoughts shifted to my mother. Is this how she felt for all these years? Did me leaving home in the middle of the night, without a goodbye, devastate her? My insides wrenched and somehow I knew the answer. And what about my dad? What he did to me was wrong, but did he deserve what I had done to him? Leaving home without so much as a phone call for six years ...

God forgive me. And please help me find them. Last week I had tried to call their old number, but it was disconnected. I wasn't sure how I'd find them, but I knew I needed to. To let them know that I was alive and well. Deeper than that though, was my concern for Dakota. She had been my closest family member, and I had left her in her darkest hour. What had become of her? Over the last few months, I'd worked through a lot of these issues in counseling, but the more I let go of the guilt and unforgiveness the deeper the longing became to reconcile with my family. I just didn't know where to begin.

I nuzzled Hope closer, letting her nearness soothe the longing inside of me. Studying her angelic face, peace washed over me. In my heart of hearts, I knew giving her to Levi and Sarah was the best thing for her. They would be the parents to her that I never had. She would be cared for, safe and deeply loved.

Levi entered the room, his face beaming, with Sarah and Joe close behind him. I kissed the top of Hope's head and handed her over to her new parents, along with the letter. Inwardly, I said a prayer, releasing her completely to God.

To My Dearest Hope,

A wise man once told me love isn't only a feeling or an emotion, but it's also a choice. And when you truly love someone, you always try to choose the best and the highest for them. When I first heard him say this, I wasn't sure if I believed this kind of love was possible. However, not too long ago I've experienced he was right. Through all of this, I've found I'm capable of this kind of love, because today, as I make my choice, I know with all my heart I'm choosing what's best for you. Not only am I choosing what is best for you, but what is best for them and for me. I guess what's the most shocking to me after all this, after all my mistakes, is that I'm able to love myself. I will be praying for you every day, and remember, if you ever feel like God has forgotten about you, just know your life is living proof that He will always leave the ninety-nine to come after the one.

Dear Reader,

I hope you've enjoyed this story. In so many ways, it is my own. I know what it's like to be abused and heartbroken. I also know what it's like to make big mistakes. Like Tamara, I ran away from home when I was sixteen years old to escape abuse, only to find myself surrounded by a lifestyle of drugs and insanity. For a while, I took a ride on that Mary-go-round until I was so empty and broken, I cried out to God to save me. In that moment, He reached into my darkness and showed me a love greater than I ever thought possible.

I believe this book landed in your hands for a reason. It's a sign to let you know that God has left the ninety-nine and has come after you! He loves you and has a plan for your life. It doesn't matter how big your mistakes or how broken you are. If you open up your heart to Him, He is willing and able to fill you and put the broken places of your heart back together. If you would like this sort of healing, I invite you to pray this simple prayer to make Jesus Lord of your life.

Jesus, I believe you are the Son of God, that you died on the cross to rescue me from sin and death and to restore me to the Father. I choose now to turn from my sins, my self-centeredness, and every part of my life that does not please you. I choose you. I give myself to you. I receive your forgiveness and ask you to take your rightful place in my life as my Savior and Lord. Come reign in my heart, fill me with your love and your life, and help me to become a person like you. Restore me, Jesus. Live in me. Love through me. Thank you, God. In Jesus' name I pray. Amen.

If you've prayed this prayer all of heaven is rejoicing in your new birth! I would love to hear from you so I could celebrate with you!

Blessings in Christ,

Elisheba Haxby
Elishebahaxby@hotmail.com

Next In Series:

Thank you for reading Ninety-Nine Signs!
If you enjoyed what you read, continue the series with the next in
the series:
Book 2: Ninety-Nine Ashes

Or read other related books:

Related to this series

Reasons: A
Contemporary Romance

Levi's Journal: A Ninety-
Nine Series...

First Chapter of Ninety-Nine Ashes:

November 29, 9:00 a.m.

Return to Sender

The line blurred as moisture pooled in my eyes, and I pressed the envelope hard against my chest.

Another dead end.

I took a long breath of the frigid morning air before closing the mailbox and heading back inside.

What now?

I kicked off my flip-flops and drug my feet across the cold linoleum floor into the kitchenette, mind spinning. My parent's old phone number was dead. An internet search of social media platforms had yielded zilch and now this. I set most of the mail on the table, but the letter I had sent to my mother a little over a month ago was still firmly clutched in my hand. Heart heavy, I stared at the red words stamped at the top of the envelope. What had I expected anyway? That finding them six years later would be easy? That they'd be exactly where I had left them, frozen in time and waiting to reunite?

I tossed the letter aside, crossed the studio to the bathroom and opened the medicine cabinet. Sighing, I reached for the bottle of antidepressants the doctor had prescribed a little over a month ago for postpartum depression. I didn't like the idea of taking medication, but they seemed to help as I walked through the grieving process. Having the symptoms of giving birth to a baby without actually bringing one home had seriously messed with my head. The first week was the worst with my hormones shifting constantly and my body swollen from the baby weight. Each time I'd look down at my empty, stretched marked stomach, I cried from the hollowness I'd felt. As the weeks dragged on, a foggy numbness had settled over my brain, muting life and its colors. I opened the bottle, tapped a pill into my hand and swallowed it with a glass of water.

I set the container back on the shelf, closed the cabinet and examined myself in the mirror. Wild hair framed my oval face, and bemused green eyes stared back at me. Would I ever be back to who I was before the pregnancy? Outwardly, I was almost there. Only six pounds to go until I was my original weight and most of my clothes fit. Inside, though, was a different story. Since the adoption, there had been a vacant part of me that couldn't be comforted no matter what I did. Was that why I'd been so set on finding my family lately? Was it some way to fill the void Hope had created?

Shaking off the thoughts, I threw my hair into a loose ponytail and went back to the kitchen. Truth was, I had wrestled with the idea of finding them for months. Lately, though, the need had intensified. I grabbed a blue mug from the cabinet, filled it three-quarters full with coffee and added an ample amount of cream and sugar before taking a sip of what had become my only vice. Leaning against the counter, I picked up the envelope once more. What was the connection between Hope and my family? They were both part of me, but neither were in my life. It would be years until I'd be able to see Hope without it killing me emotionally, but after hours of therapy and prayer, I thought I was ready to reunite with my family. Before I'd been terrified to face them with the hurt that had been between us, but in one moment that had changed. The day I gave up Hope—the instant I placed her in Levi's arms and said goodbye —I realized what I'd done to my parents by staying away for so long. Letting her go made me see how awful it could be for a parent to lose their child. As I let her go, it felt as though a part of my heart had been ripped out, leaving a hole I wasn't sure would ever mend.

But as painful as it was, I had the peace of knowing Hope was in a good place, being raised by wonderful people, given the love and care she deserved. My parents—specifically my mother, who had never laid a hand on me—had no idea where I was. I could be dead for all they knew. And even though my dad had an angry side to him that had twisted me up on the inside, a part of me still loved him.

A light tapping at the door drew me from my thoughts. "Who is it?"

"It's me, sweetie."

Joe? Why wasn't he using his key?

I set my coffee down and hurried across the small room before swinging the door open.

Joe stood in front of me, holding two Starbucks cups, a warm smile on his handsome face. "Good morning, beautiful." He offered me one of the drinks. "White chocolate mocha, extra whip."

I mirrored his expression and took the cup from him. In many ways, Joe was my own personal star, illuminating my darkest nights. "You brought me coffee before going to work? You're the best."

He slowly shook his head, his grin growing wider. "I went in early and took care of some things. Claire's covering everything else."

"We get the whole day together?" With us working opposite shifts managing the diner, that never happened.

"Yup." Joe put his free arm around me and leaned in.

I tried to duck away from him, but he held me tight. "Give me a minute. I still need to brush my teeth."

"A little morning breath isn't enough to stop me." He chuckled and kissed my cheek instead.

"Ewwww." I giggled and squirmed out of his embrace. "So, what's the plan for today? Want to grab brunch and then hit a matinee?"

"Actually, I had something a bit different in mind." A hint of mischief sparkled in his eyes.

My curiosity was piqued. A romantic adventure with Joe could be just the distraction I needed. I glanced at the stack of mail on the kitchen table. Should I tell him about the returned letter? Not now. It would only spoil his mood. "What should I wear?"

"Think a little nicer than casual."

I scanned him from head to toe, noticing for the first time the way he was dressed. He wore dark jeans and a black sweater that hugged his muscles. And here I stood in front of him with my messy ponytail and morning breath. The thing was, I didn't even feel self-conscious. This wonderful man loved me and had proved it time and again.

I set my cup on the dresser and found a burgundy sweater dress and leggings before excusing myself to the bathroom. After a quick shower, I threw on the outfit, brushed my teeth, and put on a light smattering of makeup. When I stepped out of the bathroom, Joe was sitting at the table sipping his coffee, staring dreamily out of the window.

"Nickel for your thoughts."

His perfect lips arched into a crooked grin. "Isn't it supposed to be a penny?"

I gave a half-shrug. "Inflation."

"Nothing, really." The chair creaked as he pushed away from

the table. Then he crossed the room and put his arms around me, bringing his hand to my face, tracing the outline of my cheek. "Today is about you, Tamara. I'm so proud of you."

His words washed over me, warming the center of my being. "Really? For what?" I snuggled into him.

"For what you accomplished over the last six months. Most recently, your GED."

"That's no big deal. I should have done that years ago."

He put his finger under my chin. "It *is* a big deal. Especially with everything you've been through."

Sadness trickled into my stomach as the last few months played through my head again. The nights had been the hardest when I was alone in the quiet of my apartment without the busyness of work or Joe there to hold me. There were times I cried so hard from the grief I wasn't sure I'd ever stop. The months of counseling with David, processing the trauma of what Kyle had done, hadn't been a picnic either. Working on my GED had been a mental vacation from it all.

Joe kissed the tip of my nose as he stepped away. "Stay right here. Don't move. I'll be back." He grabbed my car keys off the hook on the way outside.

Why would he take my keys? We never drove my car. I almost followed him, but he seemed adamant about me staying put. Instead, I cleaned the coffee mess, then grabbed the mocha he'd brought me and sipped as I paced the room.

Tap, tap, tap. What now? I dashed back across the room and flung the door open.

Joe leaned on the doorway, holding a single long-stemmed red rose in one hand and a muffin in the other.

I laughed out loud. "What are you doing?"

He handed me the rose, lips twitching. "That's for me to know and for you to wonder about."

"Ohhhh. Man of mystery."

"Yeah, baby." He wiggled his eyebrows.

I laughed again. He was too adorable. "Oh, behave," I said in my best British accent.

"I knew our Austin Powers marathon was going to come back to haunt me." He chuckled, took hold of my hand, and tugged me forward. "We need to get this show on the road."

The weather was crisp, but sunny with a few cotton-candy clouds floating in the sky—the kind I'd always found animal shapes in. My gaze landed on my Cabriolet, which already had the top down.

I stopped mid-step and turned to Joe, arching an eyebrow. "What's this?"

A playful grin lit his warm hazel eyes. "I thought we could take your car for a change. And you love driving with the top down."

I threw him a disbelieving look. "You can't be serious."

"Oh, I'm serious."

I smacked him on the arm. "It's freezing out."

"What happened to your sense of adventure? What happened to the girl who loved the wind in her hair?"

"That was before I met Jesus," I joked.

"Just get in the car. It'll be okay. Promise." He opened the passenger door with a wink and handed me the muffin.

I climbed in and watched him circle the front of the car. "Why do you always get to drive?"

"Because, frankly, my dear, you have no clue where we're going," he said as he settled into his seat.

"So, tell me and then I can drive." I took a bite of the blueberry muffin. Mmmm. So good. A perfect mixture of moist and sweet.

"Not a chance, darlin'." That adorable mischievous grin was back. He reached into his back pocket and took out a handkerchief. "Everything's a surprise today."

I eyed the hankie. "A blindfold. Seriously?"

He nodded, his eyes dancing. "Trust is the building block to any good relationship."

"No way." I leaned away from him, raising a hand in protest.

"Come on, T. Just go with it."

"Fine." I turned my head in surrender.

He secured the blindfold around my head. "Now, no peeking."

"I make no promises." My world was dark, but my heart felt light.

The car started, and there was motion as Joe backed out of the parking spot. Cold wind blew against my face as the vehicle accelerated. "How about some music?" I yelled over the sound of the airstream.

He shouted back, "I thought you'd never ask! I made us a mixed tape. A compilation that reminds me of us."

"Don't you mean a playlist, Gramps?"

"No, I mean a mixtape. I'm not the one still driving a car from the eighties."

"Seriously? You made an actual *tape* tape?" Cute.

"Yes. Do you want me to put it on or not?"

"Abso-freaking-lutely!" Seconds later, the country twangs of Merle Haggard filled the car. Oh. My. Goodness. He had to be joking. I flung my hand against his chest. "Joe! Put on some real music."

He let out a cough and a deep inhale as if I'd hit him harder than I had. "What? You don't like good ole' Merle? I had no idea!" He teased and then forwarded it to the next song.

Harmonious beats and rhythmic percussion thrummed out of the speakers, and I instantly recognized the tune. "Crazy" by Seal. The wind whipped the hair around my neck, sending icy chills through my body. I unbuckled my seatbelt and leaned into the current. If only I could rip off the blindfold. This moment would be so much better if I could see.

"What are you doing?" Joe's elevated voice had a hint of concern in it.

"Just getting a little crazy!" I stood and yelled at the top of my voice. In that moment, the sadness of the last few months evaporated into the wind. Giving up my baby, my missing family, the pain of what Kyle had done flew off my back and into the horizon. A burst of freedom pulsed through my veins. "Wooooooohoooooo!"

Joe joined in on the yelling and honked the horn.

A few moments later, I sat back down, laughing through chattering teeth.

"Oh my goodness, baby. You're freezing."

"N—n—no. I'm o—okay." I forced out, my body shaking.

The wind slowed as the car came to a stop. "Hold on a sec." His door opened and closed. There was rummaging around, followed by the scraping sound of the top going up.

Within minutes, the air around me was much warmer. Joe returned, wrapped what felt like his leather jacket around me and cupped his hands over mine.

I shivered. He was just as cold as I was. We were two icicles trying to heat each other up.

"This was probably not my most brilliant plan." A tinge of chagrin laced his tone.

"You can't be serious. That was the most alive I've felt in months."

He was quiet for a beat, and I could imagine the look in his deep eyes. "You're insane. You know that?"

"We won't survive," I said through a shiver, "unless we get crazy."

He chuckled and blew on our hands. "You're my kind of crazy, woman."

His arm came around me, and I curled into him. Hot air from the vents blew on us. The whole thing reminded me of our first date, except for the blindfold. Joe's finger traced the line of my neck and slid through my hair, sending shivers down my spine. Then his lips were on mine so tenderly I felt as though I could melt into him. Heat pooled in my stomach and spread through my body. "Almost Paradise" played in the background, and a little chuckle escaped my lips.

"What?" A hint of a smile lightened Joe's voice.

"I feel like I'm inside a cheesy eighties movie all of a sudden."

"Exactly what I was going for."

"Mission one-hundred-percent accomplished." I adjusted the blindfold.

"Hey, no peeking," Joe scolded. "We better get back on the road. Otherwise, you'll be blind the whole day."

If he would have just allowed me to take the darn blindfold off, I would've been content to stay right there for the rest of the day—nuzzled into him, stealing as many kisses as I could. He pulled away, and a few seconds later, gravel crunched under the tires. The vehicle rolled forward then accelerated, and the music grew louder. Joe laced his fingers through mine, and I leaned my head on his shoulder. It was a strange sensation not being able to see. But it seemed to make me more aware of my other senses, like the smell of Joe's spiced cologne and leather jacket. The music was hitting my soul like freshly squeezed lemonade on a hot summer day—sweet and refreshing. Joe had done a great job on the mix. If I were to label the tape, it would have been called *Best of the Eighties, Nineties, and Deep Worship*. A little bit of Journey, Lifehouse, Water Deep, and Hillsong United, to name a few. Twelve and a half songs later, the car rolled to a stop, and the engine died. Were those raindrops hitting the windshield?

Joe's hands came to the back of my head, untying the blindfold. Massive waves were crashing against the shore with a dark-gray backdrop. The blue skies had vanished, replaced by huge rain clouds bursting at the seams.

We were at Cannon Beach—the place Joe had taken me on our first date. I looked over at him, my heart swelling. Was that sadness in his expression?

"What's wrong?"

He shrugged and averted his gaze. "I wanted this day to be perfect, but the weather is not cooperating."

"Are you kidding me? There's nothing better than watching a

storm gathering over the ocean. Talk about raw power." I crawled over the center console and wedged myself onto his lap.

He swept a lock of hair behind my ear and ran his hand softly down my arm, causing a tingling sensation to open inside my core. Through the window, a streak of lightning lit the sky. He kissed me then, deep and slow, his hands cradling the back of my head, fingers threading through my hair. "Tamara," he whispered my name as he drew away from the kiss.

I let out a quiet moan and rested my forehead on his. Another lightning bolt flashed, followed by a thunderclap. I jumped a bit at the noise and settled back into him.

Gently, he traced my fingers, caressing them in the sweetest way. "The last time I brought you here was the day I realized that I was, without a doubt, hopelessly in love with you."

I smiled at the memory. "What exactly was it? My running off into the freezing cold water or me coming out looking like a drowned rat?"

"Both." He slowly lifted my hand and laced his fingers through mine. "I knew that day we fit together perfectly."

A wonderful feeling of euphoria swept through my body, followed by a strange moment of clarity. Every broken path of my life had actually led me to Joe. I'd wondered many times how I could survive so much, but ending up here, being so deeply loved, almost made it all worth it.

For a long time, we were quiet as we watched the waves crash against the shore and lightning streak across the sky. I was so relaxed I could have fallen asleep, but then Joe jumped. "Oh. We gotta go."

Confusion interrupted my bliss. Moving was the last thing I wanted to do, but I followed Joe's nudging and climbed back into my seat. He reversed the car, peeled out of the parking lot and sped north on Highway 101.

What was the rush about? "You going to tell me why you're speed-racing my car?"

He pushed the accelerator. "Oh please, this thing can barely hit seventy."

"Exactly."

"The old beater will be fine."

"Hey, lay off my car. This baby has treated me well over the years."

He rolled his eyes and slowed down a tad.

"Are you at least going to tell me where we're heading in such a hurry?"

Joe pressed his lips together in a thin line and made a zipping motion with one hand.

Another surprise? I supposed I could live with that. I leaned back in my seat and watched the changing scenery as the ocean came in and out of view. At least Joe hadn't blindfolded me again.

Ten minutes later, we reached Seaside, and he slowed a bit. Daydreams swirled around my mind as I took in the shops and restaurants lining the road. Maybe someday Joe and I could live in a town like this. The car came to a stop in front of the restaurant he'd taken me to the last time we were here. Joe parked, grabbed an umbrella with a small black plastic bag from the back, and exited the car. He held the umbrella over my head as we ran toward the building.

The maître d' opened the door for us and gave us a once over as we entered.

"Reservation for Phillips," Joe said.

Reservations? How long had Joe been planning this?

The gentleman scanned the large black book in front of him. "Oh yes, right this way." He picked up two menus and led us into the dining room.

Joe took my cold hand in his, and we followed him to the exact same table we had sat last time, right next to the fireplace. After setting menus in front of us, he filled our glasses with water and explained the day's special. Filet mignon with a lobster bisque. Joe and I exchanged a glance. Another wave of déjà vu hit me. Last time I had ordered almost the exact same thing, but back then I was scared to let him spend so much on me. Now I felt safe. Secure.

"We'll take two cups of hot tea to start off with," Joe told the man.

"Yes, sir. The server will be here soon to take the rest of your order," he said before walking away.

As I gazed at the fireplace, orange flames danced against the wood, and tenderness filled my insides. "Do you know how wonderful you are?" I turned my attention to Joe and stretched my hand across the table.

His hand spread over mine, a half-smile on his lips. "Just trying to give you the life you deserve."

For a long moment, I lost myself in his gaze, taking in his kind words. So much had changed between us since the last time we'd been here. Over the last few months, he'd been my rock, my safe place when the storms of life raged around me. I couldn't count how many times he'd held me together when I was falling apart.

The waitress brought us our tea and took our orders. I decided on the special, and Joe ordered a New York steak topped with mushrooms and onions with a loaded baked potato on the side.

Joe traced circles on the top of my hand. "How are you really doing over there?" His eyes held a deep concern that I was infinitely grateful for.

I thought about the returned letter sitting on the kitchen counter. A part of me wanted to tell him, but with the effort Joe had put into this date, it would be wrong for me to overshadow it with my problems. Besides, I was enjoying this day being about us and us alone. "I feel good today. I mean, even before you came over and took me on this romantic extravaganza." I gave a cheesy grin and took a sip of my tea. It wasn't a total lie. Before I'd received the letter, I had felt a little better.

"I'm glad to hear that." Joe squeezed, then let go of my hand and grabbed the plastic bag he'd brought in with him. "I got something for you." He brought out a rectangular present, wrapped in red paper, tied together with a black ribbon.

My mouth dropped open in surprise. What was this? The whole day had already been a gift.

He pushed the present across the table with his signature room brightening smile.

I stared at the perfectly wrapped package, a bit overwhelmed. "You're really pushing the romance thing to a whole new level."

"Like Hugh Grant level?" He raised an eyebrow and pursed his lips in a hilarious mock-smoldering expression.

I laughed and threw a wink. "Close."

"Open it." The anticipation radiating off him was palpable.

I let out a pleasant sigh and lifted the gift. I untied the black ribbon, tugged the tape at the corner of the red paper, and glanced up. Joe tapped the table, staring at me with a look that said, *Hurry now, you're killing me*. I ripped away the rest of the paper. Underneath was a chestnut-brown, leather-bound journal with my name engraved at the bottom. My heart expanded, filling with gratitude. What a beautiful gift. I ran my fingers over the engraving. "This is perfect. Thank you." I held it against my chest. "I love it."

"Do you remember the last time we were here we talked about our dreams?"

I nodded as I flipped through the pages of the journal. They were a rich cream color and thick, like cardstock.

"You said your dream was to write, and you shared that poem with me. It was really good, Tamara."

"I remember." The poem, based on a recurring dream I'd been having, was written out of a painful place but was never finished.

"I haven't seen you write for a while, and I wanted to encourage you to start again."

I set the journal down and flipped through the blank pages. The fresh paper aroma danced across my nose. I leaned in close and took in a long sniff, imagining I was in a bookstore, standing in front of books *I* had written. Would that ever be a possibility? Seemed farfetched, but something came alive in me at the thought. "That's very thoughtful, Joe." Would I ever be worthy of this man in front of me?

"What's wrong?" Joe's hand rested on mine again.

"Sometimes I don't understand what I did to deserve you."

"Tamara, sweetie. You are such an amazing, kind, and strong person. If you saw half of what I see, you would realize that I'm the lucky one."

"How can you say that? I've been a puddle of tears for the last few months."

"You've been through a lot, but your strength and resilience through the hard times is one of your greatest qualities. But you're so much more than that. You're smart, funny, beautiful. You're my best friend, T. My other half."

Tears rolled down my face at his words. "You see me better than I really am."

"I see you as you are." He brought his hand to my cheek, caressing away the tears. His gaze held enough emotion to knock me over. One day, I hoped I'd be the woman he thought I was.

The waitress came to our table with our steaming plates of food. The smell of flame-broiled meat, onions, and garlic wafted in the air, and my stomach growled. I set aside the gift to make room for my plate.

Joe reached for his knife. "This looks amazing." He cut into the New York Strip, popped a piece in his mouth, and let out a quiet moan.

The moment the cooked-to-perfection steak hit my mouth, I understood Joe's reaction. The meat was so tender it almost melted in my mouth. "Mmmm. I don't remember it being this good last time."

"Me either," Joe said around a mouthful.

"Then there's the fact that I don't have pregnancy hormones messing with my taste buds." My heart constricted at the words, but I instantly brushed it off. I wouldn't let sadness spoil this moment. No matter how much it stung.

"There is that, but I wasn't pregnant." He smirked and forked another bite.

His light mood took the sting out of my words. I took in a deep breath and glanced at the blazing fire. In the background, the rain pinged against the windows. Chill bumps rose on my skin. Everything was exactly as it was supposed to be, even if it did hurt sometimes. "I'm really thankful for all of this."

"I'm thankful too." His gaze landed on mine and his endearing expression melted my insides.

Heat climbed my neck, and I averted my gaze. How could a single look from this man turn me to mush?

Joe went back to his steak, and we sat in mostly blissful silence until we finished. I placed the last bite into my mouth just before the waitress approached our table and cleared our plates. "Would you like to see the dessert menu?"

"I think we're good. Thank you."

Once Joe paid the bill, we headed out for a walk. The air was damp when we stepped outside. The rain had momentarily stopped, but the huge gray clouds in the sky looked ready for another downpour. That didn't matter, though. I would enjoy every moment of this day even if we got totally drenched.

We strolled along the promenade, exploring the shops. We tried on different outfits and purchased a few knickknacks for Joe's house. Someday it would be my home, and I liked shopping for it and dreaming about adding a woman's touch to the place. It was nice to leave the sorrow of the last year behind and start thinking about the future again. But what about Joe? Most of his life lately had been about supporting me, making sure I was taken care of. He deserved to dream too.

We stepped out of an antique shop, and a large gust of wind rustled my hair. "What about your dreams, Joe?"

He stopped mid-step and turned toward me. "What about them?"

"You said earlier you haven't seen me write lately. Well, I haven't heard you talk about your dreams lately either."

He took hold of my hand and dragged me forward. "Let's go down to the beach."

Was he ignoring my question? "You didn't answer the—"

"Could you trust me for one time today?" He threw a playful smirk and continued to drag me toward the ocean. Small droplets fell from the sky.

When we made it to the sandy shore, Joe turned to me. He looked at me for a long moment, searching my face. "Earlier today, when we sat in front of the ocean holding each other ..." A flurry of wind blew around us, and the raindrops grew in size. "So many dreams filled me. One day I want to own my own restaurant, and I want it to be here, or a town just like it. I know how much the ocean means to you, and that's the thing, Tamara. Every dream that I have has you at the center of it. Starting with us at the altar, promising our lives to each other." Joe knelt on one knee.

What was he doing? We were already engaged. The rain fell heavily around us.

He reached into his pocket and withdrew a tiny black box. "Tamara Christine Jensen. I love you with all my heart. I want to spend the rest of forever giving you the life and happiness you deserve." He popped the box open and an elegant diamond solitaire ring shimmered at me.

Tears spilled down my cheeks, mingling with the rain.

"Marry me?" he yelled over the wind.

I knelt in the wet sand with him. "You crazy man. I said yes six months ago."

He slid the ring on my finger. "You deserved this kind of proposal." Then his arms were around me, his lips meeting mine with hunger and passion.

A few moments later he drew back, and I slowly opened my eyes. His dark hair was drenched, and rain dripped down his gorgeous features. The desire that shone in his countenance caused heat to pulse through me despite the frigid rain.

"You're soaked," he whispered in my ear, then stood before helping me to my feet. "Let's go get you warmed up."

On the walk back to the car, I thought about my future with Joe. I saw it exactly the way he described. Us living in a small town on the ocean. Running our own business. Raising a family...

My throat tightened around the word *family*. The returned letter and all of its daunting implications filled my mind. Over the last few months, I'd dealt with my pain with Kyle, the date rape and giving up Hope for adoption, but this one massive question mark still hung over my head. Would I be able to fully go forward with my life with Joe while having such an unresolved past?

I really wanted to, but if I was truly being honest with myself, I wasn't so sure.

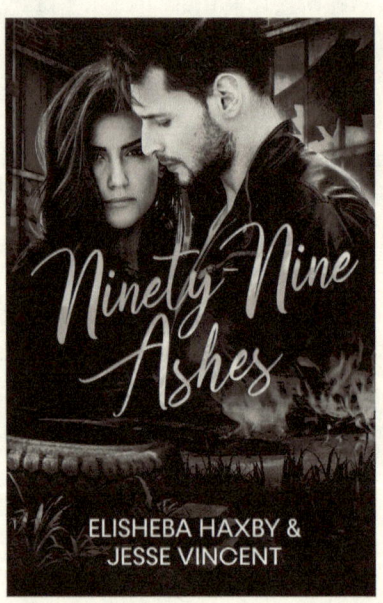

Levi's Journal

**Get Levis Journal for free by joining Elisehba's Mailing list.
(Yes the actual journal from the book!)**

Download Free: https://dl.bookfunnel.com/bmtbbwxavd

Questions for Discussion

1. What would you say the theme of Ninety-Nine Signs is? Is there more than one?
2. Have you ever had a number or sign reoccur in your life? What did it mean to you?
3. Tamara had a tendency to run from her problems, but they always seemed to follow her. Why do you think this was? Do you relate?
4. Joe had a bad feeling about Kyle and threw away his notes to protect Tamara. Do you agree with Joe's decision?
5. Joe's temper got the better of him when he laid Anthony out cold. Have you ever had someone you've wanted to punch in the face?
6. Tamara had a reoccurring dream where she felt like she couldn't outrun the darkness. Have you ever felt chased by fear or lies?
7. Tamara started writing to help cope with her pain, but then discovered she had a passion for it. Is there something you've done out of necessity, but then realized you loved it?

8. Tamara's last night at home and the memories of being abused seemed to really shape who she was. What is a significant moment in your life? How has it shaped you as a person?

9. God used various signs to speak to Tamara, but it took her awhile to realize it. Has anything similar happened to you?

10. Do you think God speaks outside of the Bible? If so, how can you be sure It's him?

11. Tamara felt the signs were good at first but then turned bad. Have you ever felt like something at first brought you hope but then ended up bringing you heartache?

12. Joe turned away from God because of a tragedy in his life. His pain caused him to question God's goodness. Are there situations that hurt so bad, it's caused you to see God in a skewed way?

13. Levi had a strong walk with God but seemed to have unanswered prayers. The deepest desire in his life was opposed the most. Can you relate? Why do you think this is?

14. One of the keys to Tamara's freedom at the end of the book was forgiveness. Not only forgiveness of others, but forgiveness of self. Are there people in your life that you need to forgive? What, if anything is holding you back? Have you forgiven yourself for the mistakes you've made?

15. Quite a few times during the book, Levi felt prompted by God to reach out to Tamara. Sometimes they felt uncomfortable. Have you ever felt lead to do something that felt uncomfortable or maybe went against "normal" social cues? If so, how did that work for you?

Acknowledgments

To Aubrey from Elisheba, for all your love and support and sacrifice. Through this journey you've been my rock and my soft place to land. I love you.

To Mom, you're the best mom anyone could hope for! Thank you for the last-minute edits.

To Mom and Dad from Jesse, for giving me life, good genes and a creative mind.

To the Rivas family, you guys are amazing and always wonderfully supportive.

To Joshua Rivas for writing the song *Ninety-Nine* and letting us use it in our book.

To Mark Ayres, for your amazing edits and writing advice without you this manuscript would be a bunch of talking heads.

To Christina Tarabochia, for helping grow our baby up, and nudging us toward going Indie.

To Kail Harbick, we don't want to beat a dead horse, but thank you for helping us remove the clichés, we couldn't have done it without you.

To our first editing group: Ruth, Chris, Jennifer, Mary, Amanda and Mark, you guys rock! All your feedback in those early stages was invaluable.

To Melanie Campbell, for your support and encouragement and for loaning your copy of The First Five Pages.

To Charlene Finley, your enthusiasm about always wanting the next chapter helped the manuscript be completed much faster.

To Maddie Buck, your encouragement and support mean so much! Everyone needs a friend like you in their corner!

To our wonderful mentor James L. Rubart, thank you for all your support and even narrating part of the audiobook.

And to our initial backers, Charlene, Shona, Chani, Diane, Marra, Lynn, Lindy, Maddie, Melanie, RD, Sarah, Linda, Deborah L., Gina, Uncle Herbert, Gary, Craig and Debbra K., Thank you so much for believing in us.

About The Authors

Elisheba and Jesse met in Youth With A Mission in 2001. Elisheba was impressed by Jesse's creative mind and his dedication to story crafting. Jesse was impressed by Elisheba's deep walk with Jesus and her commitment to emotional authenticity. They became friends and years later decided to start writing together through a set of supernatural circumstances.

Jesse carried the idea for their first book, Ninety-Nine, since 1999. At the time he knew it was a download from God, but struggled to write from an emotionally raw woman's point of view. Throughout the years when bringing this frustration to God, God simply responded with "this is not your story." Then in 2010 Elisheba heard from God to start writing and that her stories would lead people into an encounter with the love of God. She brought this word to Jesse and it clicked for both of them to work together on this project. The idea was conceived and nine months later the first book was birthed.

The journey of writing and publishing was quite challenging, filled with many hurdles and mistakes. But every step of the way God met them, helped them, and healed them. Over the many years of writing together, learning the craft, and pursuing inner healing, they decided to start a business to help other authors do the same. They wanted to combine their belief that God wants to create through His people with the need to help creatives be healed enough to partner with God and produce this creativity. To do this, they founded Above The Sun, LLC.

For more writing by Elisheba Haxby, Jesse Vincent, and Above The Sun, please visit:

ElishebaHaxby.com
AboveTheSun.org

What's Your Story?

Above The Sun is a community of hope-filled creators who believe the world can be transformed through authentic stories. Our mission is to develop authors who are committed to becoming whole in order to successfully bring their message to their unique areas of influence. If you have a book in you and you are willing to do the work to release it, we would love to connect.

Visit us at <u>AboveTheSun.org</u>